Life and Other Contact Sports

John McKinstry

ISBN: 978-0-9955545-2-8

For Alan, who never got the chance to read this (but I hope he would have approved)

CONTENTS

Life and Other Contact Sports

Let me tell you about life....

Life is rarely gentle with us.

Oh sure, sometimes we get moments where we can convince ourselves we're going to be handed a level playing field, but those moments don't last for long, do they?

Deep down we all know there are bumps coming our way – tragedies with our names painted on them – but most of us shy away from the truth of that. As a rule we prefer to bury our heads in the sand rather than look honestly at what we might have to face up to.

We know that the longer we live, the better our odds are of coming face-to-face with the worst-case scenarios. From injuries and illnesses to grief and loss, we know we're all going to be tested one day and the thought is often terrifying.

Sometimes - during the good times – it's possible for us to cling onto the notion that we might somehow manage to avoid the bumps, but in our heart of hearts we have to acknowledge that the odds of being untouched by pain and loss are more than somewhat against us.

No, life is neither gentle nor fair – life is a contact sport and it's no use pretending it's anything else.

And like in any contact sports, you have to accept that the rules will get bent or broken by your opponent when it suits them to do so.

You might want – even expect – life to play things straight, but experience suggests that just isn't going to happen.

Life *will* come straight at you from your blind side and when it hits you, it'll often do so with an excessive amount of force. Life *will* take cheap shots at you and when you go down (and you will) sometimes life will just keep beating on you.

And as it continues to pound on you, it's like you can hear life hissing at you to just stay down, because if you *dare* to try and get back on your feet, it's going to get even madder and hurt you even worse.

But you know something?

You can't stay down – you just can't.

You have to rise.

Oh, I'm not saying it's easy – believe me when I say I know it isn't.

You see, I'm a coward.

Yeah, you read that right, a coward.

I learned all of the above and I learned it the hard way.

This is my story.

PART ONE
Machismo and other such horseshit

DAVEY JONES IS COMING! Tremble with fear!
#seadevils #blueandgreen #ouryear
Posted by user - Lady Kraken

JOHN McKINSTRY

Let me tell you about superstitions…

I'm not going to waste your time telling you in minute detail about my childhood or what it was like growing up in Canada or having a guy like my dad as a father.

Most of it was probably as normal, dull and boring as your own childhood and the nasty parts of it aren't relevant at this point in the story.

My name is David Jones and there are really only two things you need to know about me.

The first is that I'm a hockey player.

Given who my dad was, this comes as a surprise to virtually no-one back home. I'm from Saskatchewan – a place so steeped in hockey that I've heard it referred to as the 'hockey player province' and I can't argue with that. Sasky has given the world of hockey some of its all-time great players and the people there take their hockey pretty damn seriously.

The second thing you should know about me is that I'm not in any way superstitious.

But I tell everybody I am.

You see, I've learned that people – from coaches to the fans – are actually pretty understanding about it if you tell them you're superstitious. I mean, you can probably remember hearing about some athlete who would only play if he had a certain, lucky number on his jersey, right? Or when players get led into the same room as the trophy they're playing for and you watch them very deliberately put their hands in their pockets to avoid accidentally touching the trophy because to touch it before you've won it is going to jinx you.

Well to me, all of that is just so much crap.

My dad told me it didn't matter what number was on your jersey, what mattered was the number of hours you'd spent practising your skating or shooting.

So I think it's nonsense, but it's useful nonsense because people can forgive a superstitious player.

They aren't so quick to forgive a gutless one though.

Sometimes – when I realise I'm facing up to something that scares the life out of me – I tell them I can't do it and I make up a reason for it, based on some lame superstition.

My favourite way of ducking out of things?

Tell them I've seen an omen (nice and non-specific) of failure or disaster and that, because of that, I can't go on.

I pulled that shit plenty of times while I was making a living playing minor league hockey back home and it always worked, although I picked up a reputation for being difficult to get on with too. One coach told me he didn't have room for some hockey diva in his squad and threatened to kick me out, but I knew he wouldn't.

I guess that's the other thing I should admit.

This is going to sound a little arrogant, I know, but the truth is that I'm not just a hockey player; I'm a damn good one.

People who knew my dad or who saw him play just put it down to genetics; I mean, how on earth could Charley Jones' son be anything other than a great hockey player, right?

Truth is, it was my brother Mason who got all the natural talent, but we both spent hours on end out on the ice with our dad, so something was bound to rub off.

I'm not a big guy, you understand, I've never been much for lifting weights, but I'm fast and I'm accurate. Top goal scorer in the Provincial Hockey League three years running. People were saying I was destined for bigger and better.

I suppose it was pretty much inevitable that I'd get a call from the Sea Devils.

The Devils are based in St Helens in Maine. Not a minor league team, but not major one either. I still recall my dad telling me that St Helens was like a training school for the big league – half a dozen Sea Devils alumni had gone on to play for the biggest teams in the world.

Of all the teams in the world, the very last one I'd have probably chosen to join was the Sea Devils.

Like I said, I'm not really superstitious, but I'd spent enough time watching my dad play at the King Centre in New England, to see the way the Devils played.

I started talking about omens pretty quickly and did all I could to (politely) get owner Jack Hannigan to look elsewhere but he seemed set on seeing me play in blue and green. He talked about my dad's legacy and about giving the fans a hockey dynasty.

He talked about how much he owed my dad.

I tried – I mean *really* tried – to find another team. Truth was, I needed the money a bigger team would bring me and the Devils were making me by far the best offer.

They loved the idea of me playing for my dad's old club and think about the fun they'd have with the marketing. Sea Devils? Davey Jones? It was a match made in heaven.

Jack Hannigan even gave me a get-out clause. Just one season and after that I could call myself a free agent if I wanted to.

It really was a great offer.

But like I said, I'm a coward.

Hockey is a full contact sport and the Sea Devils kind of relish that.

In the end, I sort of drifted into it, because there was nothing better out there.

The night before my first appearance, I was almost sick with nerves. I'd stood in my apartment looking for some omen I could point to, which I could claim had guided me away from playing that night.

I couldn't conjure up a single one.

When the car came to pick me up for the arena, I immediately looked to see if it had seat belts.

The driver – who clearly knew exactly what I was looking for – piped up and said, 'New seat belts for every seat, Mr Jones, and I've been asked to put a box cutter in the glove box. If anything happens, it's within easy reach for you.'

I dumped my gear in the back, then before getting in I popped the glove compartment to check and sure enough, there was a box cutter knife sitting there within easy reach.

I'd half hoped there would be something wrong with the transport – something I could call an omen and use as my 'get out of jail free card' to avoid taking to the ice.

I kind of knew that I'd been kidding myself though.

There was no superstition I could conjure up that would prevent my debut in front of the blue and green faithful.

I'm not superstitious but I knew exactly what could happen out there on the ice.

I had a really bad feeling about the upcoming game as we slowly made our way to the arena that night.

JOHN McKINSTRY

Let me tell you about machismo…

My sport is hockey and if you want to play hockey, then you have to accept a few things – the first of which is that hockey players redefine the standard for tough.

Let me give you an example. Go take a look through the sports stories online or in the paper and look for a story about a player in some other sport who takes a bump.

It could be a basketball player who gets fouled in the act of shooting and knocked off his feet, or maybe a soccer player brought down in a sliding tackle.

Just take a look at the expression of abject agony on the player's face. Notice how the tears spring quickly to his eyes. Observe how he rocks from side to side, wailing like a distraught infant until three or four team mates physically lift the poor soul up off his ass and carry the wounded soldier oh so gently off to the sidelines where he receives the full attention of his coach, physio and doctor.

Have a look at just how many of these wounded heroes then go back on to the pitch or court to finish their game – odds are the number will be very, very few or (more likely) none of them.

Here's how hockey differs from that.

When a hockey player takes a bump?

He plays on.

No tears, no theatrics, no leaving the ice for a little lie down. Just pop your gum shield back in and skate on.

Forget about what the opposition would say to you if you started blubbing out there on the ice – your own teammates would be anything but sympathetic.

You broke your nose?

Suck it up buttercup.

You lost a tooth?

Hell, who hasn't?

You broke a rib?

You've got plenty more.

It's about being a real man – the kind of guy who can take a bump and keep going.

And don't be under any illusions – if you play hockey it's not a case of *if* you take a bump – it's when, how many you'll take and how savage they will be.

If there's a sport out there that breeds a more macho attitude then hockey, I've yet to see it.

You know where that word comes from? Macho? It's from 'masochism' – the enjoyment of receiving pain. Maybe that isn't quite true for hockey players. Maybe they don't actually *enjoy* taking a bump (would *you* manage a big smile if someone slammed into you hard enough to fracture a few ribs?). But I'll tell you this much – they surely aren't scared of it.

A case in point was the Sea Devils big defence man, Frankie Childs.

The season before I joined the Devils, Frankie and a guy from another team were both chasing the puck. They were skating hell for leather – Frankie to clear the puck away from the Devils goal and the other guy to get the puck and try to turn it around and take another shot at scoring.

Frankie was faster and the other guy knew it.

So he dropped back slightly, let Frankie clear the puck, and then, before Frankie could do anything else, the other guy crashed into him at full speed and drove him face first into the wall.

They stopped the game because Frankie wasn't moving after he landed on the ice.

It took the big man a minute or two come around. Later on, after the game, it'd be discovered that Frankie had a broken cheek bone and was almost certainly concussed.

The assistant coach was all for taking Frankie off the ice.

Frankie's response to that suggestion was to pull the assistant coach up close and growl, 'Don't you *dare*, sonny.'

For all I know, Frankie was as scared as I would have been. It could all have been an act on his part and he could have been really desperate for somebody to hand him an excuse to leave the ice.

But somehow, I doubt it.

My dad once told me that hockey players – especially old school guys like Frankie – have a different attitude from normal people towards things like pain and injuries.

I liked big Frankie a lot.

When I met him in the pre-season training sessions before my first Sea Devils game, he told me his job was to make sure I could do mine.

'I've got your back kid,' he rumbled. 'I'm not letting you get hurt out there if I can prevent it.'

He was a reassuring sort of guy to have on your team. He was funny too – if you met the guy off ice, you'd be surprised at how goofy a sense of humour he had.

To me, he was a lot like a bigger version of my best friend, Dennis. Tough as old boots and absolutely reliable.

I really wished I could have been more like him but I've always been pretty honest about what kind of person I am.

I'm gutless.

The idea of getting thrown violently into the boards like he was is the kind of thing that wakes me up in a cold sweat.

My view of injuries is that to continue skating with them falls under the heading of 'REALLY dumb idea', because there's every chance that by doing so, all you're going to do is make them worse.

Of course, these aren't views I could share with my new teammates and expect to be accepted.

I might view all the machismo in the game as dangerous horseshit but, for everybody else, it's absolutely central to being a hockey player.

And every team stresses it; every team talks tough.

In the run-up to my first appearance in blue and green, there had already been a lot of tough talking.

And despite being a coward, I had been right in the thick of it.

JOHN McKINSTRY

Let me tell you about my best friend...

Given that I'd earned myself a bit of a reputation as a prima donna when I was with other clubs, I figured that the Sea Devils promotions guy was surprised at how little I asked for at my first game.

My one and only request was for a decent seat in the arena for my buddy Dennis to come see me make my first appearance for St Helens.

Of the several thousand people who turned up at the King Centre that night, Dennis was one of the very few who knew the tough talking I did in interviews just before the season began, was just that – talk.

Dennis knew how I really felt, hell, he was the one to practically script some of my interviews for me.

See, of all the things in life that I'm not good at, lying is probably top of the list. I go all red in the face and stammer a little. I tried to keep out of trouble at school because just one question from any teacher and they'd know straight away if I'd done it or not. And I'm an absolutely godawful poker player.

So, joining in with the build-up to the season and trying to somehow sell my cowardly self as a tough guy was doomed to failure.

Until Dennis stepped in.

'The toughest of the tough guys don't talk much,' he told me. 'They just have a way about them. They give off a vibe that says 'do-not-screw-with-me' so loud that everybody takes note.'

The rare comments I gave (the whole team was interviewed in the run-up to the first game) were generally brief and described me as being "terse" or "closed off". My favourite quote was the one that described me as being a 'barely contained ball of rage'.

Hey, it might be miles short of the truth but we've got to sell tickets, right?

Dennis sort of coached me through the press stuff. 'Assume that every single word you give costs you fifty bucks,' he advised. 'You give good glare, Davey boy. You can't change how you look so you might as well use it.'

It was good advice and he was absolutely right about me giving good glare. I've noticed over the years that when people see my face – well, the left side of it anyway – they tend to make judgements about me pretty quickly.

I have a scar – not disfiguring, but not exactly subtle either – which goes from just above my eyebrow to the side of my eye above my cheekbone.

It's whitened over time, of course, but you can't really miss it.

I've had it since I was at high school and I try not to let it define me, which can be hard because people react. What would *your* first reaction be to someone with a visible facial scar? Think *you* could avoid judging?

The worst thing about it is that, when I smile, people tell me it always looks like I'm sneering at them. Back when my mom was still alive she'd always say that the only photo of me she had ever liked was taken on my ninth birthday – back when I still had a normal smile. I've realised that most people genuinely struggle to work out when I'm really smiling and when I'm not.

Dennis is an exception to that.

He knows when I'm smiling for real – he always has. He's been my best friend forever and knows how I really feel about all the violence. He knew how nervous I was about coming to play for St Helens. He knows most of my secrets.

He knows how I got the scar – he was there when it happened and he's the one who stopped that little incident from being so much worse than it could have been.

So I followed his advice and 'worked the scar'. The Devils PR guy wasn't initially thrilled but after a few days he got with it and I found myself with an image of being an arrogant, uncommunicative jerk.

The fans loved it.

Of course, rival fans are going to give you shit no matter what you do or how you act.

I wound up with literally hundreds of posts online asking me why I hadn't spent a little time learning how to talk. I had a good few suggesting I didn't say much because I was too scared and one or two of the so-called 'experts' online began to suggest my silence was a way of challenging rival players – maybe even a way of disrespecting them (you have to love the people who stir up that level of shit in the knowledge that they'll never be the one on the ice having to deal with it).

Lady Kraken – one of the Devils' online cheerleaders – put most of them back into their box when she posted 'Actions not words. Wait till the puck drops, haters – then we'll see'.

Most of the guys in the team replied to criticism. Oh, we had to run any online comments through the PR guy but most of the team were into social media and we all had logins for the big online hockey forum. A lot of the guys recommended getting online and replying to the rival fans and the keyboard warriors but Dennis told me to let it go and not give them any of the attention they so clearly desired.

'This isn't a role you're very good at playing, Davey,' he said. 'So don't go out on stage any more than you absolutely have to.'

'There are exceptions of course but the real tough guys don't generally spend their time trying to talk tough,' he advised.

And Dennis would know.

Unlike me, he's the real deal.

He got his first pair of boxing gloves on his sixth birthday and he's had fourteen professional fights and won eleven of those by knockout.

I was at the last one.

His opponent's key strength seemed to be running his mouth, seems he even tried to talk a little trash while the referee was giving them his instructions.

Sticking your chin right in front of Dennis' fist just isn't a bright move – as he learned.

It took Dennis forty-one seconds to take care of business that night. A jab to the face, which Big Mouth palmed easily, was followed by a double jab that was equally easy to deal with.

Big Mouth actually dropped his guard – no doubt to taunt Dennis for throwing beginner-level punches at him – and that's when the real assault began.

A low left hook to the body was followed by a right hook to the suddenly unprotected jaw. Back up against the ropes and Dennis just unleashing everything in his well-stocked armoury.

The referee was stepping in to stop it at almost exactly the same time as Big Mouth's corner threw in the towel.

When I told the other guys in the team that Dennis was a buddy of mine, they kind of insisted on me inviting him along whenever we went out for a beer.

You know how at school, if you could make friends with the cool kid, then everyone would like you more? Like the coolness would sort of rub off on you? Well, that's how it went for me when some of my new teammates had a beer with Dennis.

If Dennis had been a soccer or basketball player, it wouldn't have had the same effect. But boxing? Boxing's different. Pro hockey players tend to view themselves as the toughest sportsmen on the planet but boxers tend to be thought of as worthy of respect.

A couple of the guys – including big Frankie – had seen Dennis' last fight and started ribbing him about it, asking about a refund since there had been so little of it.

Dennis just snorted and said he provided quality, not quantity and asked if anyone felt they hadn't got their money's worth.

I hardly said a word all night. I just listened as Dennis and the guys talked tough. They were comparing hits (what's worse – a nasty, low uppercut or being cross checked from behind?) and swapping stories all night. I had half wished I'd brought a notebook and pen so that I could keep a record of how Dennis handled very rude, in-your-face, challenging questions with absolute aplomb.

The guys just took to Dennis because he was absolutely the 'real deal' and having him there really helped me fit in during pre-season – but – it did leave me with one more fear.

Dennis knew what I *really* was. He didn't judge me, but he knew.

But I think he may have been the only one.

I'd done a good job in the lead-up to the start of the season and I guess most fans were pretty much convinced I was actually a tough guy.

Just like my dad had been.

I was thinking about that fact as I walked into the dressing room before my first appearance.

When people cast themselves in the role of tough guy sooner or later (usually sooner in hockey) someone will want to see just how tough that person really is.

I absolutely did not want to get hurt.

But having said that, being shown up as a coward in front of the guys from the team and the Sea Devils fans sounded almost as bad.

Let me tell you about ice hockey...

Maybe when you read that I was worried (well, terrified might come closer) about getting hurt on the ice, you thought I was exaggerating a little.

Ever watch a hockey match?

It's actually really easy to follow. Both teams can have five skaters plus their goalie out on the ice at any given moment. There are the usual technicalities and minutiae that you get in any sport but what it boils down to is that when the puck – a little disc of vulcanised rubber – gets dropped between two players in the middle of the rink at the start the game, your aim is to score more goals than the other team.

Simple, right?

Of course, you're doing this on skates.

Ever tried skating?

If you have, then did you manage to do more than walk around the rink, clinging to the wall? Spend a fair amount of time flat on your ass after slipping?

Most people suddenly develop a healthy level of respect for figure skaters or ice dancers after they try to skate themselves.

Even if you manage to do more than just walk slowly while fighting desperately for balance, how fast could you go?

The faster you skate, the less control you have, which means the risk of falling is higher.

How does the idea of falling onto the ice sound?

What would be worse do you think – getting your arm out to break your fall (in which case, goodbye arm) or going into the ice face-first?

And when you play hockey, you aren't going to be walking round the rink. Oh no. You're going to be sprinting. There are pro hockey players who can reach the same speeds as Olympic speed skaters, because you have to be fast if you want to win.

Can you see the possibility for injuries yet?

But wait – because that isn't the whole picture!

You see it would be a tough sport if all you were doing was chasing a tiny disc (maybe half the diameter of a saucer) at full speed across the ice.

But let's remember that your opposition – the other team – is unlikely to be happy at the notion that you're about to score a goal against them.

Colliding with another player – usually at full speed and quite deliberately – is one of the most common occurrences you'll see.

Think about how big a lot of hockey players are. Factor in the armour they wear, plus the speed they can skate at, and the end result is, when someone careers into you, it hurts.

Know what jousting is? Knights in shining armour on horseback, riding at one and other with their lances lowered, intent on knocking the other guy off his horse.

I remember being a little kid and watching some movie on cable with my dad. There was jousting in it. My grandfather walked in just as the good guy got knocked off his horse and when he didn't immediately get back onto his feet, Grandpa Louie disdainfully described him as a pussy.

My dad was shushing him but Grandpa Louie tended to speak his mind.

'You think if I was cross checked that I'd just lie there?' he asked and then jerked a thumb at the knights on the TV screen and said something in French that I didn't understand. At which point my dad ordered him out of the living room.

Grandpa Louie had been the one who taught my dad to skate, then to play hockey. He taught me and my brother Mason too but after a while he just worked with Mason. He wasn't a patient guy and when I refused to do things like skate right into other players he sort of gave up on me.

He would have loved the fact that I'd signed with the Sea Devils while hating the way I played the game.

Looking back though, he was probably right about one thing – jousting looked like baby stuff compared to the hits some pro hockey players took.

The sport is a lot safer now (in Grandpa Louie's day they didn't actually wear helmets) but when you get hit, it hurts.

When you check someone (the technical term for deliberately crashing into them) they're meant to be in possession of the puck but that isn't always how it goes. Sometimes – if the referee's attention is elsewhere – you get checked late, long after you've passed the puck to someone else.

So you're never one hundred percent safe from the moment

you walk out onto the ice.

A lot of checks knock you off your feet – those are bad enough – but sometimes the check doesn't just knock you over. Sometimes you get thrown up against the glass body or (even better) head first.

It's called 'boarding' and generally the fans love it.

Trust me when I say that you can hear the impact when someone gets tossed up against the boards and if you were sitting in the front row to watch the game, you'd probably jump back as the glass shakes under the impact.

Grandpa Louie always used to say that a good hit was one that the people sitting in that front row could practically feel.

Last season, big Frankie (who despite his size can skate at a speed that most speed skaters can only dream of) delivered a body check to Jeff LeRoy from the Piranhas that was so hard he actually put LeRoy *through* the Plexiglas.

Luckily for LeRoy, his helmet took most of the force of the collision and he was fine. I remember seeing that check and imagining Grandpa Louie applauding and yelling, 'THAT's how you make a check!'

Still with me on the possible risks in hockey?

Okay then, let's add in one last factor.

Some hockey teams emphasise speed and some hockey teams emphasise skill.

Others however emphasise violence.

It's a tough game (a contact sport, remember?) but some teams take that into the realm of art. Their checks are late and heavy-handed. Their players – especially their defence or 'D-men' – seem less concerned with stopping shots on goal than they are with inflicting damage on attacking players. With certain teams, if you're skating at their goal and you have the puck, then what you also have is a metaphorical bullseye on your forehead.

You might be horrified at this and ask what the referee is doing while these guys try to crucify attackers?

Well, no matter how good the referee is, he can't be everywhere and see everything.

There are plenty of things – from taking cheap shots to some utterly illegal moves – that even the best referee will miss.

When it's played neutrally, hockey is a dangerous sport but when it's played with what I'll politely describe as ill will the

21

chances of injury skyrocket.

Some teams rely on their rep for nastiness to intimidate rivals (hell, the Piranhas got through to the final last season because of it).

The thing is, once you start getting nasty, it's likely to cause a bit of bad feeling in your rivals (especially if the referee doesn't see it and no penalty gets called).

And those bad feelings bring us to another unique hockey tradition.

Dropping the gloves.

Let me tell you about dropping the gloves...

Sometimes you have to make a point.

Sometimes the opposition bend the rules and they don't get caught. Sometimes the referee just misses the shit they're pulling and other times (for some reason – inexperience or simply because he's *also* intimidated) he sees it but doesn't call it.

You can probably guess what happens if a foul doesn't get called.

That's right, the opposition do it again the first chance they can.

Like a small child pushing its luck and testing its boundaries – you'll watch as your rivals start to up the ante and see what they can get away with (and to be fair, if you had the chance – if you had a weak or wet-behind-the-ears ref – wouldn't you do the same?)

I can't personally recall the last time I saw a team that got away with something breathe a sigh of relief at not getting caught and then behave better thereafter.

No, generally if you get away with some nastiness on the ice, then you'll keep doing it. After all, if you can simply bully the other team off the puck every time they take possession then the game is probably yours.

Officially, it's the referee's job to keep order but, like I said, the ref is only human. He can't have eyes in the back of his head, he physically cannot see it all and everybody out there knows that.

So, officially, keeping control is down to the ref – just like in every other sport you've probably ever seen.

But hockey is different.

In hockey, everybody accepts that their rivals will try their luck and that the ref could well miss it.

Hockey is pretty much unique in that it has an element of what you might describe as 'self-policing'.

Most (not all to be fair, but most) teams will have at least one guy on the squad whose role is defined as 'enforcer'.

The enforcer may or may not be a great hockey player (some – like Ricky McMahon from the Piranhas – are as good at shooting the puck as they are at throwing right hooks while plenty of the enforcers out there can barely skate). It usually doesn't matter if an enforcer scores goals or not, because that isn't his main job.

The enforcer's job is to stop the other team from bullying his team.

Most enforcers are D-men and as a rule they're big guys. When they see their team eating cheap shots or fouls, when the referee seems uninterested, unsure of the rules or blind, they step in.

They don't need an excuse or anyone's permission. They just skate right up to the player who's taking advantage of their teammates and they call that guy out.

For the Sea Devils the enforcer was Frankie.

A nice guy - off ice. A guy with a dumb, goofy sense of humour - off ice. A guy who was a keen charity worker – off ice.

A six foot three human wrecking ball on the ice.

Frankie wants to call somebody out? He makes sure everybody on the ice hears him. Other players, referee, linesmen and those fans nearest him will hear the big man bellow, 'Hey tough guy! You want to go? Yeah, YOU! You want to go?'

Plenty of people have tried their luck with Frankie and almost all have regretted it.

When someone accepts the challenge, you'll see both players skate in and before the bloodshed begins, they both show they're up for this, that they're willing to get into it with the other guy.

They drop their gloves.

Hockey gloves are heavily padded. It's not uncommon to get hit across the hand either by another hockey stick or a flying puck and if your hand gets busted up then you're in trouble – so hockey gloves are heavy.

If you threw a punch at someone while wearing gloves it wouldn't quite be like hitting them with brass knuckles on but it wouldn't be too far removed.

So when you want to go, when you call somebody out, you drop the gloves – shake them off and toss them onto the ice.

Then you skate up close to the other guy and do everything in your power to batter the living daylights out of him.

Once the gloves are dropped, both parties know they'll probably get assigned a penalty as soon as it's over.

They also know that it's one-on-one and that nobody will interfere till it's over.

So nobody holds anything back.

You can't fight for long on skates and you sure as hell can't dance around. So most hockey fights are like old school, bare-knuckle brawls. Toe-to-toe, wailing away at the other guy till one of you hits the ice.

You know the old joke: 'There was a fight and then an ice hockey match broke out'? It's pretty much true. When my buddy Dennis saw some of the hockey fights (especially big Frankie's greatest hits) he was kind of appalled.

'Most of these guys aren't exactly skilful', he told me. 'Put me in front of them in the ring and I'd be confident of the win. Put me in front of them anywhere else and I'd not be so sure!'

Dennis offered (as he's probably done maybe a dozen times before) to take me to the gym he trains at and show me a few things. I turned him down of course, just like he knew I would.

'Play your game your way, Davey boy', he said. 'Don't you *ever* let these psychos catch you flat-footed out there.'

I remember laughing, nodding and then we bumped fists like we always do and I tried not to show how terrified I was of getting caught.

I'm fast.

In the minor leagues, I was ridiculously quicker than my nearest rivals and I'd avoided taking too many bumps because I was just too quick to catch.

But by pulling on the blue and green jersey and icing for the Sea Devils, I knew I was stepping up a league. There were plenty of skaters out there who could keep up with me. And I knew it.

It was a frightening thought but joining the Sea Devils was still the best career option I had by far.

Plus the Devils were well known for being a very tightknit bunch of guys and I'd have big Frankie watching my back while I was on the ice.

I'm a coward so when I tell you that I had absolutely no intention of ever dropping the gloves with anyone, you can take that to the bank.

The Sea Devils fans loved it when it got physical on the ice but I wasn't there to fight.

My job was to score goals.

The testosterone levels in the dressing rooms were sky-high when I arrived for my first appearance as a Sea Devil.

Everybody in there knew the Sea Devils' fans (the 'blue and

green machine' as they were known) wanted to see a little blood.

But I comforted myself with the knowledge that, while the fans liked violence, they were also really keen on seeing goals scored and games won.

That I could do for them.

Let me tell you about the blue and green machine...

There are loud fans, really loud fans and then there are the Sea Devils fans.

St Helens has never been a rich, well-off place. It was a fishing town back in the day and the people there have endured more than one tragedy when fishing boats were lost at sea. Winters in St Helens were as bitter as anything Canada could throw at you – a fact that the inhabitants seemed almost proud of. St Helens was the kind of place that bred tough people – hard-bitten people, survivors.

They've never had a football team there – there just wasn't the appetite for it.

Hockey was different though.

Hockey was the thing the town had a passion for and took pride in and they weren't shy about telling you that.

Damn, but these guys were LOUD.

Once the puck dropped, the blue and green machine would make its presence felt. When the Sea Devils had the puck and were on the attack, they were bellowing their approval. When the Sea Devils conceded a goal or were getting outplayed, the fans actually seemed to get louder. The blue and green machine would loudly demand that the guys on the ice dug deep and would shriek their support at them as they battled back.

There's an old sports cliché about how a really passionate crowd getting behind their team can be a game-winning advantage. The blue and green machine *are* that crowd.

Some of the players actually acknowledge what a difference the blue and green machine makes as they skate past them. They tuck their hockey stick under their arm so that they can have both hands free and they hold up all fingers on one hand plus the thumb and first finger on the other. Seven fingers held up to represent the team of six plus the seventh man – the crowd.

The fans and the players are tight in St Helens. All the barriers that separate the two groups in other places don't exist there. The players regularly interact with fans online and they turn up for fan club meetings which are usually public and often full and frank in nature. They'll cheer when you're winning and they'll cheer when you're losing but in return they expect you to put heart and soul into every game you play while you're wearing the blue and green jersey. Woe unto anyone who ices for St Helens and then seems content to just phone in their performance! It's their passion and once you pull that jersey on, it has to be yours too.

My dad once told me about how he went to a fan club meeting. The Sea Devils had actually won the game (one nil with the game's only goal coming in overtime) against a rival team they should have comprehensively hammered.

My dad told the assembled crowd that he and the guys had been exhausted after playing three road games on the trot. He admitted they'd been tired and their hearts hadn't been in it.

He told the blue and green machine that he and the rest of the team knew the fans deserved better and they *would* provide it.

This, remember, was after a game they won.

The blue and green machine made a point of packing out the next game at the nearby St Pierre Arena against the then top-of-the-league Serpents. They lost by a single goal against the team that had won just about everything in the last two years. The whole team played out of their skins that night and my dad (when he called home just after the game like he always did) said he'd just had the game of his life.

I've often wondered if all the effort he put in - going that extra mile for the fans - exhausted him too much. I've asked myself if maybe he was too tired and sore to have been behind the wheel of a car after the game because that was the night of the crash.

There's no way to tell of course, but it meant I always got a rush of memories when I heard the chants and songs the blue and green machine sang. I loved them with a passion. These guys were the kind of crowd that any sportsman would kill to play in front of but I knew it was almost inevitable that, when I took to the ice, someone would greet me with the chant they used to have for my dad. As soon as that happened, I knew it was going to take everything I had to focus on the game instead of thinking back to the funerals I'd attended while I lived in St Helens.

They were going to want a reaction - hell, they were going to want me to be a carbon copy of my dad, but that wasn't going to happen.

Back in the day, when the blue and green machine began to

chant: 'Send! For! Jonesy! Send! For! Jonesy!' my dad would skate out with a flourish and do his damnedest to get them a goal.

My dad was a showman as much as an athlete.

Me? I'm pretty much a simple, meat-and-potatoes, get-the-job-done kind of guy. I don't do razzle-dazzle, but I *do* score goals.

I'm a sniper not a play maker.

Someone has to run the puck up through the other team's defence and into striking distance of their goal.

That isn't me.

Odds of getting checked, boarded or simply knocked off my feet are way too high for my liking when you do that.

But if someone else can get the puck up past the opposition's defence, then I have a knack of being able to drift up that end of the ice. I'm pretty good at getting up close and into perfect position to receive a pass or to pounce on a rebound.

I'm exactly the kind of player that most D-men despise. I don't take many (if any) risks but, if you can keep feeding me the puck, I can put it in the back of the net often enough to make the opposition fans weep.

The best moment of my career before signing with St Helens was when I put six goals past the net minder of a rival team and his coach (seeing the guy's morale and confidence had taken enough of a beating) pulled him off the ice and put the backup goalie in instead.

The opposition's enforcer was absolutely furious, of course. He was all set to drop the gloves and that was the point where I skated back to the bench complaining of a muscle pull in my arm.

It was late in the third period. It would have taken a miracle for the opposition to overturn six unanswered goals and my then coach knew damned well that, if he let me skate back onto the ice, I'd probably get a beating that'd make me a non-starter for the game the following night.

So – much to the irritation of a certain six foot two enforcer – I stayed off ice for the rest of the game.

I wasn't injured of course.

I was just giving the coach an excuse to bench me.

There were catcalls and boos for the remaining few minutes of the game but there was nothing the opposition could do.

When both teams went back onto the ice at the end of the match to shake hands, their enforcer pulled me in close and whispered, 'You're a gutless son of a bitch, you know that? Your dad would have stood his ground.'

I pulled my hand free and gave him my best smile. 'True,' I said. 'My dad never was that bright.'

He looked disgusted and skated off.

I said a prayer that night – an Act of Contrition – apologising to my dad for what I'd said about him.

He left a hell of a legacy. And I knew I had a big pair of shoes to try and fill.

I also knew that the blue and green machine would expect me to try.

Some of them still had (and still wore) hockey jerseys they'd bought back in the eighties when my dad was still playing.

I couldn't be a showman. I just didn't have it in me.

But I could score goals.

The blue and green machine liked goals almost as much as they liked to see the gloves dropped.

No player really succeeds at St Helens without winning over the blue and green machine and my strategy for doing so was very simple. I was going to sneak as close to our rival's goal as I could, then hammer as many pucks into the net as possible.

I knew that some of the fans would be disappointed that I didn't play exactly like my old man but I figured that after a few games (and a few goals) they'd accept that I was a very different kind of player. And accept me.

I had it all worked out: skate safe, avoid trouble and be clinical about burying the puck in the back of the net.

It seemed like a winning strategy right up till our opponents for game one of the season were announced.

When I discovered who we were playing in game one, I knew that my strategy had just been shot full of holes.

My new strategy was very different.

My new strategy was to just make it off the ice alive.

Let me tell you about the Dragons...

It would be in no way unfair to say that there was something of a rivalry between the Sea Devils and Dragons.

In point of fact, the word 'rivalry' may be a little too mild a term to describe the nature of the games played between the two clubs. One TV pundit put it beautifully when he suggested there had probably been Ozarks of hillbilly clans locked in a blood feud who were more likely to be forgiving than Devils or Dragons fans were.

The Douglasville Dragons were the one team that the blue and green machine did *not* like to lose to. The St Helens fans were never more vocal than when they played their most despised rivals. Sea Devils versus Dragons was guaranteed to be a real needle match. And any hopes I'd had that the venom was restricted to the fans pretty much vanished as soon as I walked into the locker room to get changed.

The dislike between the two teams wasn't faked to sell tickets like some pro-wrestling show. Oh Lord, no! The two groups of players had a real and active dislike for one another and with good reason.

Three years before I joined St Helens, their top goal scorer was a guy called Tony Patton. He was a big guy, a power forward who would fearlessly run the puck straight into the opposition's defence.

He was tough, he was consistently scoring goals and (to the horror of the blue and green machine) he was poached by the Dragons just after the halfway point in the season.

In his first match against his old club he scored three of the four goals in a four–nil thrashing of St Helens.

This – understandably – didn't go down all that well with either the fans or the players from St Helens. It might have been brushed over had it not been for a little victory dance that Patton did after he put the puck in the net for the third time.

He made a point of beating his chest and shouting, 'WHO'S NUMBER ONE?' as he skated past the Sea Devils fans who were loudly booing him.

That chest beating and the trash talking were a step too far and that was when things got all kinds of nasty.

Patton was still loudly telling the world that he'd scored the 'best damn hat-trick of my career' when big Frankie skated slowly and very deliberately over to his ex-colleague and got right in his face.

The arena actually got quiet as the two men had words – none of the officials dared restart play – they were all staring at the two ex-teammates standing centre ice as they traded words.

Then Patton gave Frankie what could be best described as a disdainful shove.

Two seconds later the gloves were off and there was blood on the ice.

They took a grip of each other's jerseys to help keep their balance and Patton scored first – landing a jab in Frankie's face, then another.

Watch the video of that fight sometime and you'll see the look on Frankie's face. He winces when he gets hit (especially that second punch because it bloodied his nose) but, apart from that, he's just glaring at Patton, staring at him like he's some kind of inferior life form.

Dragons fans will tell you that Frankie was taken aback at how fast Patton could punch but truth is, Frankie just stood there and took a couple of shots. He was staring at Patton as if to say, 'Is that it? Is that all you've got?' Then, just as Patton tries to manoeuvre around to launch a hook, Frankie got down to business.

The jab Frankie started in with wasn't exactly a perfect punch. My buddy Dennis would probably have called it scrappy.

But it stopped Patton in his tracks and it was just the opening salvo in the blitzkrieg Frankie then unleashed.

Right hook followed right hook as Frankie rained down blows on Patton and as Frankie's third big punch connected, Patton's feet went from under him and he was down on the ice.

Now, most of the time – not always in fairness – but most of the time, if you put the other guy down in a hockey fight, you've won and that's the signal to stop beating on him and take yourself over to the penalty box.

But on this occasion, once Patton's ass hit the ice, the assault didn't stop.

Whatever Patton had said to Frankie had clearly pissed of the Sea Devil's enforcer more than just a little and he continued to slam punches into Patton.

Cue two Dragons players launching themselves at Frankie in a bid to knock him onto the ice.

Cue two Sea Devils players skating right into those Dragons players to intercept them.

Cue a bench clearance about thirty seconds later with every player from both teams (including the goalies) on the ice throwing punches.

It would be far from unfair to suggest that relations between the two clubs have not really improved since then. If anything, they'd probably deteriorated.

Last season before I arrived, the two teams met four times. Every one of those four games saw frequent penalties - three of which led to multiple game suspensions – and one almost career-ending injury.

Before I arrived, the Sea Devil's golden boy was Danny Kane. I'd be skating on the same line as him when I made my debut for St Helens and I liked him, although his attitude was one that I just couldn't understand.

See, Danny was almost hyperactive in the changing room. He was pacing up and down and he was talking so fast that at times I didn't catch what he was saying.

He was excited.

Really, really excited.

Hyped, stoked, ready to get out there on the ice and do or die.

The one thing he wasn't was scared and that made no sense to me because Danny had been the one who'd been hit so hard the previous season that he'd been lucky not to wind up in a wheelchair.

He had scored two goals and was skating up the ice again, banging his stick to signal that he was open and to pass him the puck so he could try for his hat-trick.

The puck was duly passed to him.

It had literally just touched his stick when two Dragons players - one of whom had been practically stalking him since they knew he was a danger to them - both went in for the check. One hit him high while the other caught him low.

Even the Dragons fans – normally more than happy to mock the fallen – went silent as a stretcher was brought onto the ice.

'It's not going to be two goals tonight. It's not even going to be three goals tonight!' Danny proclaimed as he pulled his jersey on. 'I'm going to put SIX goals past them boys! I am going to make their fans WEEP!'

Everyone laughed and applauded or banged their sticks on the ground at that.

I joined in but I couldn't get my head around it.

Why wasn't Danny scared?

Okay, technically St Helens were the better team. We had the speed and the skill and that counted for a lot.

But the Dragons had their strengths too.

They had assembled a roster full of tough guys and hard cases. Not exactly the most skilful of hockey players but as brutal a bunch of goons as you could hope not to meet on the ice.

Oh, and they also had their secret weapon.

One player who, on his own, had pretty much guaranteed Douglasville win after win but not because he scored goals.

On a team packed full of brawlers, he stood out because of both his size and his ferocity.

We called him the Ogre.

Let me tell you about the Ogre...

Do you know what an ogre is?

If you're not sure, then the best place to look is in a book of fairy tales.

Not the sanitised version of fairy tales though, not the stories populated with singing cats and dogs where a happy ending is always guaranteed.

No, if you want to discover what an ogre *really* is, you need to go back to the real fairy tales, the tales of the Brothers Grimm, where people would end up beaten, mutilated and killed and where there was absolutely no guarantee that the ending couldn't turn out to be written in blood.

Those are the stories where you'll discover what an ogre is.

Ogres are monsters.

Huge, immensely strong, flesh-eating monsters.

Ogres were the ones to ambush unwary travellers and beat them to death with clubs, hammers or just their bare hands.

Ogres were the creatures in the fairy tales who stole and ate babies.

'Ogre' therefore was the perfect nickname for the Dragons top D-Man, Ollie Brooks.

Brooks wasn't just big – he was huge.

A monster of a man at six feet seven in height who had the kind of muscles that even the most serious bodybuilders and power lifters would sell their souls for.

He always shaved his hair off at the start of a new hockey season but he allowed the beard he was sporting no more than a quick trim. His huge shoulders and immensely powerful arms were covered in tattoos of skulls, demons and daggers.

Image was all to Mr Brooks.

He dressed a certain way, acted a certain way and woe unto anyone who did not treat him a certain way.

Pretty much nobody in the Sea Devils' dressing room planned on treating the Ogre as he wanted to be treated and most of the team had been fairly public in telling him that on social media and through our PR junkets.

'Why would we respect Brooks?' Danny Kane had rather

pointedly asked during an interview for a local radio station. 'He doesn't score goals, can hardly pass the puck worth a damn and spends most of his season in the penalty box!'

This wasn't actually an unfair commentary on the Ogre.

On paper, Ollie Brooks shouldn't have been in a pro hockey team. Take a look at his stats and you'll see what I mean. In four years with Douglasville, he'd managed to rack up a rather unimpressive three assists and one single, solitary goal.

He had also managed to get himself banned for more games than any other Dragons player although some commentators suggested – given some of his misdeeds on the ice – that in and of itself was impressive as it meant he'd never been banned for life from the game or faced assault charges.

Looking at those stats, you'd come away with the impression that he was a liability and, to an extent, you'd be right.

But what the stats don't do is spell out the sheer fear factor the Ogre gave off and the impact on the morale of just about any team in the league as soon as they saw Brooks take to the ice.

There were virtually no fouls in the game of hockey that Brooks hadn't committed.

He would board people using his massive bulk to slam them up into the glass and, while he made plenty of legitimate hits, he would also board people from behind. Being on the receiving end of a cheap shot from a guy the Ogre's size just didn't bear thinking about.

He had cross-checked, using his stick to smash people into the boards and he had dropped the gloves with every tough guy in the league. He had speared one opponent with his stick and had been banned for an elbow to the jaw that could have put the player he hit into a coma.

If an ogre from the fairy tales ever ran into Brooks, I reckon it'd take one look, tuck tail and run.

Of course, once the puck dropped, tucking tail and running wasn't going to be a realistic option for anyone wearing a blue and green jersey.

As I tied my boots on, I remember wondering if there was some superstition I could concoct to allow me an escape clause that night because, although I genuinely didn't believe in superstitions, I was getting a genuinely bad feeling. My stomach felt like it had been tied in knots as I started to put my pads on.

I had no idea what the mood in the Dragons dressing room was like but in our room it felt like the team was getting ready to go to war.

I'd never been in a big clique or gang at high school (the role I tended to have back then was of victim since I was usually the one who got picked on) but I figured that if I had been, if I'd been part of one big gang laying plans for a full-scale brawl with another gang, that's how it'd feel.

The mood in the room could best be described as bloodthirsty.

Usually the guys told me that big Frankie was the calm one before the game. They would sort of get themselves centred, get their game faces on in the room and Frankie being so calm and collected helped them all get mentally prepared.

But not that night.

You see, Brooks and Frankie had kind of a history – Frankie being the first guy to ever put the Ogre on his ass.

They'd dropped the gloves half a dozen times since then with Frankie usually losing.

Watching Frankie getting his game face on was just plain scary.

When I first walked into the dressing room, he was already there – that wasn't unusual. Frankie was almost always the first guy at the rink all the way through the pre-season.

What was different was that he wasn't sitting in the middle of the group cracking goofy jokes.

That night he was off in the far corner on his own, shadow-boxing.

Dennis could probably have told you if he was any good – I was never much of an expert – but he looked like he was in the zone.

He wasn't moving about much – wasn't dancing like Dennis would have done. Hockey fights aren't like boxing matches. Once you get a grip of one another there usually isn't much dancing around – you're toe-to-toe with the other guy and nobody dances about much because when you're on skates that just isn't an option.

Frankie was feigning how he'd shoot out his left hand to grab a nice, tight hold of the other guy's jersey, then mimed throwing a right hook abut jaw level.

He feigned jabs and uppercuts and the look in his eyes was one of absolute commitment. If I'd seen Frankie bearing down on me with that look on his face, I'd have run for my life.

Ollie Brooks' reaction to seeing that same look however was likely to be a bit different to mine.

I remember that I'd just dumped my bag on the bench when I heard the first thump.

I heard another and another and, when I turned to look, I saw Frankie driving his fists into the wall.

He wasn't Superman. The wall itself didn't shake then crumble. Frankie was a big guy, but he was just flesh and bone like you and me.

But he didn't flinch.

And, man, he was hitting *hard*.

No matter how tough you were, if you got caught cleanly by big Frankie, you were going down.

As his punches struck the wall, his expression changed completely.

Frankie, the goofy, upbeat guy was morphing into Frankie, the Sea Devil's enforcer.

As the speed of his punches picked up, he was snarling, growling, and hissing words under his breath.

'Brooks is going *down*!' I heard Danny Kane suddenly declare and a second later most of the guys were banging their hockey sticks on the ground in a weird version of applause.

When Frankie turned round, the look in his eyes was dead, like a shark would give you before it tore a chunk off of you.

The knuckles on his left hand were bleeding.

Danny pointed out the blood and Frankie shrugged, said it didn't mean shit, wiped his hand clean and taped over his knuckles.

'The Ogre is going down!' Danny repeated excitedly.

Everyone was nodding. The level of aggression in the room was off the chart.

We all knew the Ogre was going to cut up rough with someone.

We just all thought it'd be with Frankie.

Let me tell you about Coach Williams...

I had just finished putting on my armour and had taken my Sea Devils jersey out of my bag when all the chatter in the room suddenly stopped.

Most of the coaches I'd had in the past had to bang a hand on the door for a while to get everyone's attention. Pre-game, everyone has nerves and most dressing rooms are loud with talk and nervous laughter. One coach I knew brought a whistle into the room and blew it till the hubbub subsided.

The head coach of the Sea Devils, however, had no need to resort to that kind of thing.

When Coach Williams walked into the dressing room, he didn't need to ask for your attention – you just automatically gave it to him.

He had played for St Helens himself years ago at the same time as my dad. Even now, he was still a big guy, maybe six feet tall and heavily built. There might have been a hint of grey in his hair and beard but you'd never mistake him for some kind of gentle, elderly uncle. He had a little semi-circular scar under his left eye – a memento from when someone had high-sticked him and nearly taken that eye out. The beating he laid on the perpetrator earned him a four game ban and a big fine. The blue and green machine started a collection and actually paid the fine for him.

He was a solid, dependable and often very blunt-spoken man who had no patience whatsoever with fools.

He eyed Frankie when he walked in, his gaze going straight to the tape on Frankie's hand.

'That better not slow your punches or rob them of their stopping power, Frankie-boy,' he said quietly.

'It won't be a problem, coach,' Frankie replied meekly, like a school boy caught in the act by the headmaster.

'It better not,' Coach Williams told him. 'If you want to vent some fury we have a perfectly good punch bag in the gym. And if you make a mess of the wall,' (he nodded to the little spots of blood on the wall) 'then I expect you to clean it up after you're done. Clear?'

Frankie nodded and our coach looked slowly around the room – his eyes resting for a second on each player in turn – before walking into the centre of the room.

'Alright, gentleman, pay attention to me, this is how it's going to go tonight.'

Some coaches got all happy-clappy when they delivered a team talk. Others just rained down verbal abuse on you and told you that if you didn't score goals and knock the other team onto their asses, that you were less than a man.

I didn't much care for either approach.

The happy-clappy ones – who told you that you were just awesome before you'd actually hit a puck across the ice – made me sigh and roll my eyes. The others were just bullies and I've got too many bad memories to ever find being yelled at motivational.

Coach Williams didn't do either of these.

Oh, it wasn't that he was in any way incapable of delivering a blistering mouthful of abuse. He was in fact well known for making his views on referees and opposition players fairly public (and his voice carried – sometimes to the other side of the arena).

But, as I'd learned in pre-season, that was our head coach's public persona.

In the dressing room, it was just him talking to us. He never needed to shout because we were all ears.

'I could draw you some complex-looking plans,' he began. 'I could highlight some nice, technical way to implement our system and lay some pro level strategies on you. And, you know what? I probably will do that; but not tonight. The complex strategies, the chess game on the ice, are for when we play a real hockey team, not some bunch of apes in red jerseys.'

That brought smiles and a bit of laughter.

'Tonight we're taking to the ice against a team who throw a party and run up the flags if it manages to get to the end of the game without a ban. You aren't meant to put skates on a gorilla – in my opinion that's a form of animal cruelty - but that seems to be what our good friends in Douglasville have done.'

The smiles got broader as Coach Williams warmed to his theme.

'Some of the guys we're playing tonight will refuse to insult you verbally. That's not out of good manners, it's because they don't have an IQ high enough to allow them to talk and skate at the same time.'

Even I was grinning at that point.

The coach waited for us to simmer down before going on.

'They're a team of goons, plain and simple. The one quality player they have is their goalie. Besides him, the others aren't in our class. Some can barely skate. They're thugs, but you have to – all of you – remember, that they're dangerous thugs.'

He paused and looked pointedly over at Danny.

'It's taken me months to get you guys together and I'm not looking for any early injuries to mess up my nice plans for the season. Is everybody crystal clear on that?'

We all affirmed that we were.

That part of Coach Williams' talk – as you can imagine – resonated rather strongly with me.

'Nothing fancy tonight guys. No complex plans or weird formations. Tonight we play things strictly in accordance with my golden rules. I know that some of you know them, while you new guys don't, so I'm going to spell them out for all of you. Everyone listening?'

Every head nodded.

'Rule number one. We give nothing away for free. They want to pass the puck? We're in their face trying to intercept. They want to run with the puck? We're right on them and looking to check. They want to take a shot at goal? We're right on them, screwing up their concentration and their aim. We give nothing for free. They want it? It has to cost them.'

We all nodded, me with a lot more reluctance. There was little chance of me trying to block, much less check, a Dragons player.

'Rule number two. Our heads never go down. If they score - hell, even if they put a dozen damn goals past us – we don't quit. We keep our heads up at all times – no matter what.'

Again, everyone nodded (although I had to admit that if we went twelve-nil down, I doubted I'd be anything *other* than demoralised).

'The third and most important rule is the one I want you all to have in the front of your minds every time you step onto the ice. The third and final golden rule is the one I want burned into your minds in letters of fire! You all listening to me?' He raised his voice sharply and we all barked a loud affirmative at him. 'The third rule is that we look after our own. Out there on the ice? You watch each other's backs, you stick up for your team mates and you do all in your power to protect one another.' He paused and again looked around the room, making eye contact with each player. 'We clear?' he growled.

There were loud shouts of 'Yes Coach!' and he repeated his question, only a lot louder, bellowing 'ARE WE CLEAR?'

Loud cries of 'HELL YES COACH!' filled the room accompanied by the loud crack-crack-crack of hockey sticks being beaten against the floor in acknowledgement.

He let the noise go on for a few seconds before raising his hands for silence.

'Cruel World starts shortly gentlemen. Get your shit together. We've got a team of goons to hammer.'

Let me tell you about hockey armour...

Hockey is a contact sport – if you play it, you wear armour.

Sadly, we don't get to wear quite enough padding to keep us completely unaffected by a full-force body check, but we do get to buckle or strap on some protection to cut down on the probable injuries we'll take.

You know, I've heard people who follow other sports question the bravery or manliness of people in sports like hockey and maybe football, just because of the pads we wear.

I saw some guys online talking about rugby and comparing it to hockey and gridiron. According to the commentator, rugby players were just plain tougher because they wore no protective gear at all but still tackled each other full force.

I can completely respect that.

From what I've seen (and the guy who started the conversation had attached some video links to the kind of hits rugby players take) rugby looks to be a tough sport.

But let's keep it in perspective here, it isn't hockey.

In hockey what we're chasing is the puck – a small disc of hardened rubber.

Hockey players get really good at hitting the puck so hard they can send that little lump of rubber across the ice at speeds of up to one hundred miles an hour. Think I'm joking? Look it up and once you've confirmed that I'm right, type "injuries inflicted when struck by a hockey puck" into your search engine and read what comes back.

If a rugby ball hits you full force in the chest, then I guess you're going to be winded.

If a hockey puck was to crash into your chest travelling at that kind of speed?

Well, let's just say that I've a *big* believer in wearing armour.

The only trouble with wearing armour of course is how long it takes to put it on.

Once you've got your skates and pads on, it's not quite so easy to get to the bathroom, and as Coach Williams left the dressing room, my bladder suddenly let me know that emptying it might be a really smart idea.

I hesitated.

The other guys were getting set to walk out as a group and I didn't want to look like I was acting the diva by not joining in. But I *really* needed to go.

There had been absolutely no way in hell I'd have walked out while Coach Williams was talking but once he'd gone it was different.

As I dithered, it was Frankie who came to my rescue.

'You okay?' he enquired.

I admitted I needed to pee as quietly as I could and Frankie rolled his eyes and said he'd cover for me – just to hurry the hell up.

'So long as we're there for Cruel World starting, we're good,' he assured me and I got to the bathroom as quick as I could manage while wearing skates.

Frankie was waiting as I made my way back in.

I grabbed my jersey and pulled it over my head then picked up my stick and helmet.

'Alright Superstar,' Frankie said. 'Time to meet the Dragons.'

Let me tell you about the build-up...

There's a definite rhythm to the start of any Sea Devils game.

There are almost always some fans there early, mainly the ones who want to watch the teams warm up just before the game begins.

When I made my way onto the ice for warm-up, I heard some clapping and raised my hand to the fans – many of whom were wearing old-school blue and green jerseys from the period when my dad played. Given their ages, I guessed a lot of them had been fans at that time and had probably bought those jerseys back in the late eighties – and still wore them.

The age of a jersey was sort of a badge in the blue and green machine as it gave an indication of how long you'd been a fan. Some of the fans yelling out welcomes to me as warm-up began had clearly been following St Helens for at least a couple of decades. One or two had their kids (or maybe it was their grandkids) with them.

Like I said, people from St Helens took their hockey *very* seriously.

My stomach did a backflip as I took in how intently the St Helens faithful were watching me and it was suddenly all I could do not to skate straight off and go and hide in the dressing room.

They were watching me and weighing up every little thing I did.

And I knew that most of them would be comparing me to my dad, wondering if I would play like him, fight like him and give my all for them like him.

'Hey! Superstar!' Danny shouted. As I turned Danny promptly sent one of the warm-up pucks my way.

I almost didn't go for it.

Almost.

But I'd been playing hockey for practically as long as I'd been walking and sometimes your body moves before you even have the chance to think about it.

I trapped the puck neatly as it came my way, exploded forward the way my dad had first taught me years ago and, as Danny hollered his encouragement, I drove the puck forward at our goalie and lifted it slightly as I took the shot.

Hockey goalies – you know them, the ones who have to wear

those scary-looking full face masks – have a big stick in one hand and their free hand is covered in a big, heavily-padded glove, kind of like a baseball pitcher's mitt. Most goalies are pretty good on their glove side and our keeper – Robbie Murphy – was no exception. Robbie was damn good on his glove side.

Which didn't stop me burying the puck neatly in the back of his net.

Robbie gave me a glower (he didn't even like to miss a glove side save in practice) and Danny laughed, skated over and we bumped knuckles.

I made a point of ignoring the fast-moving skaters wearing red jerseys who were all staying obediently on the other half of the ice.

We'd already had plenty of time in pre-season to get used to the way we played. Our warm-up at St Helens was literally that – a chance to stretch, take a few practice shots and get your head in the game.

A siren pierced the air - the signal that it was time to get off the ice.

It didn't feel like we'd been out there any time at all. As I followed Danny back to the home side of the arena, I could see that the King Centre had seriously filled up. Fans from home and away had made their way to their seats.

As we assembled again in the tunnel that led from the dressing room to the ice, we stepped aside for the two kids – both shaking with nerves – who were about to skate onto the arena.

The music got a little louder and a little more insistent as the two kids – members of the L'il Devils, our Pee Wee team – skated out to a round of applause from the crowd.

Both of them carried a flag.

The flags were dark blue to represent the sea (where at one point most of the jobs in St Helens had been) with a stylised, green-skinned monster on it.

People in the crowd were clapping along to the music. Like I said, there's always a rhythm to these events. The mascots skate on, the music gets louder and every fan worth their salt knows it's time to leave the bar or stop that heated discussion over who the greatest D-man was in club history and get to their seat.

It's nearly time for Cruel World.

As we watched the mascots, one of them – he must have been only five or six – slipped.

This little kid fell on his face, the Devils flag slipped out of his hands and when he raised his head he looked like he was about to cry his eyes out.

The crowd – and I mean both home *and* away fans – suddenly began to clap and shout their encouragement.

One of the linesmen had skated on to see if the kid was okay.

I couldn't hear what was being said but the kid suddenly, violently, shook his head and managed to get hold of the flag and back up onto his feet.

As the kid pushed himself forward, he managed to snap the flag out so that it was flying properly again as he skated on.

A big cheer went up – again from both sets of fans.

It was actually a nice moment.

It wasn't destined to last though.

Soon the two L'il Devils had skated off and the loud rock track that had been playing came to an end.

Then – as it always did – the King Centre went quiet.

Everyone knew what was coming next.

I wanted to turn and run. I really did.

Call it a premonition if you believe in that kind of thing. I don't – but I had such a bad feeling that I felt like I might actually be sick.

The silence went on for a minute or two. No music, no chatter, no clapping.

Then – finally - the lights went out and a cheer that was practically a roar came from the blue and green machine.

It was time for Cruel World.

JOHN McKINSTRY

Let me tell you about Cruel World...

Every Sea Devils fan knows Cruel World.

It was effectively adopted as the club's anthem back in the early eighties and it's still the music the team take to the ice to today.

It starts slowly and softly.

An acoustic guitar is all you hear in the intro. It's probably best described as brooding – maybe even ominous – and when it starts, the King Centre lights up.

Just about every fan holds up their cell phone to display either a blue or green background. There are groups of fans who deliberately arrange themselves so as to be able to show alternating blue and green lights.

Hundreds – sometimes thousands – of these blue and green lights mark out the fact that this is Sea Devils territory.

And that's when the rivals have to take to the ice.

Even the friendliest of rival teams will probably describe St Helens as a tough rink to play at.

As Billy Wade – the man who has been the "Voice of the King Centre" practically since it opened – announces 'Ladies and Gentlemen, please welcome tonight's opponents, the Douglasville Dragons!' the boos were already echoing loudly from the stands so loudly they almost drown out the music.

The rivalry between St Helens and Douglasville was after all anything but friendly.

The Dragons skated on, some of them egging on the crowd's reaction by banging their sticks against the Plexiglas as they skated past the home fans.

The music – that brooding guitar track – slowly fades and the drumbeat starts.

The St Helens crowd join in.

Clap.

Clap.

Clap-clap, clap-clap.

On the album the drumbeat is still soft but in a packed out King Centre the noise is thunderous.

Clap.

Clap.

Clap-clap, clap-clap.

Then the whisky-drenched voice of singer Jimmy Crowe starts to intone softly that we are, all of us, born into a cruel, cruel world.

Jimmy and his band, Shipwreck, had an unexpected hit with the song back in eighty-seven. The whole band is from St Helens and when Jimmy sings, you can hear that lilt in his voice that a lot of folk from St Helens have.

The members of Shipwreck were all hockey fans. Jimmy would play gigs wearing his St Helens jersey so, when the song became a hit, it was a no-brainer that they'd play it at the games.

I'm the only one in the tunnel not using my stick to tap along to the song.

I love the song because it reminds me of my dad and all his achievements and I hate it because every time I hear it I'm reminded that he's gone.

My grip on my stick is like a vice and as the music starts to get louder, I know my breathing has gotten faster too.

An electric guitar joins with that insistent drumbeat as Jimmy sings that we're all born to fall.

That we're all born to die.

I tell myself that it's just a damned song and breathe out hard like the therapists taught me to.

But as I try to focus, I know that this isn't just a song. It's an anthem.

As Jimmy's voice whispers that they tell us not to rise, I know this song embodies everything it means to wear the blue and green jersey. It's about never quitting. It's about refusing to accept defeat.

When Timur Volkov played for the Sea Devils, he apparently disapproved of Cruel World and told Coach Williams that he didn't want to have to hear it in practice. Cruel World was a loud rock track and not at all to Timur's taste.

While several players skated prudently away (waiting for the inevitable explosion from the St Helens coach) Timur went on to say that he preferred to practise in silence.

Coach Williams did not simply eviscerate the Russian power forward however.

He had him wait where he was on the ice, while the coach popped off to get something.

When Coach Williams returned, he had printed off a copy of

the lyrics to Cruel World, which he asked the Russian to memorise so he could sing the song from that point onwards during practice.

Volkov objected strenuously, saying that singing along to some dirge-like piece of music would not do anything to develop his skill.

To his surprise, Volkov found our head coach completely agreed. The song would not affect his skill. Singing the song had nothing to do with techniques or tactics, the coach had explained.

But, it had *everything* to do with pride.

A year later, Volkov returned to the King Centre as acting captain of the Wolves. On paper, the Wolves should have walked all over lowly St Helens as they had a collection of star players in that team.

Trouble was they didn't *play* as a team.

Volkov later confessed that when he'd heard Cruel World on his return to St Helens, he had finally understood its importance.

St Helens were a tight-knit team who worked together, whereas the Wolves were a bunch of individuals – many of whom saw their own teammates, rather than the opposition, as their rivals.

The Sea Devils hammered the Wolves six-two that night and Timur apologised to Coach Williams for ever doubting him.

As the music continued to get louder, I found I was fighting the urge to join in with the others and bang my stick against the ground to the beat.

Timur had apparently hated how dark the song's lyrics were.

As the spotlights began to sweep the ice, I could hear the lyrics the Russian player had found so distasteful start to pound out.

Jimmy Crowe's voice rising from a whisper to a snarl as he told us our wings would be broken to prevent us from flying and our lives would be pain until our moment of dying.

I crushed down a mental image of my dad in a burning car trying to free himself from a seatbelt that had jammed and wouldn't open.

I had known the memories would return to me and thought I'd been prepared for them but I wasn't. All I could think of was the night my dad had gone to the St Pierre Arena and my brother Mason and I had both been due to accompany him. I had gotten a cold and my mom kept me home but Mason had gone along.

Some people had actually described Mason as the lucky one.

The eighteen-wheeler that had struck my dad's car had slammed into the passenger side killing my big brother instantly.

My dad though had been alive and unable to move when the car caught fire.

The music was getting louder and louder.

I had heard the song week in, week out when my dad played but had never consciously played it since.

I can remember my dad skating out onto the ice with the song thundering out.

My mind filled with images of my dad and my brother and my body became almost completely tensed up - I was grinding my teeth and clenching my fists.

I felt like something inside of me was going to burst.

Then I suddenly brought my stick down hard on the ground.

Frankie clapped me on the shoulder as I joined in with the others and the blue and green faithful in the audience.

Clap.

Clap.

Clap-clap, clap-clap.

The song began to build its crescendo as Jimmy Crowe bellowed 'We shall rise!'

Clap!

Clap!

Clap-clap, clap-clap!

See us rise. Jimmy yells as the guitar soars and the bass hammers out that rhythm. See us rise!

Then the music stops and you can hear Jimmy Crowe draw in a big, deep breath.

That's our cue down in the tunnel and the atmosphere is electric. We're waiting for the next words of the song, because, as soon as we hear them, it's game time.

A heartbeat later, the Shipwreck frontman bellows out the words we've been waiting for.

'THE DEVILS ARE COMING!'

The guitar and drums come crashing back in and Billy Wade yells, 'Ladies and Gentlemen! Your home team! The Sea Devils!'

Skating out onto the ice with Cruel World still playing and the blue and green machine cheering like lunatics was an unbelievable feeling.

Even a coward like me couldn't help but be affected by it.

When Billy Wade introduced me to the crowd ("Making his first appearance tonight, wearing number twenty one – his father's old number! – please welcome, Davey Jones!") and I skated into the line-up, it felt like everything was going to be alright.

But then the lights came up and from across the ice, I could see that the Ogre was ignoring Frankie and staring right at me.

JOHN McKINSTRY

Let me tell you about face-off…

Bullies look for signs.

They look for those tell-tale giveaways that you've seen them and that the fear has started to pump through your veins.

Trust me on this. I'm as gutless as they come and, by default, I'm an absolute expert in the signs you give to show you're terrified. It doesn't matter how good an actor you are – when you're scared, you're scared – and your body language announces that fact to the world.

I raised my hand quickly to my face as if I were adjusting the visor on my helmet.

What I was really doing was getting my arm in front of my face to try and hide the involuntary swallowing motion I made.

If bullies notice you gulp suddenly when you see them, it's only going to egg them on.

That I knew from bitter, personal experience.

I wasn't sure if Brooks had seen me swallow nervously or not and I was spared any further wondering as, at that point, Frankie glided past me and put himself right between me and the Ogre.

Brooks switched his gaze from me to Frankie and suddenly grinned.

It was only when you saw them both together that you appreciated the height difference between them.

Brooks was just *huge*.

He said something to Frankie and in reply, Frankie gave him a shove.

The King Centre went quiet as both sets of fans stared in silence onto the ice – probably wondering if the inevitable brawl was going to happen early.

But Brooks just laughed, blew Frankie a kiss and skated off.

Frankie skated over to me.

'You watch yourself out here tonight, Superstar. Ogre's got his beady eye on you.'

I nodded and fought the urge to turn and skate off the ice at speed.

I should have realised.

My stats weren't exactly a secret after all. The online

community in St Helens – especially the ridiculously vocal Lady Kraken – had been extolling my virtues for the last few weeks.

The Dragons knew exactly what I could do if I got the puck and they weren't any keener on losing than we were.

I was focussing on my breathing - every therapist I'd ever visited had been real big on breathing exercises – when the referee called us over for face-off.

Face-off means exactly that. The two teams of skaters face off – each player against a skater from the rival team. The two skaters at centre ice will wait for the referee to drop the puck between them. When that happens, we're off.

But until the puck drops, you're one-on-one against a rival player, waiting for play to begin.

As we lined up for one blood-freezing moment, I thought Brooks was going to line up against me. He skated towards me and then grinned and veered away to face off against Frankie instead.

The Dragons player I wound up facing off with was Jerry Rice, one of their top scorers and almost as fast on the ice as I was.

We both touched our sticks down on the ice – eyes on the two team captains at centre ice. The referee was talking to them and holding up the puck, ready to drop it between them.

'Hey, Superstar.' I looked up at Rice's words and followed his gaze as he nodded over to the Ogre who I realised was staring at me.

When Brooks saw he had my attention, he mimed running a finger across his neck in a throat-slitting movement.

My stomach felt like someone had just dumped a pitcher of iced water into it and I suddenly needed to pee again really badly.

But it was too late to turn and run.

Before the panic could engulf me, the puck dropped and we were off.

Let me tell you about the best save of the night...

My first shift on the ice nearly got me killed.

The puck was won by Danny who rocketed forward with it. The Dragons immediately moved straight into defensive mode – all five of their skaters rushing back to protect their goal as Danny hurtled forward, controlling the puck perfectly as he went.

The Dragons were – unsurprisingly – at their best when they played defence.

But they were vulnerable if you were fast enough. And Danny was fast enough.

He must have realised that he had some (very big) defenders bearing down on him but he still managed to get a shot off. Whether it was nerves or not, he put his shot straight at the Dragons goalie who swatted it almost contemptuously aside.

Pierre Gagnon was in his third season with the Dragons and was about the only member of the team you could describe as a proper hockey player. Whilst most of the Dragons come across as angry, explosive-tempered thugs, Gagnon was cold and clinical. Nothing seemed to affect the Quebec-born goalie – a fact he took pride in. He held the league record for fewest goals let in during penalty shoot-outs and was described by one and all as a consummate professional who never displayed either nervousness or frustration.

Goalies who get rattled or frustrated are easier to score against. The air of calm that Gagnon projected was what makes him so damned dangerous.

But no goalie is invincible.

The puck was taken swiftly up ice again by Jerry Rice. He skated around one of the Sea Devils (a nice bit of play, I have to admit) and then, before he could set himself up for a shot on goal, Frankie crashed into him and checked him into the wall.

Dragons coach, Mario Daniels, was on his feet screaming at the referee to call it, insisting it had been an elbow Frankie had used. (It wasn't – if Frankie had used his elbow, then Rice would have been lying out cold on the ice.)

As I skated over for the next face-off, I felt someone bump into

57

me.

It was the Ogre.

'Soon as little Francis over there gets himself sin binned, it's going to be open season on you.' His voice had a hint of a Boston accent and his tone was conversational. 'This isn't going to be your night, Superstar.'

I skated away and he let me go – content to have delivered his threat.

Some bullies like to watch you sweat before they give you a beating and the Ogre was clearly one of them.

The next face-off was in Sea Devils territory.

The referee was taking his time before dropping the puck and, as I skated into position, Brooks followed me.

I wanted to bolt and run.

The referee was about to drop the puck when the Dragons player in front of him jumped the gun and started to move before the puck was released. The referee stopped play and insisted on a different player to come and face off.

As the players changed over, Brooks shoved his elbow into my shoulder.

'You nervous around me, Superstar? Tell you what, why don't I put you out of your misery right now? You want to go? Want to drop the gloves with me, Superstar?'

I tried to tune Brooks out as the referee held up the puck again.

'Don't you *dare* ignore me, boy!' the Ogre growled, a hint of genuine anger in his voice.

The puck dropped and before the Ogre (who was clearly looking at me rather than at the game) could react, I was moving.

Brooks was a big, scary guy but, damn, was he slow!

I was past him and racing up the ice before he could turn. If I'm really honest, my sudden burst of speed had a lot more to do with putting distance between me and Brooks than rushing to support Danny as he swept the puck forward. But, either way, it meant Danny and I were suddenly on the attack with every Dragons player back on the wrong side of the blue line.

I could see immediately though that Danny's set up was all wrong.

He was so elated at having skated past the whole Dragons team that he wasn't thinking – he was skating straight at the goal, rather than attacking it from an angle and Gagnon was already in position for what would probably be an easy save.

One of the things I liked about Danny when I played alongside him in pre-season was how generous he was. He wasn't a glory boy – he just wanted the puck to go into the net – he didn't much care who tapped it in.

I'm not generous and I *do* like people to know that the team is a goal ahead because of me, but I guess I just wasn't as good a team player as Danny.

That was what I counted on as I banged my stick on the ice behind him and yelled, 'Behind you.'

We had practised this move over and over in pre-season.

One of us would run at the goalie but, instead of shooting the puck, they would suddenly pass it backwards and let the other guy coming up behind them take the shot.

It was almost instinctive by that point and Danny boy didn't even slow down as he ran at Gagnon.

He faked as if he was going to shoot and then smoothly passed the puck behind him – trusting I'd be in position.

I was.

Like I said, I'm not a power forward and I've no urge to run the gauntlet of another team's D-men.

I'm a sniper.

Get the puck to me and my results sort of speak for themselves.

The puck shot back almost perfectly – coming straight to my stick.

I could see Gagnon shifting as I let fly.

The Dragons' goalie recognised he'd been suckered and immediately pivoted to try and tackle the new threat.

I lifted the puck high – aiming at the top corner of the net.

It shouldn't have been saveable, that should have been my first goal for the blue and green.

Gagnon's reflexes would have put a cat to shame however.

He got his glove to it and knocked it to the side with maybe an inch to spare. A little closer and it would have been in but the Dragons' goalie had earned his money.

Both Danny and I tried to get the rebound but Gagnon quickly flicked it out towards another Dragons player so we skated round him and back towards our end of the ice.

Danny was jubilant.

'Going to put SIX past them tonight, Danny boy!' he crowed.

I was silent as we skated away from Gagnon.

I could see the look the Ogre was giving us as we passed him. His attempts at intimidation hadn't worked.

And as we line changed so I could get a seat for a minute and catch my breath, I knew he'd take steps.

I was left wracking my brain to think of an excuse not to go back out onto the ice, but I couldn't think of a single damn one.

Let me tell you about my first assist...

In hockey when they look at a player's stats – especially a forward's – they don't only look at the number of goals scored.

Often the most valuable player isn't the one who scores but the one who consistently sets up other people for the goal.

When you help out on the goal – pass the puck to the guy who scores – it gets recognised. It's called an assist and my first for the blue and green happened with seven minutes of the first period to go.

We were on the power play.

Danny had been checked from behind and the offending Dragons player had to sit out the next two minutes.

For those two minutes, St Helens would have five skaters on the ice to the Dragons' four. It was a golden opportunity and something we'd been practising in pre-season.

Sanity meant Douglasville had to defend like devils till they got their man back from the penalty box. And, sure enough, I saw the Ogre take to the ice as Douglasville quickly line changed – putting their toughest four players onto the ice.

As we moved down the ice to face off in the Dragons' zone, Brooks skated by Danny and me. He shoved Danny hard.

'Ribs sore, sonny?' he asked with a grin.

You know one of the worst things about being a coward? You know damned well when you should speak up and man up.

Right there, I should've had Danny's back. I should have told Brooks to go to hell or try his luck with both of us.

I didn't.

I kept my head down, my mouth shut and just kept skating.

Which of course, didn't save me.

As I moved up to the face-off, Brooks shouldered into me. 'Thought you guys from Sasky had bigger balls,' he said. 'Was your dad like this too? A pussy, I mean?'

I could feel my face flush and Brooks laughed, turned his back on me and skated on.

It had only been a matter of time till someone tried to use memories of my dad to get at me.

Dennis – experienced in dealing with the trash talk of lesser boxers – had told me to accept it was going to happen. It was a case of when and not if.

Eyes on the prize, Dennis had counselled. What the person casting my dad's death in my face wanted was for me to lose my temper and, with it, my accuracy. You want to make them cry. Dennis told me to say nothing and just think of putting the puck into the back of the net.

I had – only half-jokingly – told Dennis I had a natural advantage. I was so gutless that the notion of losing my temper didn't occur. I was too scared to do that.

As I skated forward, I told myself I wasn't my dad. I was different, almost certainly inferior in most people's eyes and had no desire to do things the way he had.

Someone tapped me – hard – on the shoulder.

I spun, expecting an attack, but it was Frankie.

'You're spacing out, Superstar,' he growled. 'Get your damn head in the game – this face-off is yours.'

I nodded and skated into the middle of the circle while the other skaters encircled me.

The referee was looking on as one of the linesmen held up the puck. I faced off in the centre against Rice and set my stick on the ice.

Before the puck could be dropped, Rice moved forward aggressively and the linesman yelled at him to change.

If you moved prematurely then you had to move away and let another member of your team come to the centre to fight for the puck.

Rice rotated back into this team and was replaced by the Ogre.

We set our sticks on the ice.

'This isn't going to be your night, hotshot,' I heard Brooks mutter. 'In point of fact...'

The puck dropped and I got my stick to it and hit it square to the right.

Lief Jacobson, a four-year veteran with St Helens, caught the puck and rushed the goal.

I missed the outcome of that as Brooks had grabbed for me and I'd skated sharply away.

I heard the words 'Gutless piece of ...' as I put distance between me and Brooks.

I turned, scanned the ice looking for the puck.

A Dragons player had it and was rushing up the ice.

I was the only St Helens player in position to stop him.

I skated right at him, flailing my stick from left to right on the ice to try and block the puck if he took a shot.

I should have tried to check him and that was clearly what he was expecting. The only reason he slowed was because he was expecting a hit – if he'd realised how unlikely I was to try and check him, he'd have skated right through me.

In my peripheral vision, I could see some of the Sea Devils fans, up out of their seats and yelling at me. I knew what they wanted and expected but they were going to be disappointed.

In front of me, the Dragons player suddenly made the decision to go for it.

He shouldered past me.

To be fair, he nearly unbalanced himself doing it – he clearly expected me to try and actually stop him and so used more force than was required.

Nonetheless, he got past me.

He'd gotten maybe three feet past me when Frankie crashed into him like a blue and green battering ram and drove him up against the boards.

The referee blew his whistle and the clock was stopped.

Thirty-four seconds of our power play had been used up.

As the referee signalled a penalty on us (Boarding against Frankie) Coach Williams was on his feet bellowing that it had been a fair hit.

And as I looked across the ice, I saw the Ogre grinning at me. He made that slow, throat-slitting gesture again and, when I saw Frankie skate off to the penalty box, my heart absolutely sank.

It was now four on four. Frankie couldn't protect me and the Ogre was gunning for me.

Face-off in St Helens' zone and Brooks - unsurprisingly – matched me.

The puck was dropped and went wide.

I skated away as fast as I could and, as I skated, I saw Lief had the puck. He spotted me and launched the puck my way.

For a second, I considered letting it go past me.

Brooks couldn't just crash into me if I didn't have the puck (well, not without a significant penalty, at any rate). He wanted me to have possession because that made me a legitimate target.

What made me go for it was the absolute knowledge that being as far away from Brooks as possible was desirable. Being at the other end of the ice kept me away from him.

Besides, getting the puck was reflex, something that had been hammered into me by my dad and my grandpa.

So I kept going, caught the puck and blasted a slap shot at Gagnon.

It went wide but not by much.

I slowed, turned and the Ogre was suddenly in my face.

The clock had stopped and there were sixty-two seconds of the power play left.

Brooks wasn't hesitating – he shoved me and snarled, 'Want to go, pussy?'

I skated around him.

'Gutless Wonder!' Brooks yelled after me.

I could hear the boos.

Mostly from the Dragons fans.

Mostly but not exclusively.

After that, Brooks was my shadow as we faced off again and I again won the puck but failed to score.

Any time the puck came my way my goal was to get rid of it as quickly as I could.

I took a pass from Danny with twelve seconds of our power play to go and practically as soon as the puck came to my stick, there was a blur of movement and Brooks had launched himself at me.

My speed saved me.

I was quick enough to pass the puck straight back to Danny and accelerate forward. As I exploded forward Brooks crashed into the Plexiglas. He'd missed me by inches.

Billy Wade's voice announced over the PA that the Dragons were back to full strength.

We were now at a one man disadvantage for thirty-four seconds till we got Frankie back.

Danny took a shot at goal, Gagnon deflected it and the puck went wide with both teams chasing it.

A scrabble for the puck began at the glass as Lief got to it first but was trapped there as a red-shirted goon held him against the glass while another goon tried to tear the puck free from him.

Twenty-seven seconds till Frankie got returned to the ice. I was counting the seconds off under my breath as the puck came free and Rice was suddenly running at the St Helens goal.

He put it low. Robbie Murphy got his stick to it and the puck went wide again.

Nineteen seconds to wait as Douglasville captured the puck and attacked again.

I looked for the Ogre and didn't see him.

I hadn't seen Douglasville line change so he still had to be on the ice.

Dennis' words ('Don't let them catch you flat-footed') went through my mind and I shifted sharply to my left, even though there was nobody in a red jersey near me.

I heard the sudden crash behind me as Brooks flew into the boards exactly where I'd just been standing.

It would have been an illegal check if it had landed. It would probably have gotten a serious penalty for Brooks.

And it would have taken me out of commission for the rest of the game.

Dear sweet Jesus but I wanted to get off of the ice!

Eleven seconds till Frankie was released.

As I skated past the penalty box, I could see he was already on his feet – eyes on the clock and counting down the seconds till he could get back on.

I skated sharply to centre ice, moving abruptly from the left wing.

Brooks skated past me.

Grinning.

Five seconds till Frankie was back on the ice.

I was shouldered into by someone in a red jersey. Jerry Rice hissed the word "Pussy" as me as he jostled me.

I skated past him.

Two seconds.

'DAVEY!'

My eyes went to the person shouting my name.

Lief had the puck and was boxed in.

I accelerated forward by reflex.

Cheers from the blue and green machine told me better than any clock that Frankie was back on the ice.

As I caught the puck I saw the Ogre skating right at me.

I sped up and shifted to get away from him.

I went right around the Dragons, goal with the Ogre chasing after me.

He was only looking for me and I was really just looking for the quickest way I could to get rid of the puck so that he wouldn't have a legitimate excuse to pulverise me.

My dad always taught me to never look at the ice or the puck when you skate. You should know by touch where the puck was and your head should be up and your eyes searching for an opportunity.

When I saw Danny suddenly break free of the player marking him, I didn't hesitate – I blasted the puck across the ice straight to him.

I wasn't looking for an assist – just to get rid of the puck.

Danny's positioning however was perfect.

He hit the puck as soon as it was close enough and not even Gagnon could reach it in time.

The blue and green machine were on their feet howling victory as Danny put St Helens one-nil up.

Danny's face was jubilant as he skated away and, as he passed me, we bumped knuckles.

'What a pass! Keep them coming, Davey boy,' he enthused. 'We've got another five to score!'

The others were skating over to bump knuckles with Danny and I was just waiting for the chance to line change and get off the ice for a couple of minutes, when something crashed into me and sent me flying.

I managed to avoid landing face-first on the ice and turned around to see Brooks bearing down on me.

My heart sank as the Ogre pointedly threw his stick aside.

I knew exactly what was coming next.

'Told you this wasn't going to be your night, sonny.'

The Ogre's tone of voice was no longer conversational.

He circled to my left and I was very aware that the King Centre had gone quiet.

Brooks snapped his hands sharply downwards with a practised ease and his gloves fell onto the ice to reveal big, heavily-calloused fists.

'Let's get this done,' the Ogre growled at me as he raised his hands up high like a boxer.

Both sets of fans were waiting expectantly for me to drop the gloves as well.

What they apparently weren't expecting was for me to turn my back on Brooks and skate away from him, but that's exactly what I did.

The booing started almost straight after but that was fine with me.

The choice between being booed or beaten bloody by a man like the Ogre wasn't exactly a difficult one for a coward like me to make.

JOHN McKINSTRY

Let me tell you how it feels to be bullied...

I could hear the catcalls from the Dragons fans as I skated away. I could live with that. Any time you're doing something that has the rival fans shower you with abuse is generally a good thing.

I tried not to make eye contact with any of the home fans as I skated away though.

I knew damned well that at least some of the boos would have come from St Helens fans, disappointed that I'd backed away from the Ogre.

It wasn't an unfamiliar feeling.

My fingers reflexively came up to my face and touched the scar there.

You don't need to play hockey to run into bullies – as I was well aware.

I could remember exactly how it felt to have an audience of other kids (all excited at the prospect of seeing a little blood) chanting 'Fight! Fight! Fight!' as someone flailed away at me.

It had been years ago but I'd never forgotten how it felt – no victim ever does.

That same stupid sense of shame at not getting into a fist fight to satisfy the audience I'd had at high school went through me as I skated away from Brooks.

It didn't matter that, logically, I'd done the smart thing.

I'd have lasted seconds against the Ogre and we both knew it. My job was to score goals – not to go toe-to-toe with a brawler like him.

It was easy to rationalise.

None of my reasons were the real ones though.

The real reason was I was just too scared to drop the gloves with the Ogre.

I passed Lief as I skated away and tried real hard to avoid reading too much into the fact that he looked away and couldn't make eye contact with me.

Grandpa Louie would have turned in his grave – I have no doubt.

Guilt, which was what I was suddenly full of, is a singularly useless emotion. It doesn't seem to help, and it hurts deep down.

As I looked around the ice I saw the Dragons' line change.

It was a very minor detail, a standard thing to do.

But it was about to become a very important factor in my life although I didn't realise it at the time.

What distracted my attention and jolted me out of the guilt-trip was to see the Dragons fans all suddenly let out a cheer and come to their feet.

I dimly realised they were all looking behind me.

I was starting to turn, but it was already too late.

In my periphery I was aware of movement.

The Ogre, it seemed, wasn't finished with me.

All I registered was a blur of movement and then the impact as Brooks – skating at full speed – collided with me.

For a horrible second it felt like I was flying.

You know the old joke about it not being the fall that kills you but the landing?

That's the best way I can sum up the experience of being hit so hard that I was knocked off my feet and thrown up against the Plexiglas.

The world went black for second as I hit the boards and then fell backwards, barely conscious, onto the ice.

I couldn't breathe.

It was terrifying. And the terror actually helped. I panicked so badly that it kept me from dropping into unconsciousness.

If you can't breathe, you're going to die.

What I remember most about that hit was how quiet the world suddenly became.

I managed to draw in a ragged breath and, after a second, get my eyes open.

I was on my back and struggling to rise.

In front of me all hell was breaking loose.

Frankie and the Ogre had dropped the gloves and were pounding on each other at centre ice. Jerry Rice was grappling with Danny and, in the background, Coach Williams was screaming furiously at the referee and looked ready to get on the ice and throw a few punches himself.

As I turned onto my side, a thick stream of blood trickled from my mouth onto the ice.

I was struggling to get onto my knees and, as I slowly moved myself, my helmet fell off.

That became an important factor in what was about to happen.

The brawl between Frankie and the Ogre had captured everyone's attention. A brutal left hook from Brooks had rocked Frankie so badly that it looked like a fight-ending punch but Frankie rallied, smothered the next two of Brooks' punches then caught him with an absolute peach of an uppercut.

All eyes were on them.

Including mine.

I wasn't even aware that Billy Fryar was on the ice till he was right on top of me.

JOHN McKINSTRY

Let me tell you about cheap shots...

When you drop the gloves with someone, it's meant to be a straight, fair fight.

It's one-on-one, *mano y mano,* and when one of you goes down, as a rule, the referee steps in to bring things to an end.

It's got to be the epitome of macho - two guys wailing away on another till one of them hits the ice.

And – like just about anything macho in my opinion – it's not exactly the smartest of choices.

Hockey fights aren't boxing matches. You aren't paired off against someone guaranteed to be the same height, weight and skill level. You could find yourself out of your league and in a no-win situation really easily.

A hockey fight has its uses but bottom line is, it's a stand-up brawl. Neither person really defends themselves – they spend all their effort knocking the other guy down before he can do that to them first.

If your goal is to take an opposing player out of commission, then there are much safer ways to do it than by dropping the gloves.

Look up the rules of whatever brand of ice hockey you follow (the rules vary from place to place and Olympic ice hockey is very different in some respects to what you'll see played at the arenas in North America and Canada). Focus your attention on the section of the rules that relate to penalties and you'll get presented with a virtual list of all the different ways that hockey players can, and do, ruin each other's day.

They cover everything from spearing (thrusting your stick at another player) to kicking (yes, it does happen and if the thought of someone lashing out a kick while wearing a razor-sharp hockey skate doesn't scare you, then there's probably something wrong with you).

For my money, the worst offences were the ones I'd describe as cheap shots.

Checking someone up against the boards is brutal but at least if they see it coming they can brace themselves.

Check somebody from behind and the odds of really injuring

them go way up – that of course is exactly why certain players do it.

Cheap shots come in a variety of forms and what they all have in common is that they are so much safer than starting a brawl.

The Ogre was far from innocent of using them, but – when interviewed after the game – he claimed to be very much on the side of the angels.

Mr Brooks had a tough-guy reputation to maintain and he told reporters he had – after enduring significant verbal abuse on the ice from me – offered to fight me fair. He'd dropped the gloves and shown willing. My response – to skate away disdainfully – had set off his temper and he'd acted accordingly.

He added that he hadn't anticipated how physically weak and unable to handle the normal impacts of an ice hockey match I was.

There had, he reassured the reporters, been no game plan or co-ordinated, pre-mediated effort in what had happened to me.

When you have the Ogre on your team, you just know that when rival teams do their threat assessment that he'll be top of their list.

Smaller players like Billy Fryar tend to get overlooked.

At five four, Billy Fryar was the shortest player on the Dragons' roster and one of the smallest guys in the league.

Being smaller never makes you less of a threat, however. I'd been taught *that* particular lesson back at high school and had never forgotten it.

Billy Fryar skated on just as Frankie and the Ogre went to war at centre ice.

As I was rolling onto my side and spitting the blood out of my mouth, he paused, looked around the arena and then started to move towards me.

He didn't start to sprint till he saw me try to haul myself up onto my knees.

I've seen the tapes of that game. He can mutter all he likes about being indecisive and skating forward whilst still looking at the brawl between Frankie and the Ogre to his heart's content but I saw him zero in on me, then suddenly break into a run – straight at me – as I rose.

I got up onto one knee and, like everyone else, my eyes were on the brawl which Frankie had started to take the worst of.

I felt, rather than heard, Fryar's approach maybe a heartbeat before his knee smashed into the side of my face and I was driven backwards where the back of my head – unprotected given my helmet was rolling about on the ground a few feet away – connected hard with the ice.

It was the cheapest of cheap shots – a Dragons speciality – and the end of my first game with my dad's old club.

Let me tell you about being stretchered off...

The thing that stuck with me most about the incident with Billy Fryar was when I was jerked into consciousness as I was being taken off the ice.

I was on a gurney and staring up at the lights in the King Centre ceiling.

Everything – every part of my body – seemed to hurt.

There was yelling all around me.

I could hear Coach Williams unleashing a stream of verbal abuse at someone at the top of his lungs and I idly wondered if they'd bleep out the many f-words or just transmit his outburst unfiltered.

A light suddenly appeared right in front of my eye and I groaned. What I wanted to yell was words to the effect of get-that-damned-light-out-of-my face but only a groan came out.

'David? Davey?' an unknown voice asked. 'Can you hear me Davey?'

I dimly understood the person talking was a paramedic and I tried to reply but, dear God, my whole jaw felt like it was on fire and again all I could manage was a groan.

I tried to raise a hand – maybe give the guy a thumbs up to show I'd heard him - and as I feebly lifted my arm the tone of the paramedic's voice changed sharply.

'No!' he barked. 'You stay where you are, son. This game is over as far as you're concerned.'

This guy was clearly used to being around hockey players but what did he think I was going to do? Leap up off the gurney, drop the gloves with Fryar, then score the game-winning goal?

'Sure,' I managed to say, slurring the word a bit. But I think he understood because he looked a bit surprised at my response. I guess he wasn't used to hockey players actually doing what a paramedic told them.

If you'd asked me (and if I'd been able to provide you with a coherent reply) at that moment in time, I'd have told you that what I'd just experienced was the most painful thing that had ever or could ever happen to me.

And I'd have been wrong.

The most painful moments of my life were still ahead of me and, as they got me into an ambulance bound for St Elizabeth's hospital, I was heading straight towards them.

Fate was about to introduce me to Lady Kraken.

PART TWO
The non-contact jersey

If you believe that that horrific hit by Fryar on Jones was accidental, then you probably believe in the tooth fairy as well!
#vengeancewearsblueandgreen #seadevils
Posted by user - Lady Kraken

JOHN McKINSTRY

Let me tell you about the post-match analysis...

Years ago, I remember my dad showing me a cutting from a local Sasky newspaper.

It had the report on the big hockey match of the weekend in it and to go along with that report there was a small, grainy, black and white photo of Grandpa Louie.

In the photo, my grandfather looks like he's leaning slightly away from the player whose jersey he had taken hold of. Both men had clenched fists and it was clearly a snapshot taken during an on-ice brawl.

Apart from a slight grimace on Grandpa Louie's face, you could be forgiven for thinking this incident had been settled in a quick and professional fashion.

It wasn't.

I hadn't been born when Grandpa Louie played that match but later – when I went to elementary school – the teachers and parents of my Sasky classmates all still talked about it.

I'm sure that people have exaggerated the events of that match in the years that followed. I'm equally sure that neither that photo nor the report of the match beside it came remotely close to the reality of what my neighbours enthusiastically called the bloodiest fight of my grandfather's career.

See, Grandpa Louie was good on the ice. He was another of those Sasky kids who seemed to have been born with skates on. In his prime, he was probably as good, if not better, than my dad.

But unlike my dad, Grandpa Louie was no goal scorer.

Grandpa Louie played defence his whole career and as a D-man his focus was on protecting his goal and his teammates.

That season he missed two games – one through injury and one through suspension – both times a guy called Bobby Wren wreaked havoc on the ice against my grandfather's team. Wren basically bullied the opposition, bragging that he owned them when he played against them.

When Grandpa Louie finally took to the ice against Bobby Wren, everybody knew that the two of them were destined to go toe-to-toe and they duly did. Grandpa Louie demanded (and was promptly passed) the puck and he ran it to the other team's goal. The other team's defence actually stayed away from him as he rushed the goal with Wren, the only defender in front of him.

The check Wren put in was the excuse for the two of them to do what they had been planning to do all along.

The fight that followed marked both men forever.

It was where Grandpa Louie lost his four front teeth and took such a hammering that my normally placid grandmother swore she would leave him if he didn't quit hockey.

My grandfather loved to tell the story of that fight to my brother and me when we were kids.

When we heard Grandpa Louie talk about beating Wren senseless on the ice it was okay, because he was our grandpa, he was the good guy and we were meant to cheer the good guy on, right?

My dad put up with this for years but I still remember when he made a point of taking Mason and me to a game when he was still playing local league (right before he got the call from St Helens).

Bobby Wren was in the audience that night and my dad introduced us to him.

Bobby Wren's career had ended in that game.

I'm sure people still recognised him and bought him a drink in the bars locally but I wondered how much of a consolation that had been to him after Grandpa Louie beat him to the ground.

It had been the one, single punch that my grandfather threw after Wren hit the ice that did it.

They didn't wear helmets back then and Bobby Wren's head got bounced off the ice at a crazy angle. It damaged the optic nerve in Bobby's right eye and after the doctors had made their gloomy prognosis, Bobby was let go by his team - they couldn't get insurance for him.

He wasn't bitter.

He was friendly when we were introduced, shook our hands and gave a crooked smile that showed he'd also had a fair amount of dental work done.

Bobby Wren spoke slowly, sometimes pausing at odd moments. I liked him.

It was the first time I'd ever wondered if maybe my grandpa wasn't such a nice guy after all.

I got so worried about it I finally asked my dad if it was still okay to like Grandpa Louie.

He didn't blow it off, he took my question seriously.

Yes, he had said, it was absolutely okay to still like Grandpa Louie because he really *was* a good person. He had kept in touch with Bobby Wren and the two of them had become friends years after their big brawl on the ice.

What I should do, though, was start to realise that the report on that hockey match combined with my grandfather's stories did not give the full picture and that neither the reporter who wrote the piece nor the fans who read it had had to live with the injuries that came out of that fight.

That thought was going through my mind during my first night in hospital.

When the doctors were done checking me for any immediate injuries that could stop me breathing (one or two of the doctors – probably as a genuinely innocent way of trying to build a little rapport with me – started to explain what they were checking for and, man, I so wish they hadn't) they left me in a room with a TV up on the wall.

In addition to the two busted ribs I'd suffered, not one, but two head injuries. My neck was in a brace and they told me there would be some further investigations the next day.

The scariest moment of the night was when the last doctor left me. On his way out, he told me he had been watching the game and had seen the two hits laid on me.

'Trust me when I say it Mr Jones,' he said quietly. 'The way your head moved when you took that knee? The strain on your neck? You are jackpot lucky not to be injured far worse than you actually are. Do you know how easily that hit could have damaged your neck or your back? I'd say you dodged a bullet tonight, Mr Jones. Whatever your lucky charm is, keep it close, because that second hit in particular had the potential to leave you in a wheelchair.'

It maybe won't come as a surprise if I add that sleep didn't come easily after hearing that.

I turned on the TV and couldn't help searching for a report on the game.

The commentators who covered the match were full of the enthusiasm you'd expect from people trying to sell the game and build the ratings. They exclaimed loudly when they saw the hit.

They chuckled wryly as they noted the Ogre stalk me on the ice.

'Looks like this is going to be a real baptism of fire for Davey Jones!' one enthused as he watched me avoid the Ogre's first attempt to put me into the boards.

The reports took their time showing and then reshowing the hits that led to me being stretchered off.

'OH MY GOD!' one yelled as footage of Fryar slamming his knee into me played. 'Look at that impact!'

In Grandpa Louie's day, all you would get as a record of a game was a black and white photo.

Nowadays it's different.

I got to see the footage – from multiple angles and even in slow motion – over and over again.

Logically – since my stomach was in knots watching what could have been a career-ending hit – I should have turned the TV off.

But I didn't.

I watched the Fryar hit over and over and that doctor's words came back to me.

Jackpot lucky.

Damage to neck or back.

Wheelchair.

Maybe if all I'd had was a grainy, old photo I'd have gotten more sleep that night.

But somehow I doubted it.

Let me tell you about the nightmare...

My mom told me when I was a kid that she never remembered her dreams when she woke up.

I think she found it cute that I could recall all of my dreams in minute detail.

After the accident – I can't remember why – I had asked her again about her dreams and if she still didn't remember them. She told me not to be silly and changed the subject so I never found if she really *did* have the luxury of not remembering her dreams. I really do hope that was the case but I always doubted it. She was in therapy for years – just like I was – and I know she often took sleeping pills to be able to get some rest.

My mom might, just maybe, have shared her pain with my dad but she'd never have burdened me with it and I doubt her therapist would ever have learned about it.

I always loved my mom and hoped she was spared the kind of dreams I had.

It took years for the dreams to fade but one of them – the nightmare – never really went away.

As I got older I no longer had the nightmare every single night but it was always there and even years later it could still ambush me and leave me awake in a terrified, cold sweat when I finally managed to wake up from it.

The nightmare hasn't changed in one single detail since the night I first had it.

I'm in a car but the car isn't moving.

My hands are always free in the nightmare. At least at first.

It's dark outside the car but as I sit there – able to move but not moving – it seems to get brighter and brighter.

I can't feel the heat of the flames that are slowly engulfing the car but, at a certain point, the light is so bright that I turn and look at it and know instinctively I have to get out of the car. Or I'm going to die.

That's always when I try to move and discover I can't.

I struggle and scream for help.

No-one comes.

85

Finally I realise it's the seat belt that's holding me in place.

I know all I have to do is unbuckle it and I'll be fine.

But when I reach for the button to unlock it, I find there isn't one. The seatbelt is attached to the floor of the car and can't be opened.

The lights get brighter and I fight and claw at the seat belt.

But it won't budge.

I usually wake up at that point.

When I was a kid, I'd wake with a scream but as a grownup I just sit bolt upright panting for breath like I've run a marathon.

Sitting bolt upright when your neck is in a brace isn't something I'd recommend.

I wasn't exactly surprised the nightmare returned that night, although I *was* surprised at how strong it was.

Therapists told me it would fade in time but, to be fair, the therapists had never really been able to help me with this.

In truth, the only person who ever helped me had been our local parish priest.

Father Jackson was the only one who didn't seem intent on coddling or patronising me. Everyone else kept telling me the same old, glib lie that adults always tell children – it'll be okay.

Father Jackson knew that was just crap.

He'd been a soldier before he joined the priesthood and his advice was the only kind that had helped.

'Say a prayer,' he had told me.

I'd asked what kind of prayer and he'd just shrugged and told me it didn't really matter. Just say a prayer, send it out to the people you've lost and tell them you still miss them.

It didn't stop the nightmare coming but afterwards it helped. Sometimes I even managed to get some sleep.

I chose to say an Act of Contrition that night.

In fact, I said several.

Not for what I'd done but for what I was about to do.

It was sort of a pre-emptive apology to my dad for quitting and walking away from both the Sea Devils and ice hockey forever.

The last doctor's words – jackpot lucky, wheelchair – had bored themselves into me.

I've covered me being a coward already, right?

I figured my dad would probably understand. Oh, if he was still around he'd probably be disappointed because hockey was his life.

But I think he'd have been supportive.

But whether he would or wouldn't have approved, I knew that I'd made my decision.

I didn't want to end up paralysed.

I didn't want to die.

I was done.

Let me tell you about signing autographs...

I never, ever liked signing autographs.

Oh, I'd done it before. In point of fact, before playing for St Helens I'd probably signed hundreds with my last few clubs. If you're a professional athlete then you need to accept that signing an autograph for a fan sort of comes with the territory.

I didn't dislike doing it because it was a burden on my time or anything. Hey, I'm a sports fan too and I'm someone who has a photo of the Sea Devils team that qualified for the playoffs in eighty-nine, signed by every member of the team and the coach.

No, I hated signing stuff because I didn't feel I'd actually done enough to be worth someone wanting my signature.

If you met a Hall of Famer then that person has clearly done things and achieved things in the sport. That person signing their name for you sounds meaningful.

But me?

I'd played minor league hockey and, while I was good at it, I was no Stanley Cup winner.

For me, signing autographs just felt wrong – like some twenty-year old sitting down to write their autobiography before they're old enough to have done anything worth writing about.

Beyond some minor league hockey, my only claim to fame was having a sport celebrity (albeit a minor one) as a father.

So it never felt right that I should be signing an autograph but it was expected of me so I did it any time someone asked.

And that was a lot of people while I was laid up in hospital.

A lot of the hospital staff asked for one and I obliged, while hoping they couldn't spot just how fake the smile I gave them actually was.

I actually got to the point where I sort of enjoyed it because at least when I was fake-smiling my way through an autograph signing I had someone to talk to.

Visiting hour can be a chore if you have nobody to come and visit.

Oh, some of the guys from the team stopped by. Danny was the first and he seemed guilty at not having somehow managed to sense what the Dragons were up to and save my ass. I told him not to sweat it – nobody could have seen it coming – but he stayed distraught and I knew that part of him had to have been looking at my injuries and realising that if the Devils hadn't hired me, odds were good that the person in the hospital bed would have been him.

Plus Danny hated (really hated) the fact that despite some rather significant penalties being awarded against Douglasville, we had still gone on to lose three-one.

Danny aside, I had a couple of club officials pop in (mainly to confirm that the club would be picking up the tab for my stay in hospital) and that was about it. The team had an away game and had to travel. Danny had turned up sort of on behalf of the others who promised to catch up with me when they got back home in a couple of days.

My only other visitor was Dennis.

He had been horrified to see the hit on me and had stuck around St Helens (despite being due to start training for his next big fight the following day) to check I was okay. I told him I appreciated him stopping by and I meant it. Once he left though, that pretty much exhausted my circle of potential visitors.

So there was nobody else to really talk to.

Most of the time that's absolutely fine with me but in hospital it meant I had lots and lots of time to fill.

Lots of time to dwell on how lucky I'd been and to think about how likely it was that I could somehow play hockey but not get hit again.

Not very likely, I decided.

Time really hung heavy and even signing a puck or match programme broke up the monotony a little.

Even though I felt like more of a fake than ever before as I did so.

I'd already decided to quit so it felt like I was signing things under false pretences.

The only thing that kept me from absolutely climbing the walls was a tablet.

When Danny visited me, he brought it, along with a charger, as a gift. Danny had spent some time in hospital the year before so he knew how valuable a tablet could be. He knew exactly how dull and frustrating spending even a few days in hospital could be and that being able to surf and interact with people on social media helped.

Of course it can also be used to search for the injuries the doctor told you you'd suffered (and all the associated complications and horror stories) as well as to search for any video of the hits that had put you in the hospital in the first place.

I must have watched Fryar's hit on me again and again as I lay there with my neck in that stupid brace.

The doctor's words (jackpot lucky, wheelchair....) kept echoing in my mind as I watched the footage.

And as you can probably imagine, logging into social media sites provided me with even more fuel for my decision to quit.

The first post I saw on the league website had been put up by someone whose screen name was DragonChylde666. It read: "And the Oscar for best performance in a hockey match goes to Davey Jones from St Helens for this swan dive."

The next user, Firefiend21, posed the question "A four-match ban? For that? God have mercy, is the league going to add extra match penalties because the person who got clipped is some cry-baby who doesn't belong on the ice alongside people like Fryar and Ollie B?"

Another user named DouglasvilleGal05 had started a petition to have the ban on Fryar reduced or overturned (when I checked it, it had over two thousand signatures).

Plus I was being discussed on several other sites where Douglasville fans really let rip. Do a search for the hashtags "cry-baby", "glass jaw", "pussy" or "coward" and you'll see some of the milder things they said about me.

And while the blue and green machine *was* outraged (Lady Kraken questioned the eyesight, hockey knowledge and parentage of anyone who called Fryar's hit on me a clean one) there was a definite sense of disappointment from some of them that I hadn't dropped the gloves with the Ogre.

Okay, it was a minority, but those were the posts I spent most time rereading – the ones from our own fans who had already lost respect for me.

Want to know the craziest thing?

I'd made the decision to quit. Reading posts from some dyed-in-the-wool Dragons fan didn't really make me feel worse but mild censure from St Helens fans did.

I wanted to change their minds.

They hadn't seen half of what I could do after all. I figured if I'd put the puck in the net for them a few times I could win the majority of them over.

Every time my thoughts drifted in that direction, I'd come across another post from a St Helens fan that changed my mind right back. Like FisherKing13 who noted that I really wasn't my father's son and that he'd watch videos of my dad and hope that St Helens hired a decent replacement for me asap.

Saying that I felt conflicted didn't do it justice.

After a couple of hours of surfing, I switched the tablet off.

Screw them all.

None of them had to ice against people like Brooks and Fryar. I doubted that many (if any) of the keyboard warriors out there had ever had to go toe-to-toe with a monster like Brooks.

Who in the hell were *they* to judge?

I'd have probably managed to work myself up into a nicely self-righteous mood if it hadn't been for the fact that I felt genuinely guilty at letting some of the fans down.

I screwed my eyes tightly shut.

I had made my decision and I *was* going to quit.

I'd just have to learn to live with the fact that it felt very much like running away with my head down in shame and my tail well and truly between my legs.

Those were the thoughts that were careering through my mind when there came a very polite knock on the door of my room.

I wasn't in a great mood by that point and I was more than half-tempted either to pretend not to have heard it, or (even better) to yell at whoever was on the other side of the door to go the hell away and not come back.

I've sometimes wondered how my life might have turned out if I *had* done something like that.

But I hadn't.

My folks raised me right and, whilst I might be a coward, I was a coward with good manners.

So I called out to the person at the door to come on in. I didn't know then that by doing so I was going to have my life turned upside down and learn what real pain was.

The guy who nervously entered looked like he was in his late thirties or maybe early forties. He was fairly neatly dressed – shirt and tie - but his clothes, while smart, where rumpled as if he had slept in them.

And he looked exhausted.

He was, as I'd thought, hoping for an autograph. But not for himself. He wanted one for his hockey-mad daughter.

His name was Russ.

And he was Lady Kraken's father.

Let me tell you about perceptions...

It's easy to conjure up a picture of someone in your mind, isn't it?

It could be some guy in a call centre when you need to phone up for something. It could be an article you read in the paper or a post you read online. Whatever it is, as you talk to the faceless person at the other end of the phone or read the column or article, you think you've got a handle on the person. You can picture what they look like, what age they are, even what kind of personality they have.

You hear about fans of an actor who played a really nice, friendly character on TV or in the movies and, when they meet the person in real life, they're shocked at how unpleasant that person actually is.

They don't really have the right to be surprised though. All they had was a *perception* of what the real person was like – the actor who plays the nice guy on screen never claimed he was a nice person after all. He was just an actor playing a part.

But we all do it. Don't we?

Lady Kraken was a name we all knew.

She was loud, persistent and utterly, unrepentantly partisan. This woman was a Sea Devils uber fan, who undoubtedly bled blue and green.

She was sharp too.

Her knowledge of the game (and St Helens' history and statistics) was pretty much encyclopaedic.

She had managed to draw most of the guys (including Coach Williams) into a conversation online at some point. She seem to post all the time – Danny had joked that hockey was probably more important to her that her day job (and given the frequency of her posts, we reckoned that hockey had probably cost her her job at some time).

And she could be brutally critical.

She had singled out Robbie Dee – another of our D-men – for her wrath. She had highlighted his (frequent) poor games and compared his stats to our other defence men. She had posted videos of Robbie's performance showing his – in her opinion, uninterested – expression.

She wasn't calling for his scalp though.

She wanted him to get off his ass and improve.

Her last post on our website summed it up perfectly. "Robbie Dee – WTF are you playing at? You were invisible on the ice in the first period. You let Jones get hung out to dry and then out of the blue you become God's gift to D-men! You ran the Dragons ragged man! Then in the third period you went back to being invisible! YOU CAN DO THIS, DEE! We've seen how damned good you can be so stop hiding the fact!"

Robbie was a pretty good-looking guy but he was pretty thin-skinned. He didn't like criticism and he'd highlighted that post on all his social media accounts with the words: "What do you know about hockey, honey?" beside it.

Robbie's fans – a lot of them young ladies who were more interested in seeing the annual calendar with its shots of Robbie flexing his pecs than in his stats from the league – sent a barrage of abuse Lady Kraken's way.

Lady Kraken's reply was: "Goodness! I didn't realise there were still so many puck bunnies amongst the blue and green faithful! Wonder how many of the bimbi actually appreciate how piss poor Robbie's stats are, or how good they *could* be?"

She blew kisses to people who sent her abuse and when one young lady dared to question her knowledge of the St Helens team, she invited her to forward on her address so she could send her a get well soon card ("You want to challenge my knowledge of the game or my team? Aww! Aren't you just adorable, thinking you're even close to being in my league! Give me a call when you work out what 'icing' means, sweetie, and maybe we'll talk!")

None of us had met her but we all figured her to be in her late twenties or early thirties. Robbie Dee was convinced she was an obese, dungaree-wearing lesbian. But then Robbie aimed bile like that at any woman who didn't fall at his feet immediately and worship him. The fact that Lady Kraken had called out the exact issues that Coach Williams also wanted Robbie to improve probably didn't help Robbie get a better opinion of her.

We all had perceptions of her.

Turned out we were all wrong.

When Russ told me who his daughter was, I told him he looked either really good for his age or that his daughter was a lot younger than any of us had ever guessed.

That was when Russ nervously and very respectfully asked if I'd like to meet her.

I had to admit that piqued my curiosity and I had agreed, thinking that he could maybe bring her in at visiting hour the next day.

But Russ – while telling me he was very conscious of the fact that I was injured and didn't want to "be a bother" - went on to tell me she wouldn't need to make an appointment because she was actually at St Elizabeth's.

I asked if she worked at the hospital and he replied no, she was a patient over at the Whyte Centre.

Lady Kraken, as it turned out, was fifteen years old and the Whyte Centre had been her home away from home for quite a while.

The Whyte Centre dealt with only one type of patient.

It was St Elizabeth's oncology unit.

JOHN McKINSTRY

Let me tell you about Lady Kraken...

Here's a question for you.

If you agreed to go round to an oncology ward to talk to a fifteen year-old girl who had just been through chemo, what would you be expecting?

Maybe that the girl would be some tragic, willowy, borderline angelic figure? Maybe that the ward would be a quiet, beautifully lit place of hope?

I guess we all of us want to hope that hospitals are perfectly equipped and comforting places, because at some point in our lives we realise we're likely to have to spend time in one.

The Whyte Centre was far from perfect.

It was clean, functional and far, far too small.

It had been set up with funds from Diana Whyte – a local businesswoman whose folks were taken from her by the big C.

There were four beds in the ward and you didn't need to be any kind of genius to work out which one belonged to Lady Kraken.

The occupants of three of the beds had normal stuff on their bedside tables - cards, magazines, books and not a lot else.

The fourth bed, however – the one furthest from the door – had a blue and green scarf above the little bedside table. There was a Sea Devils calendar and posters of the team on the walls and the person sitting on the bed (head down as she typed furiously on her tablet) wore a hockey jersey instead of pyjamas and she had covered the loss of her hair with a Sea Devils cap.

The only incongruous detail was a doll. A very girly, blonde-haired doll in a pretty white dress, which was posed sitting down on the bedside table beside a copy of "Lone Wolf" (Timur Volkov's autobiography) and a couple of hockey pucks with scrapes and cuts on them (indicating they were game pucks).

I had walked slowly to the door of the ward and made my way slightly nervously into the room in Russ' wake.

I didn't know where to look.

Was it okay to make eye contact? Could it be misinterpreted if I smiled at anyone?

One of the ladies on the left-hand side of the room smiled over at me and I returned her smile as best I could. She only looked to be in her thirties. Her hair was gone and there was a little plastic tube in her nostrils.

I tried hard not to stare at it.

I hesitated again as I saw Russ walk up to his daughter.

She was just a kid.

I figured she was probably incredibly delicate and wasn't even sure how to start a conversation.

As I was licking my suddenly dry lips and trying to think of something inoffensive and gentle to say, her head snapped up from her tablet and a pair of piercing blue eyes were suddenly boring into mine.

'Newsflash, Superstar,' she snapped. 'It's cancer – not the 'flu. You can't catch it just by breathing in the same air as us.'

Her accent was pure St Helens and her tone was scathing.

Lady Kraken, as I quickly discovered, didn't do tragic, willowy or angelic.

She was a brutally honest, frequently foul-mouthed young woman who said *exactly* what she thought.

As she stared at me, I opened my mouth to reply but couldn't think of anything remotely intelligent to say, so I closed it again.

Her expression softened a little and she nodded at the chair beside her bed.

'You taking a seat or not?'

'Umm, sure,' I said weakly. 'I guess…'

The blue eyes narrowed again and she glared.

'If you've something better to do, some prior engagement, then don't let me keep you. If you want to talk, that'd be fine but if all you're doing is bringing the pity party, then you can find your own way out.'

I walked over to the seat she'd indicated and sat down.

'So… umm, how are you doing?' I asked.

The look she gave me could have stripped paint.

'Well, Mr Jones,' she said in a badly-feigned cheerful voice, 'I'm just recovering from my last chemo session – how do you *think* I'm doing?'

She didn't actually add the word "dumbass" to the end of the question but she did bat her eyelashes at me before dropping the fake-cheerful act to glare at me again.

When she was online, Lady Kraken tolerated no fools and took no prisoners.

It was only when you met her in real life that you understood just how much she held back when she blogged and posted. Online she was tough but in real life she was brutal.

I had no idea how to talk to her.

The idea of getting up and walking out was beginning to feel like a really good one when she picked up her tablet again.

I thought she was going to immerse herself in it again and just blank me when she turned it so I could see it and I saw that it was a video of my first shot at Gagnon.

'So unlucky,' she said. 'The angle was right, the shot was fast and accurate and that should have been your first goal for us. That Gagnon! Damn, but he's good!'

'I know,' I said, suddenly able to form sentences again now that we were on the safe ground of hockey talk. 'In the team talk before we played, Coach Williams called him the only real hockey player the Dragons have.'

'No shit?' she asked, genuinely interested.

'Yeah. He told us it was just cruel to put skates on a bunch of gorillas but that was what Douglasville kept doing.'

She laughed at that.

I felt good about that, like I'd actually broken the ice.

But then she started to cough.

It went on and on and I didn't know if it was ever going to stop – but I wanted it to. Her whole body shook and Russ came over to put an arm around her.

When it finally ceased, he passed her a plastic cup of water. A nurse popped his head around the door to ask if she needed anything.

She handed the cup back to her dad then directed that glare of hers at the nurse.

'What I need, Stan, is for you to get out of my face. Me and Mr Jones here are talking hockey.'

Stan nodded 'Sure thing, devil-girl. If you get someone from a decent hockey team like the Wolves in here, will you let me know?'

She gave him the finger along with a mouthful of abuse that would have done credit to Coach Williams when he was in an antichrist sort of mood.

The nurse grinned then he made himself scarce.

Lady Kraken turned her attention back to me.

'Tell me, Mr Jones.'

'It's Davey,' I told her, and extended my hand.

She stared at my hand for a moment and I wasn't sure if I'd upset her again or not but after a pause she took it.

Her grip was so, so weak.

'I'm Kelly Anne,' she said.

'Nice to meet you, Kelly Anne.'

She snorted.

'Yeah, right! I'm just a ray of freaking sunshine, aren't I?'

I grinned. 'Absolutely. Not in any way a foul-mouthed, bad-tempered pain in the ass.'

She smiled back at me.

'Don't make me kick your ass, Jones,' she said. 'So, tell me more about Coach Williams. What's he really like? And is Robbie Dee as big a jerk in real life as he is online?'

I'd planned to pop over and spend ten minutes or so with the girl in the Whyte Centre.

It was after midnight when Stan finally told me – no excuses – it was time to leave.

Let me tell you about the dolly...

Everything Kelly Anne owned seemed to be hockey-related and the only colours allowed anywhere near her were blue and green.

The one exception to this was the pretty white dressed dolly that sat on her bedside table.

Even if the doll's dress had been blue or green, it was such a feminine thing that it stood out like a sore thumb amidst the hockey paraphernalia.

I figured it was none of my business and if the girl wanted a dolly with her while she was in hospital, then why not?

When I woke up the next day, I planned to go visit Kelly Anne again.

She had invited me (rather imperiously) to pop round and her dad had initially looked a little wary – clearly noting that his daughter was asking a lot of someone she'd only just met.

But I'd told them I'd be delighted to visit with her again the next morning. And I'd meant it.

I really am not a good team player and – as my few friends can attest – I'm not exactly the most sociable of souls. But I found that I was actually really looking forward to some more hockey-talk.

First of all though, I had to wait to see the nurse and then a doctor.

The nurse was okay – he helped me get up and cleaned – but the doctor was real frosty with me.

As he examined me, he commented on what I did for a living. 'Hockey,' he said in a doom-laden voice, 'is a dangerous occupation and not one I associate with smart people.'

I bit my tongue as he started to outline his own workload – filled as it was with people who *genuinely* needed him after suffering *real* accidents.

Maybe, he had suggested, I should reconsider my chosen profession and allow him to spend his time on people who deserved it.

The temptation was to remind him that the club was covering all costs and ask him what in the hell was his problem but it didn't exactly feel like the right time to say that.

He told me it looked like I was unlikely to need surgery but it had been a close call.

As it was - he told me with a certain degree of gloomy relish - I was facing a long, painful period of rehab.

For that I could have hugged him!

Long rehab meant I would continue to be paid but wouldn't be able to play until signed off as fully fit.

The idea of quitting was still there but, if you could keep getting paid while you recovered, then why not? I'd been hurt doing my job and was unlikely to pick up a new contract while injured.

I hadn't decided what I'd do but I knew I was going to be off ice.

I wasn't planning to tempt fate.

So all in all I was in a pretty good mood as I made my way slowly round to the Whyte Centre and Kelly Anne's ward.

After the mouthful I'd been given last night after my hesitant entrance, I'd planned to arrive as confidently as I could.

But as I approached the door, all I could hear was a loud, hacking cough.

I looked into the ward and the lady in the bed opposite - the one who had smiled at me the night before - looked up, caught my eye, and shook her head.

I stayed outside the ward as the coughing continued.

I didn't know if I should stay or go. What was I meant to do?

I glanced back into the room as the coughing began to die down. I heard Stan, the nurse from the night before, say 'That's it, devil-girl, get it up," and then the unmistakable sound of someone hawking and spitting.

A moment later, Stan came to the door. He had a steel dish in his hand and I tried not to notice the blood in it.

'Give her a minute or two before you go in, okay?' he told me.

I nodded weakly and he wandered away.

I made myself count down slowly from one hundred and then glanced into the room. The lady on the bed opposite had clearly been waiting for me and she gave me a nod.

As I walked in, I noted that Kelly Anne wasn't looking my way.

Instead her eyes were locked on the pretty doll beside her bed.

I thought for a moment she was going to pick the doll up and cuddle it. And after a second, she did pick it up but her intention was not to hug it.

As she picked it up she muttered something, (I didn't catch all the words because I was too far away, but the last one was definitely "bitch") before bashing the doll's head against the side of the bedside table.

'I take it the doll is a Dragons fan?' I asked as lightly as I could.

I realised she couldn't have been aware I was there. When she turned – looking startled – I saw that the expression on her face was very different to what I'd been expecting.

She looked scared.

Then she caught herself. It was like a mask sliding into place as her expression shifted and that glare returned and was directed at me.

'Oh, Miss Timm here isn't a hockey fan,' she said.

'Miss Timm?' I queried.

'Sure,' Kelly Anne replied. 'That's her name – Vicky Timm. Vicky? I'd like you to meet Mr Jones. Davey? This is Miss Timm.'

So saying she bashed the doll's head against the bedside table again.

'Vicky Timm, huh?' I said as I walked over. 'Something tells me you didn't choose her yourself.'

'Gosh, I wonder what could have led you to that conclusion, genius?' she growled and then tossed the doll down carelessly on the table.

I took one of the chairs beside Kelly Anne, then picked up the doll and had a look at it. There was a dent in the side of its head which the long blonde hair more or less covered.

'You gave this a hell of a bang,' I pointed out.

'I'd do a lot worse if I could. Just don't have the strength.'

'I could probably find you a piece of rope – you could lynch her?' I kept a straight face and, after a moment, got a faint smile from Kelly Anne.

'Don't tempt me,' she said. 'My dad doesn't want me to mutilate Miss Timm here.'

'Your dad bought you it?' I asked surprised.

'Of course not, dumbass – you think my dad doesn't know me?'

'So if Russ didn't buy Miss Timm for you...'

She sighed and lay back in the bed.

'Just after I was first diagnosed, my dad's boss and his wife came to see me. You could tell they didn't want to be there. Mr Sanderson and my dad don't exactly get along and I'd never even met Mrs Sanderson before. They came to see me because it was sort of expected they should show their faces. If their car had gotten a flat on the way over and put paid to their visit, they'd have been delighted. And so would I.'

'What does Russ do?'

'He teaches math over at Blue River High School. Mr Sanderson is the Principal there. If they ever do a reality TV show called Americas Next Top Asshole, he'll be a shoo-in to win it.'

'So you're not a fan of his?' I grinned.

She grimaced. 'He's the kind of dick that has to be a principal because he's absolutely no damn good at actually being a teacher. My dad sort of tolerates him.' She closed her eyes as if in pain. 'Dad has had to ask for a lot of time off to come see me. His boss has pretty much made him beg for it each time. As a result, I have to try and bite my tongue on those glorious occasions when I get to share some of my remaining time with Mr and Mrs Sanderson when they decide to bolster their social standing by visiting the sick.'

'So Sanderson gave you Vicky here?'

'No, his wife did. He sat there and checked and rechecked his watch and his only contribution to the conversation was to ask if I was being a good girl for the doctors.'

'Bet that went down well,' I said.

Her eyes snapped open and she nodded at the little stack of pucks. 'I really, genuinely considered pelting him with those,' she said with feeling.

'But you managed to restrain yourself?'

'Barely. I think my dad positioned himself between me and the pucks to prevent me taking steps to bring that visit to a premature end.'

I laughed.

'After which, Mrs Sanderson – who in my opinion is the spitting image of an ex-beauty pageant contender with her pearls and her floral-pattern dresses – hands me Vicky here, like she's handing me a guaranteed cure for the shit that inside of me, ripping my lungs and stomach to bits. She tells me I need to remember that all women – no matter what's happening to them – are still beautiful. In the interests of full disclosure, their visit was just at the point where my hair had started to disappear.'

'Charming,' I said with feeling.

'Oh, it got better. Mrs Sanderson is really, really keen on Jesus. She's a member of that new church out by the city hall building, the one that was in the news when their pastor said it was in the Bible that it was a woman's place to suffer. And so we should all just shut up and do our suffering quietly so as not to disturb the poor menfolk.'

'You've got to be kidding! Isn't that kind of thinking a couple of centuries out of date?'

'You'd think. Anyway, Mrs Sanderson tells me I need to do as the doctors tell me - because you know that would never have occurred to me - and I need to lie here quietly and wait for God's judgement.'

I didn't know what to say to that. It wasn't unusual to experience that feeling with Kelly Anne – I often found I didn't have the words to express how I felt.

One thing though was that I found my grip around the doll had tightened as my fist started to slowly clench.

'I wouldn't upset my dad for the world but, on the three occasions they've popped in, I've had to fight the urge to tell them what I think of them.'

'Why do they come back if they're so unhappy about it?'

'Cards from the school. Anyone could deliver them but it's a status thing. Mr Sanderson wants to show everyone what a good, caring head of the school he is, so he brings them and makes a huge deal of the effort involved.'

I set the doll carefully back on her bedside table.

'I can see why you don't like this thing,' I said.

'Oh, Vicky has her uses.'

The tone in Kelly Anne's voice changed when she said those words. I almost plunged in with some dumb joke about the uses I could probably find for the doll but her suddenly quiet, intense tone made me hold my tongue.

Kelly Anne stared at the doll in silence for a moment or two and then said 'It'd be really easy, Davey, to just be a victim. Sometimes – when it hurts badly – I think that must be easier than being myself. Just lie here and wait to be judged. You know what they say, don't you, Davey? After someone with the big C dies, the first thing their relatives are told is that at least the person isn't in pain anymore. Some days, that can sound, oh, so appealing.'

I got it then.

I understood why she so vehemently banged the doll's head against the table. It was a way to remind herself that *she* wasn't going to be a victim.

Again, I felt so useless that I just didn't have the words.

My eyes landed on the book on her table – Timur Volkov's autobiography – and then suddenly I realised that I *did* have the words; the same words I'd heard sung at the start of every, single Sea Devils game.

'They tell us we're despised,' I sang the words quietly and badly. I've never been much of a singer, but I think she got it straight away.

Her eyes locked with mine.

I reached out my fist to the table and rapped it against it.

Tap.

Tap.

Tap-tap, tap-tap.

She extended her own hand to the table and made a fist.

Tap.

Tap.

Tap-tap, tap-tap.

'They tell us we're despised.' I sang the words again and she licked her lips, then joined in. 'They tell us not to rise.'

Tap.

Tap.

Tap-tap, tap-tap.

'But we *shall* rise,' we both sang the words. 'See us rise! See us rise!'

Our knuckles had started to hit the side of the table harder as we sang.

Tap!

Tap!

Tap-tap, tap-tap!

'The Devils are coming.'

We both said the line softly – a cancer ward isn't exactly the place where you go to bellow the words to rock songs after all.

I extended my clenched fist to hers and she met it with her own.

'You want to talk a little hockey, devil-girl?' I asked her after a moment.

She nodded, wiped a hand over her eyes and then reached for

her tablet.

We sat there and we talked hockey for a couple of hours and it was a good conversation.

It wasn't until later that day when I was back in my own room that I realised I'd have to tell her sooner rather than later about my decision to leave the Sea Devils and hockey forever.

I had the nightmare again that night.

This time, though, it wasn't me in the burning car.

It was Kelly Anne.

I just stood there, unable to move as the flames engulfed her.

JOHN McKINSTRY

Let me tell you about Kelly Anne's idea of feedback...

How do you respond to feedback?

When you do something wrong and you get caught doing it – I mean caught dead to rights, busted – how does it feel?

It might have been back when your teacher caught you out when you were a kid at school or it could have been when you screwed something up in the office and the boss caught you doing it.

How did it feel?

Nobody I know likes to be made to feel stupid and while most people say they're sorry in my experience, they're usually sorry not about their mistake but because they got caught.

I'm good on the ice but nobody's perfect.

I've had coaches at almost every point in the life. From Grandpa Louie and my dad through to my first coach as an amateur player back in Sasky and the many so-called professional coaches I had to put up with after I turned pro.

Don't get me wrong – I'm sure some of my pro coaches were actually pretty good. It's just that I was born into a hockey family. By the time I hit my teens, I'd already endured every tirade possible from my grandpa and heard pretty much everything worth hearing about hockey from my dad.

I spent years in the lower leagues.

I knew damn well I could do better – that I was a cut above the other players- but I never chose to move up.

I didn't want to be genuinely tested.

I entered that world knowing that I probably already knew more about hockey than most of the people around me. I got used to there being a little or nothing the coaches could say to me.

And when they did try (in fairness, I'm prone to being lazy if I can get away with it) my response was often far from professional.

Putting hand on heart, I knew that I had more than earned my diva reputation.

I'd sulk, I'd skate off when someone was talking to me, or I'd claim to have some superstitious reason for not doing what I was told. I once told a coach I couldn't do additional laps of the ice because my dad had done extra laps the day of the car crash and it reminded me too much of that night.

I know. I know.

Classy of me, wasn't it?

My dad would've been disappointed in me and my grandpa would've just kicked my disrespectful ass.

Truth of the matter was I just didn't feel like working out that day but the coach scared the crap out of me. He'd caught me slacking off and wanted to make a point. If I'm honest, he was probably well within his rights to propose a bit of extra ice time for me – I deserved it – but I didn't feel like working up a sweat.

That coach – like most of the ones I had – didn't have any desire to push me if I brought my dad into the equation. Most people would promptly back down, rather than hand me a little constructive criticism.

Kelly Anne of course *wasn't* most people.

It was my third day at St Elizabeth's and, according to the nurse, I'd be getting discharged later that afternoon.

I decided that visiting with Lady Kraken (who had, I noted, received tidal waves of online abuse for her last blog post which had been titled: "Why the league must expel Fryar") was how I wanted to spend my time.

She was not in the best of tempers when I arrived at the Whyte Centre.

I could hear her swearing at the top of her lungs several minutes before I actually reached the ward doors.

Stan, the seemingly unperturbable nurse, was just outside the ward and he was grinning broadly.

When he noticed me his grin got bigger.

'Sea Devils lost five-nil to the Wolves last night,' he told me. 'And devil-girl in there isn't best pleased.' Then he clapped me on the shoulder and said, 'Hope you're wearing body armour, bro.'

'Don't suppose the fact I wasn't actually on the ice myself last night will help me?' I asked.

'You mean, do I think you mentioning your lack of presence on the ice will prevent her taking your legs off at the neck? Let me see, you're the star player, the big signing and the one who's meant to score all of St Helens goals this season!' He tried – and failed – to suppress his grin. 'You'll let me know if that weak-ass excuse works for you, right?'

I sighed. 'You could try and enjoy it a little less.'

'Not a chance, devil-boy,' he laughed. 'I'm a Wolves fan and had fifty on them to win! You enjoy your visit though!'

'Thanks.' I said and walked into the ward.

Kelly Anne was in full flight as I entered.

She had her tablet in her hands and was pointing at it as she expelled a stream of expletives. Her audience seemed to be the lady in the bed closest to the door who had gotten me to wait the day before.

'It's Face-off – not KICK off!' Kelly Anne all but screamed. The older woman had a faint smile on her face and had evidently been on the receiving end of one of Lady Kraken's rants before. 'You know what though, Sheila? It is absolutely okay for *you* not to know that – you know why that is? It's because you know you know squat about the world's greatest sport! You know who it ISN'T okay to not know that? The referee! The goddamn referee is MEANT to know basic stuff like this, but it's patently obvious he didn't! In fact, I doubt he knew any of the rules! In fact, I doubt he knew his ass from a hole in the ground! In fact...'

She noticed I'd walked in and her eyes narrowed dangerously.

'You,' she snapped, 'were not on the ice last night!'

I nodded.

'True,' I said.

'We lost!' she wailed. 'We lost on home ice to a short-benched Wolves team that we had a chance to beat!'

I nodded again.

'Also true,' I said.

'If you'd been playing, then we might have won!' she hollered.

I nodded once more.

'Anything is possible,' I told her.

My mild tone seemed to spur Kelly Anne on to further heights of foul-mouthed melodrama.

As Kelly Anne began a tirade on the Wolves, the referee, the linesmen, the league and the Dragons for taking me out of commission, I glanced over at the lady named Sheila who was now smiling broadly. She winked at me as Kelly Anne's voice rose.

If you could use passion as a fuel, then Lady Kraken could have acted as a nuclear reactor.

I glanced around. The lady opposite Sheila was also grinning and clearly enjoying Kelly Anne's stream of venom.

The fourth lady – I realised I'd barely noticed her on either previous visit – had turned her face to the wall and very clearly wanted nothing to do with the discussion.

As Kelly Anne finally paused for breath, I held up a hand and nodded across at the fourth woman. Kelly Anne glanced over and her expression was instantly contrite.

'Sorry, Jane,' she said.

The other woman didn't respond.

I walked over and pulled up a seat beside Kelly Anne. I nodded over at Sheila.

'So that's Sheila?' I said, and looked over at the lady opposite. She laughed and then coughed hard before introducing herself as Rhonda.

I turned to the fourth lady – the one with her back to us – but Kelly Anne caught my arm and shook her head.

I didn't push it.

Instead I asked, 'So, I'm guessing you have a view on last night's game?'

'Goodness, Mr Jones!' she exclaimed in a badly-feigned attempt at being winsome. 'I don't know if I should offer my thoughts and inexperience. After all, the referee clearly knows hockey *so* much better that I ever could!'

Sheila and Rhonda were both grinning and I nodded at Kelly Anne's tablet. 'I take it you've downloaded the game?'

The glare that question earned me seemed to amuse Sheila and Rhonda no end.

'You want to swap places with Miss Timm so that I can bang *your* head off the table, wise ass?' Kelly Anne enquired.

'No, I'm quite happy to leave the head banging to Vicky,' I replied. 'Why don't you talk us through the game, devil-girl?' I asked her.

Sheila and Rhonda both called out agreement.

'You can explain what happens at kick off again,' Sheila added mischievously.

'It's Face-off!' Kelly Anne snapped, but she was tapping on her table and a moment later I heard the familiar music for the local hockey highlight show.

I already knew from talking to her over the previous couple of days that Kelly Anne's knowledge of the game wasn't faked. Some of her online critics accused her of just popping names or statistics into a search engine and then spewing out the results but, the truth was, she seemed to know every team in the league brilliantly well. She knew the history, the players, the coaches and the awards and trophies they had won.

She was also a wonderfully animated host and would freeze the picture on her tablet to explain in plain English what was happening in the game.

Sheila and Rhonda had clearly been humouring Kelly Anne at first, but I could see that she was quickly winning them over. Hockey – especially when you have such a knowledgeable guide – can be immensely addictive and the two older ladies began to ask questions.

I listened as Kelly Anne answered every one with pinpoint accuracy. How many career goals had Timur Volkov had? How many penalty minutes had Frank managed to rank up? How many games did Coach Williams play back in the day?

'Your memory is phenomenal!' Sheila told her and Kelly Anne grinned. 'I know, my dad always says I have a kind of photographic memory. It would've been really useful if I was likely to live long enough to get to college.'

Sheila just nodded and continued to listen to Kelly Anne's breakdown of the team stats. But that comment rocked me and it took a lot of effort not to let it show.

If I hadn't been so stunned by her casual acceptance of her own end, then I might have been more alert to how dangerous the conversation could be to me as Rhonda began to ask about my dad.

Kelly Anne began to reel off stats about my dad (all of which I knew to be exactly right) as she searched online for footage of him

I heard the cries of "Send! For! Jonesy!" coming through the tiny speakers of her tablet.

Sheila in particular was very taken by the footage. She sat there in rapt attention as Kelly Anne painted a picture of the game we were watching. St Helens was playing the River Fall Fists and when they went one-nil down, the blue and green machine started the chant to get my dad out onto the ice.

'He was playing injured,' Kelly Anne added. 'He'd had a hamstring problem for about a week before he iced against the Fists.'

Memories flooded through me – painful ones.

'It wasn't his hamstring,' I said quietly.

Kelly Anne looked over at me. 'The St Helens website described it as...'

'He took a bad check the previous game,' I said in a tight voice. 'The doctors told him to rest but the game was for a quarter final spot. No-one forced him to skate but he knew he shouldn't – he was getting up in the night and pissing blood. He just hated disappointing people. He told the coach to spread the story that it was just a hamstring he'd pulled. He should've stayed on the bench but he never could resist leaping into the spotlight.'

Sheila turned to me and said, 'He looks like quite a player – although I'm obviously no expert. Is that how you play? Like your dad?'

That brought a snort from Kelly Anne.

'He's *nothing* like his dad,' she assured the older woman.

If you were going to be talking to a cancer patient in an oncology ward, what kind of tone do you imagine you'd adopt? Soft? Gentle? Reassuring? Those are the ways in which a good, decent person would talk to that patient, right?

If you were a decent sort of person then a tone of barely-restrained anger is probably *not* what you'd plan to employ. It's also unlikely that if you wanted to be seen as a decent sort of person that you'd look daggers at the patient, but I was doing both as I suddenly snapped, 'And what does *that* mean?' at Kelly Anne.

Memories of my dad always touched a raw nerve with me and I was used to people backing down if I became upset.

But Kelly Anne didn't back down, she just shrugged.

'I mean you're nothing like as good as you dad was,' she said simply. 'You're a sniper – that's all.'

'That's all?' I repeated, aware of how aggressive I probably sounded but unable to stop myself.

'That's all,' she said simply. 'You could be as good as him – in fact, you could probably be better – but you won't be. You'll go down as someone who had potential but who never managed to live up to it.'

Sheila was motioning at Kelly Anne but the hockey fanatic in front of me didn't seem to notice or didn't realise she was stepping over the line with her remarks.

I took a deep breath and tried to get a leash on my temper.

Kelly Anne shrugged at me.

'I've seen video of almost every game you ever played,' she told me. 'I'm a fan but I know what you are.'

'Just a sniper?' I asked.

'No, you're also a wuss,' she told me calmly. 'You shy away from making checks; you skate away from just about anything physical. When you iced against the Dragons you were practically sprinting away from the Ogre. The only scar you have is that one,' she pointed at the mark below my eye. 'And I never read about you getting that in any hockey match.'

'That's because I didn't get it in a hockey match,' I snapped.

She seemed unperturbed at my tone.

'That's what I mean. You have a grand total of eighty-three penalty minutes in your entire career and you've never once been penalised for roughing or fighting. You've never received a game ban and never once dropped the gloves.'

'So?'

'So, you're a sniper. You'll score lots of goals and St Helens needs that. If you would get more physical and make and take checks? You'd be one of the best power forwards in the game. You would be better than your dad by a long chalk. But you won't do that because you're too scared to.'

'Don't you think that's a fairly ... personal remark to make?'

Her blue eyes narrowed angrily.

'I'm not your mother, Jones. If you want to be coddled you'd best ask someone else.'

I slowly let out a breath.

'You can be a truly unpleasant creature – you know that?' I asked acidly.

'Don't ask my opinion if you don't want to hear it. When you know you only have limited time, you have to decide if you'll fill it by bullshitting people or by being honest with them. I'm honest. You could be great but you're scared of taking a bump. If my opinions offend you then the door is the big, wooden thing in the wall behind you.'

I glared at her for a moment and the notion of storming out like a sulky teenager did dance briefly through my mind.

Then suddenly, I started to laugh.

'Jesus wept,' I managed to finally say, 'there is just *no* give in you at all, is there?'

She glared – clearly still expecting a fight - then finally gave me a faint smile.

'Meant what I said, Davey. I'm your biggest fan. Your goals are going to lift us to the top of the table and if you ever chose to take a bump or two? To make a few checks of your own? You'd be near as damn unstoppable!'

There was a wishful tone to those last few words.

I really didn't want her going into my skills on the ice again. She had nailed me – absolutely got me bang to rights – and I didn't want to go back over it. I wasn't exactly proud of being gutless but I knew what I was. I just hadn't realised how obvious it was to others.

'You know they're discharging me later today but I'd figured I could pop by tomorrow if you wanted to talk more hockey?'

To my surprise she shook her head.

'You'll be busy,' she said. 'Team will want to get you checked out and into rehab, right?'

'I'm sure they'd be okay with me taking a little time out,' I replied weakly.

'Get your ass back on the ice, Jones,' she replied firmly. 'Get fit, get through rehab and get back to scoring goals. *That's* your priority.'

'You sound like the Coach.'

'You couldn't give me a nicer compliment,' she beamed. 'I'm not saying you can't visit but the team needs you.'

I tried to imagine how she was going to respond to the news I was quitting.

'Yeah, well, can't let the team down, can we, devil-girl?'

She shook her head firmly, we bumped knuckles and I left the Whyte Centre feeling like more of a coward than I ever had in my entire life.

I could have told her about my decision – I could have at least hinted at it to maybe lessen the impact for when I did tell her, but I didn't.

As I waited to be discharged from St Elizabeth's, one treacherous thought began to worm its way into my head.

She knew me.

Knew I was gutless.

Maybe she'd already worked out I was planning to quit?

If that was the case then I'd be spared having to tell her myself.

And of course, as soon as my brain began to consider all the fantasies – the situations where I'd be spared having to have that nasty conversation with Kelly Anne – there was one rather obvious one.

If she got real sick again she'd probably not know about my decision till it was too late and I was gone.

I gritted my teeth and actually shook my head at that.

No.

Hell no!

But it was just *so* seductive.

No need to hurt her feelings, no need to endure that withering scorn or see the furious, hurt look in those eyes.

And if she got really bad, she might even…

You can follow my thought process, right?

When the nurse came in to hand me some papers to sign, I was kneeling down, head bowed, praying that God wasn't going to call Kelly Anne home any time soon.

You know what though?

I understood, even as I prayed for her, that my desire not to have to actually *see* her die was a lot stronger than my wish for her to live.

I wasn't just a coward when I was on the ice, you see.

I even managed to be gutless when I was saying a prayer.

JOHN McKINSTRY

Let me tell you about the black jersey...

Hockey is a contact sport.

Injuries happen and, when they do, you need to be able to recover quickly.

The sheer number of games you play in a season is far higher than in most other sports. I saw a joke online that said at the start of the season a football player would be bracing himself for a gruelling schedule of sixteen games.

Hockey players call that October.

One of the main reasons my dad was so keen to get me, Mason and my mom along to games was that, if he didn't, then he'd hardly ever see us.

If you take a bad bump and are out for a few weeks then your team *will* suffer so you've got to be able to bounce back fast.

Of course, throwing somebody who's in rehab for an injury straight back into team practice wouldn't be macho and tough – it'd be unbelievably dumb.

But you've got to get back on the ice and fast.

So in hockey the goal is to get back out and skating again as soon as possible but to avoid getting you injured again, you have to skate wearing what they call the non-contact jersey.

The rule – and there are absolutely no exceptions to it – is that the person wearing the non-contact jersey must not be touched.

Saying you didn't see them or that you skated into them accidentally is not acceptable – the person wearing that jersey cannot be checked or touched in any way.

The idea is to rebuild your skill and your confidence in a safe environment.

Me personally? I wish I could have worn that jersey in every game!

The jersey is always a different colour to the uniform you wear in order to make you stand out and to remind the other guys on the ice that – even in the heat of the moment – they can't touch you.

At one point the St Helens non-contact jersey was white but then someone highlighted connotations of white flags and surrender – things that don't sit well with most hockey players – and it was changed.

On my first team practice about a week after leaving St Elizabeth's, I was back in the King Centre to skate with the team. They wore blue and green jerseys and I wore black.

There were greetings from the guys in the locker room and fist bumps and snarled comments about payback when next St Helens played the Dragons (a fixture I was hoping fervently to still be on the injured list for).

I'd spent a few days skating with Jessica – the team's physio. She was using my gloomy doctor's prognosis as a blueprint for my recovery. There was no reason not to skate with the team – provided I wore the black jersey.

It's hard to describe what it's like to watch all the guys around you pull on the blue and green uniform while you have to wear black. Some of the guys actually look away. Frankie – who was skating with the team even though his ban for fighting the Ogre had one more game to go – looked as glum as he obviously thought I felt. 'Don't worry about wearing black,' he mumbled. 'You'll be back to normal in no time and then you can dump that thing or wipe your ass with it.'

Frankie's comment tells you all you need to know about how most players feel about wearing the non-contact jersey – you aren't a real hockey player until you take the damned thing off.

If there had been even a hint that I'd need to attend team practice without it, I think I'd just have gotten in my car and driven back to Sasky.

For insurance reasons I also couldn't skate alone so Jessica was on the ice with me at all times. If you ever had someone in your class at school who had learning issues and had a teaching assistant with them all the time, then you've got an idea of how I looked to the guys.

My dad always said the black jersey could make you better – if you let it.

Every time he had to endure wearing it, he told himself he'd really develop his skill and that when he took the black jersey off for the last time, he'd have some new trick or improvement to share with the blue and green machine.

If my first session wearing black was anything to go by, then the odds of me improving as I did my rehab, were zero.

I began the session by slipping and falling.

Okay, even professional players do still slip at times but not as they step onto the ice to do a few circuits of the rink.

Nobody gave me a hard time about it, but damn, was my face red! (My grandpa would have laughed his ass off if he'd seen that.)

After I managed to put only three pucks out of twenty on target, due to how bad I ached, I was told to leave shooting for a few days.

While the guys drilled, I did gentle circuits of the arena with Jessica.

Everybody tried to cheer me up at the end of practice – none of them seemed to realise that the prospect of a long, slow rehab was exactly what I wanted.

It meant I'd be at no risk of further injury while I chatted with an agent about how to get out of my contract and leave hockey far, far behind.

JOHN McKINSTRY

Let me tell you about my rehab…

The first person from the online community to "welcome" me back was somebody whose screen name was Born_In_D-Ville.

"Know what happens if you get a second neck injury shortly after your first one?" he posted. "Don't worry – it's not a trick question. Ollie B will show you the answer real soon!"

You've got to love the keyboard warriors.

Born_In_D-Ville wasn't alone – he was just the first one to post a little hate for me online.

As a rule I didn't actually spend much time on social networking sites but I had a lot more free time as I went into my rehab programme with Jessica. Plus, since I wasn't playing, I'd been asked to do a little PR and part of that was online, so I got to see a lot more than normal of the bile those guys spewed.

Born_In_D-Ville set the tone. Another user with a screen name of DragonClaws31 wished me well in my imminent retirement from the sport, due to start on the evening of my next game against Douglasville. One or two Dragons fans posted images of wheelchairs and another posted a picture of a Wanted poster with my face on it and below that, the message: "NOT WANTED! By our team or his!"

And I lost count of the online warriors who proudly told the world they could (and given have the chance, would) kick my ass.

Most of the people who made threats or hurled insults did it from behind the anonymity of an onscreen name and an image (mostly of a snake or a dragon) instead of a photo.

Brave, brave little keyboard warriors!

I'd happily confess to being gutless but even I'd never mouth off at someone like that and then run away and hide online.

Frankie had told me at the start of the pre-season that some so-called fans would try some of this crap to intimidate and upset me.

I asked if anyone had ever tried it with him and he laughed and said, 'Of course!' He was the enforcer – when *he* got suspended or injured, all the little heroes crawled out from under their rocks to hurl abuse his way.

His initial response (taking a photo of his ass and posting it to them with the message: "Pucker Up") understandably didn't get signed off by our PR team (although Frankie told me they laughed themselves hoarse when they saw it).

In the end he posted the message: "Dear Keyboard Warriors, please note that lions don't lose any sleep over the opinions of sheep" and left it at that.

'If I had to go round and kick the crap out of every Jackass who sent me abuse online,' Frankie told me, 'it'd turn into a full-time job and I'd never get to play hockey.'

I kept that in mind as Jessica took me slowly through my programme to get me back to match fitness again.

If you think that having a whole group of people posting hate online won't have an effect on you, I have to tell you you're wrong.

It's corrosive.

Try and imagine what it's like to constantly read people's remarks about you winding up in a wheelchair, or worse, and tell me that won't have an effect on you.

But – as I discovered a few hours into my first day of rehab when Born_In_D-Ville tore into me – I had one huge advantage. A foul-mouthed, hockey-obsessed, one woman tornado called Lady Kraken.

Despite wanting to, I hadn't gone back to visit her. I kind of felt she'd be more inclined to talk to me once I'd started skating again.

She didn't seem to mind my absence.

She *did* seem to mind some of the abuse I was taking.

"Wheelchairs? Did you seriously post pictures of wheelchairs? CRAWL BACK UNDER YOUR ROCKS YOU PONDLIFE!" she posted.

Our PR guy had told me that managing social media was a full-time job.

Lucky for me, Kelly Anne had plenty of free time and was more than equal to the online warriors.

"You want to *fight* him?" she posted in reply to a user called Teeth_of_the_Dragon who had proudly announced how easily he'd kick my ass. "GOSH! How BRAVE of you! You want to fight someone in rehab from a neck injury! Hey, I've got a better idea, hero! Why don't you wait till he's *out* of rehab? Then we can put the pair of you in the ring and your entire little tadpole fan club can come and see you go one-on-one with Jonesy! Or do you only challenge people when they're just out of hospital?"

The hate that should have come my way went to her instead.

And yes – given that I was talking to different sport agents with a view to getting one to represent me and get me out of my contract with St Helens – I felt as guilty as hell.

At the end of my first week of rehab, I joined in with a quick exercise Coach Williams had cooked up.

We did a lot of set piece training – the goal was to get us to reflexively carry out a series of moves to get us past the defence and set us up to score.

All I had to do was accept the puck when Danny (who had the job of actually running the defence) fed it to me.

I must have done it dozens of time in pre-season.

My skating was improving and I caught the puck and was actually moving almost normally as I tried to shift into position to score.

That was when Robbie Dee suddenly charged at me.

He gave a big yell as he threw himself at me and I froze like a rabbit in the headlights, the puck forgotten as I flinched, closed my eyes and waited for the hit.

Which of course never came.

The man wearing the black jersey cannot be touched.

Oh, Robbie shoulder checked me – very mildly – as he veered swiftly away from me. It was nothing but a love tap but I shuddered as he tapped me.

My head was full of images of wheelchairs.

Coach Williams called an end to practice at that point. Robbie gave me a knowing sort of grin as he headed to the locker room – kind of like he'd always suspected I was gutless, and now he had proof.

I was spared having to walk straight back into the locker room when the coach told me he'd like a word.

I followed him as he skated across the arena and came to a halt beside the Plexiglas where the Ogre had checked me in my first game.

He reached out a fist and knocked it on the glass. 'Pretty solid, isn't it?

'Yeah,' I said non-committedly.

'Wouldn't do for someone your size to go through it and land in somebody's lap,' he added.

I gave a faint smile, 'Guess that's true, Coach.'

He nodded and then said, 'I've been reading some of the crap people have written about you this week, son.' He hooked his thumb towards the Plexiglas and asked, 'How many of the critics do you think have actually taken a body check like that for themselves?'

I shrugged. 'Not many I guess.'

'Virtually none of them. Funny how they still seem to feel qualified to tell you what you should have done though.' He turned to me. 'You have any injury experts amongst the online gurus, son? People telling you how close you came to dying?'

'Not dying,' I said, after a pause.

'They tell you about winding up crippled?' he asked shrewdly.

Images of wheelchairs danced through my mind. Coach Williams looked away and I'm almost positive he did it to avoid seeing the shiver that suddenly went through me.

'I could lie to you, Davey,' he said after a moment. 'I could tell you this is an aberration and will never happen again. I could tell you that it's all about the hockey and nothing to do with players taking a dislike to you or seeing you as a victim. I *could* tell you all that... but I've never been a fan of telling lies.'

He tapped the glass again.

'This is the reality, son. Hockey is a contact sport – you cannot play it and realistically expect not to take a bump. If I told you anything else I'd be lying. If you play, then you *will* take a hit – it's that simple.'

I tried to make my reply light-hearted.

'The joys of being a hockey player, eh?'

'Which would you rather be, Davey – a player or one of the spectators? How long do you think you could last as some anonymous online "know-it-all" who really knows nothing?'

I shrugged.

'You're not a physical player, son. Hell, I knew that when I hired you. Your job isn't to brawl with idiots like Brooks – it's to put the puck in the back of the net.'

'My shooting *is* improving and...'

He raised a hand to silence me.

'You can be as good as Gretzky himself, son - it won't change the fact that you'll still take bumps. There's more money involved in this league than you're used to. There's more pride invested in what we do here than you're used to. The bumps are coming and flinching and shutting your eyes will only make them harder to take. Ask Frankie. Ask your buddy, Dennis. When the bump comes, you keep your eyes open and try not to flinch.'

'Just try and take it on the chin like a real man, huh?'

That was the first – and last – time I ever tried being flippant with Coach Williams.

The look he gave me made me hang my head in shame, then look away.

I heard him sigh.

'It's not complicated, Davey. If you see someone about to check you, or throw a punch at you, and you freeze and tense up, then it'll hurt a whole lot more. The more unwilling to take the hit you are, the more likely you are to flinch.'

'I'm not real good at being physical, Coach,' I told him in a rare moment of honesty.

'I know that, son, but you've got to stop praying it'll never happen and just accept that it's part of the game.' He clapped me on the shoulder. 'You think about it, okay?'

I nodded.

But while I heard his words, all I was really thinking was that I needed to decide on an agent and get my ass away from a sport that seemed likely to kill me.

Rehab continued and I became aware of how closely Coach Williams was watching my progress as we moved into my second week with Jessica.

I still hadn't gone to see Kelly Anne and was starting to get frustrated with the agents. They all seemed to want to meet and greet, to build up a decent relationship – as one of them put it – before actually agreeing to take me on as a client.

The Monday of my second week of rehab pretty much followed the pattern set in week one.

Robbie Dee seemed to be my shadow that day and at one point, I was a step away from grabbing him and yelling, "You see me wearing the non-contact jersey, you asshole? BACK OFF!"

Monday was painful but I got through it.

Tuesday was different.

On Tuesday, the online abuse continued but there was not a single reply to it from Kelly Anne.

When Wednesday arrived, there still no posts or comments from Kelly Anne.

Born_In_D-Ville posted: "Hey Jones! Has your bodyguard gotten fed up with you too? Seems like everyone hates you!"

I suppose I should really thank Born_In_D-Ville because I was kind of running on autopilot that week and his taunt woke me up.

Wednesday night – despite how tired I felt – I headed out to St Elizabeth's.

I was about to be introduced to the harsh reality of the oncology ward.

Let me tell you about the lynching...

Russ was standing outside the door to Kelly Anne's ward when I arrived at the Whyte centre. He looked exhausted and Stan the nurse was pressing a cup of coffee into his hand. Not a paper cup from the vending machine but a real mug.

As I approached them, I could hear Stan gently telling Russ that he'd be no good to his daughter if he collapsed with exhaustion.

Russ was about to reply when he saw me.

'Is it okay if I visit Kelly Anne?' I asked.

Stan was already nodding but to my surprise, Russ wasn't.

'You're welcome to,' Russ said after a pause. 'But we all know you're really busy and if you have other stuff to do, then...'

He caught the glare I was giving him and sighed.

'I'm sorry, Mr Jones,' he said, 'it's just been a bad few days and I've been warned today about preying on people's good nature when it comes to getting them to spend time with my daughter.'

I heard a snort of derision from Stan at that.

'First off, Russ, my name's Davey – not Mr Jones. Secondly, it's not a chore to hang out with someone like Kelly Anne. Thirdly, if I ever run into your asshole of a boss in person, I'm going to throw him out of the damn window!'

As Russ tried – and failed – to stop a smile from creeping over his face at my last remark, I heard Stan say, "Amen, devil-boy!' He held up a fist and I bumped knuckles with the nurse.

'I'm on the injured list, Russ,' I told him. 'I doubt anyone will chew me out for being late to practice. Grab some sleep – I'd be happy to go hang out with Kelly Anne.'

Stan clapped Russ on the shoulder and nodded.

Russ raised the mug, 'Soon as I finish this Stan,' he promised.

Stan nodded and left us.

Russ took a sip of his coffee then looked back towards the door to his daughter's ward.

'You know what I hate most about the big C? It's how unkillable it seems to be. It's like a monster in a horror movie. You can stab it, shoot it, drive a stake through its heart but somehow – just when you think the good guys have won and the monster is safely dead – it suddenly sits up again ready for the next round.'

He took another sip of coffee then carefully set his mug down on the table nearby.

'You ever lose someone to the big C, Davey?'

I nodded soberly.

'My grandma,' I said.

'Did you see what she was like before she lost her fight?'

I shook my head slowly as the memories resurfaced.

'I was only really a kid,' I said. 'And she didn't want us to visit her. She told us a hospital was no place for kids but years later, my mom told me it was because she wanted us to remember her the way she'd been.'

Russ nodded a little sadly at that.

'I'm sorry for your loss, Davey, and I can understand why people do things like that. The big C sucks out the best parts of a person, it changes them into something they're not.'

He paused and then finally sat down.

'Just want to prepare you,' he said, as he massaged the bridge of his nose with thumb and forefinger. 'I thought there had been an improvement, we all did, but...'

'My grandpa would tell you there's no point trying to finesse the big stuff,' I told Russ gently. 'Least said, soonest mended was a favourite phrase of his.'

'She isn't improving,' Russ said at last. 'She had some tests Tuesday morning. Upshot is, she begins another course of chemo on Thursday.'

He said it all so calmly, so matter of fact, that we could have been discussing the weather.

Me, I felt myself go cold.

And remembered those treacherous thoughts I'd had before being discharged.

'Her chances?' I tried to keep my voice calm. 'They good?'

He picked up the unfinished mug of coffee and took a sip.

'I never jinx myself by talking about the odds. You know how many times she has already beaten them? I'm just letting you know that she isn't herself right now and when the chemo starts, she might be even less so for a while.' He looked me in the eyes. 'I really appreciate you coming but if you choose to stay away, I'll understand. And so will she.'

'I'm just being selfish here, Russ. See, I don't think she'd be happy to hear I was free and couldn't make time to visit. Fact is, I think she'd get out of bed and kick my ass. And I'm a coward, Russ, can't take the pain, so I've got to protect myself from your daughter's wrath!'

'Davey...' he began.

'I got this, Russ,' I told him. 'Go home and get some sleep. I'll talk a little hockey with Lady Kraken in there.'

He nodded, set his mug down and stood up. He looked like he was going to say something – something difficult – then he thought better of it as I saw him swallow down whatever it was he'd been thinking.

Instead he said, 'You're a good man, Davey – thank you.'

A moment later, I walked onto the ward.

Sheila looked up as I came in and smiled (although the smile was at best polite and maybe only a little removed from a grimace).

The ward was quiet and that just felt wrong

Kelly Anne was lying on her side on the bed, her eyes on the doll sitting on her bedside table.

'You and Miss Timm mind if I visit?' I asked. I thought I'd spoken quietly but my voice suddenly seemed far too loud.

'Hey, Davey'.

Her voice was quiet. All of the energy that normally surged through her was gone.

'I ran into your dad. He told me it'd be okay to stop by, so long as you want some company.'

'I'm not good company tonight, Jonesy.'

'Are you ever?' I tried to keep my tone light and got a faint smile.

'Dad tell you my news?'

I nodded slowly.

'Got a nice, big syringe full of poison with my name on it,' she said dully.

I noticed that her eyes hadn't left the doll.

'She's fucking loving this,' Kelly Anne said.

'Vicky?'

'Vicky,' she confirmed. 'Sitting there all fancy and prim and proper and being a good girl. Waiting for judgement. I don't have the strength to pick her up and bang her head off the table and I swear she knows it. I know she's only a doll but I swear the weaker I get, the bigger the smile on her face gets.'

I reached over and picked up the doll.

'I think staring at Vicky here is what Coach Williams would call unproductive. Why don't I just put her in the drawer?'

'No, when I go into chemo, the odds are pretty good that I'll get a visit from dad's asshole boss. I'm… not myself in chemo. I might forget to take her out again and then Mr Sanderson might get all upset and huffy.'

I made a mental note to punch Mr Sanderson in the face if I ever met him.

'Want me to bang her head off the table for you?' I offered.

She shook her head and after a moment I set the doll back on the table top.

We sat there in silence for a while.

'I'm not sure how many more times I can do this, Davey,' she said quietly.

'Put up with my company?' I tried to make my words sound light.

'Chemo,' she said simply.

She just could not take her eyes off that damned doll.

I felt the first spark of anger.

'Look at me,' I said suddenly.

She turned her head slowly round to face me.

'You're no victim, devil-girl.' I hooked a thumb at the doll. 'That *isn't* you. And if staring at that thing isn't helping you then it's hindering you!'

'Coach Williams say that too, Jonesy?' she asked. 'Maybe that works for pro hockey players but I'm just plain old Kelly Anne.'

'No, you aren't,' I retorted firmly and leant in. 'You are Lady fucking Kraken and let me tell you something, if Lady fucking Kraken saw that doll staring at *her* then she'd do more that bang its damn head off the table!'

I'd started speaking firmly but quietly and by the end I was almost yelling.

I watched as the expression of Kelly Anne's face shifted – hardened.

Like the mask being slipped back on, I was aware of a change in Kelly Anne from her suddenly sitting up onto one elbow to the harsher tone in her voice.

'And just what, Mr Jones, do you think Lady fucking Kraken would do to Miss Timm here?'

'I think she'd lynch the damn dolly,' I told her.

'Sadly I don't have a noose,' she said, fighting not to smile. 'They don't tend to stock them on cancer wards – might be seen as being in bad taste.'

I looked from her to the doll and then back again.

'Wait here,' I told her.

I had a feeling Stan would be more than happy to help.

Turned out I was right.

JOHN McKINSTRY

Let me tell you about my grandpa...

Are you able to cry? To shed a few tears when you're in pain or upset?

When I was a kid, I was quite sure that my grandpa was, for some reason, unable to.

My grandpa was a hockey player – a bone fide tough guy – and he didn't hold with men crying.

It's one of the many reasons why I know I'm not as good a man as my dad or my grandpa – I *have* shed tears quite willingly and publically – and Grandpa Louie would never have done that.

I saw him take a hit playing pond hockey one year. My grandpa had joined the game - out on a frozen lake back when my family still lived in Sasky – playing defence of course.

He took a stick to the face.

It was completely accidental – the culprit immediately froze and began to apologise profusely but once Grandpa Louie had taken a minute to get his bearings and spit out some blood, he just laughed, clapped the culprit on the shoulder and yelled, "Play on".

The high stick had broken my grandpa's cheekbone and badly chipped a tooth.

He must have been in pain but there were no tears. It was the same anytime he took a hit. From getting a few ribs broken to having his knee collapse under him, my grandpa seemed unable to shed a tear.

He didn't boast about it.

I never heard him yell 'I will not cry' or anything like that. It just wasn't in his nature to do something so weak as to cry.

My brother Mason and I grew up *knowing* that Grandpa Louie would not shed a tear. It was as set in stone as the law of gravity.

Until the day of my grandmother's funeral.

I barely remember my grandma. I can recall a warm, elderly lady who seemed as gentle as my grandpa was fierce.

I remember the pretty, brightly-coloured scarves she wore when her hair fell out and me being ushered into her bedroom one day so she could hug me and say goodbye.

And I remember the funeral.

Mom had taken Mason and me in a separate car from dad and

grandpa's.

There were lots of people crammed into our little local church. But nothing happened at first.

Everyone had arrived except dad and grandpa.

We waited maybe ten minutes. I could see the priest looking out at us concerned and my mom shaking her head at him.

Finally she tapped me on the shoulder and told me to go and find them.

The hearse was parked just outside and, when I glanced at it, the driver pointed me to the side of the church.

I walked over and as I approached I heard crying.

My grandpa – the toughest man I'd ever known – was crying his eyes out.

'I want it to be a person!' he bawled. 'I want it to be a person, Charley, so I can beat it!'

He smashed his fist into the stone wall of the church.

'It should be a person, Charley! A person! I should have a chance to fight it! To beat its bastard brains out!'

A volley of punches slammed against the wall as Grandpa Louie wept like a child.

It was as he turned to say something that he saw me.

For one horrible moment I thought he was going to beat me to a pulp because he launched himself at me and grabbed me by the shoulders.

But he didn't want to beat on me.

'You don't tell them, Davey!' he said in a terrifyingly intense voice. 'You don't tell anyone you saw me like this. Okay? It's just the wet anger, Davey, but you mustn't tell. Promise me!'

I nodded frantically at him and he hugged me briefly and then stood up and dashed away the tears.

'Just the wet anger,' he repeated. He took tissues from my dad and wiped his eyes then cleaned the blood from his hands.

It wasn't the last funeral I attended.

My brother and father were taken from me in the car crash. My grandpa and mom both suffered heart attacks.

At every funeral I went to, I felt dead inside.

I never thought the wet anger was something I'd experience myself.

But I did.

The day after Kelly Anne, Stan and I had lynched the dolly -

leaving Miss Timm swaying gently from side to side from the bed frame - I went back to see Lady Kraken.

I had gone to our PR guy and asked for some Sea Devils merchandise as a gift for Kelly Anne. Sensing a positive story, he asked for some details. Given that Kelly Anne had never once mentioned her illness, I assumed she wouldn't have any desire to be a features news story, so I apologised and explained it was a "private kind of thing".

I thought he'd hand me grief but instead he just opened up a store cupboard and told me to take whatever I needed.

So I arrived at the Whyte Centre with a big bag of goodies of the blue and green variety.

But I stopped at the doorway of her ward.

Do some research on chemo and you'll notice one of the most common side effects is nausea.

I was prepared for that.

What I wasn't prepared for was the sight of someone throwing up what looked like blood.

I couldn't look away, but dear God, I wished I could.

When she was done she just lay still on the bed. Looking over at her I was so sure she was dead.

Stan – face serious for once – told me I could go in but to give her time.

So I did.

I stepped away from the door and I tried to block out what I'd just seen and heard.

But the sounds of that little girl crying as she threw up never ever left me.

At that moment I understood perfectly how my grandpa had felt before my grandma's funeral.

I could feel the tears in my eyes and my right hand suddenly clenched into a fist.

'There's nobody to fight here, Davey,' a calm voice from behind me said. 'Or at least not with your fists.'

I hadn't seen Russ and, as he walked over to me, I took a deep breath and slowly allowed my hand to unclench.

When I was feeling a little calmer, I asked him, 'How do you cope with this, Russ? How do you get through this stuff?'

'What makes you think I'm coping?' he replied quietly. 'I have bad moments too, Davey. Sometimes bad nights.'

139

'So how do you get through them?'

He paused before replying.

'I say not today,' he told me at last. 'I can't say something like "You'll never break me" because we probably all break sooner or later. So instead I say, not today – you will *not* break me today – then I try to be as good a dad as I can be in the time we have left.'

Later Russ and I went into the ward and spent time with Kelly Anne.

By the time I eventually went home, I – just like my grandpa – wished the big C was a person.

So I could beat it to death with my bare hands.

Let me tell you about the streak...

I stopped calling the agents.

It wasn't a deliberate decision on my part; I just found I didn't have the time to keep chasing them.

In the lower leagues things got done fast. You usually got a yes, no, or a you-have-got-to-be-freaking-kidding pretty fast.

In the league I had joined, however, things were more serious. The agents knew there was a chance that the people they took on could wind up in the majors. They were careful who they took on and they really wanted new signings to jump through a few hoops for them. They wanted their signings to fit the bill as being "motivated self-starters" and "career-minded professionals".

I had a fairly good idea how my grandpa would have responded and, while I didn't mind playing the game a little, I had started to find their constant desire to "develop a two-way relationship" and "build rapport" tiresome.

Besides which, I simply had more important things to do.

After her first night there was no improvement in Kelly Anne – in fact her condition worsened.

I stopped by every night after training. I told her how my rehab was going and how the team was doing.

I did most of the talking.

The third night I was there, she abruptly motioned that she was going to be sick. Stan was too far away, so I instinctively grabbed the little metal bucket by her bed and managed to get it in front of her just in time.

You ever want to get some perspective in your life? Try holding out a shiny, metal basin for a fifteen year-old girl to vomit blood into. Then tell me you still have problems.

By the fifth night Stan told me I'd gotten so competent at helping his patient that he felt relaxed when I arrived at the Whyte Centre.

I listed that compliment as being only *just* behind the time my dad told me how proud he was of me when I scored my first-ever goal in a pond hockey match.

A week after that first chemo session, Kelly Anne was talking more.

A lot more!

She was pissed at missing games live and she was *really* pissed at the streak of bad luck that seemed to have plagued St Helens since the start of the season.

She was hungry to hear what Coach Williams was saying to the guys – the drills we'd had to practise and the changes in tactics he'd been trying.

And she asked – repeatedly – when I was going to be back in the line-up.

I ducked the question by telling her about the progress I was making and I hated myself for the moment I knew was coming when I would tell her I was going to quit.

A week and a day after that chemo session, Kelly Anne was informed she would need to be given another.

That night I spent a little time checking in with Russ and Stan and then with the other ladies on the ward. Sheila and Rhonda were both very enthusiastic about the suggestion I made to them.

The other lady however – Jane – barely looked at me as I outlined my plans.

Jane looked like she was in her early thirties. She was petite with very blonde – almost white – hair and she clearly was very uncomfortable about making eye contact.

'Do what you like,' she finally told me in a hollow voice before turning her back on me.

I felt myself automatically apologising to Jane. I knew there was a story there but nobody had clued me into what it was and it didn't feel right to ask.

But she had agreed so I went ahead with my little surprise for Kelly Anne.

Stan had agreed to delay her when she was chatting to her doctor that evening and Russ – who was in on it – delayed her further.

When Kelly Anne was helped into the ward by Russ, the first thing she saw was a huge TV with the pre-game commentary already in full flow.

St Helens were playing the Piranhas that night and Sheila, Rhonda and Stan were all wearing the blue and green jerseys I'd brought them – to show they were honorary Sea Devils fans. ("For one night only," Stan had warned. "Can't let a picture get out of me wearing the blue and green!")

But he *did* let her take a photo of course.

Stan was the kind of guy who went the extra mile - he genuinely gave a damn.

We got one photo of all of us together.

Well, all of us except Jane as, by unspoken agreement, we had left her alone.

It was a good game – if you were a Piranhas fan. An endurance test if you were a Sea Devils fan.

It ended (despite St Helens putting twice the number of shots on goal as their rivals) in a three-one loss.

Robbie picked up a ban for high sticks then mouthing off at the referee ("Dumbass" Kelly Anne had snapped) and in the dying seconds, Danny – who had scored our only goal that night – was taken off with what looked like a shoulder injury.

Kelly Anne had her head in her hands by the end.

'How long are the hockey goals planning to punish us?' she asked with a little of her old melodrama. She pointed a finger at me. 'We need goals, Davey! Goals! That's how you snap a streak! You need to be back on the ice!'

'The man's in rehab, devil-girl,' Stan said. 'He's no use to you right now. Besides, you guys got MUCH bigger problems than his absence!'

I think it was probably the broad grin accompanying his remark that inspired the stream of vitriol Kelly Anne replied with.

Rhonda was trying not to laugh when Kelly Anne finally paused from outlining to Stan what she thought of the Wolves.

Rhonda asked me, 'Is this what the aftermath of every hockey game is like? I mean, I'm new to this, but if being potty-mouthed is a tradition then I'll be happy to join in.'

She put a hand on Kelly Anne's shoulder as she spoke.

I grinned at her and said, 'I grew up in a hockey family, Rhonda – to me this is all perfectly normal!'

Stan nodded. 'Totally normal,' he agreed. Then he fingered the blue and green jersey. 'Well, apart from this aberration!'

Kelly Anne opened her mouth to reply and came up short. She looked panicked for a second but both Stan and I were already moving.

It took her a few seconds for the vomiting to pass.

Nobody looked away.

Sheila and Rhonda both knew intimately what Kelly Anne was

going through.

I noticed Jane turned round when she heard Kelly Anne being sick. The look in Jane's eyes was one of absolute sympathy. When Jane saw me looking her way she held my gaze for a second before slowly turning away again.

When she was done and Stan had taken the pan away, Kelly Anne looked ashamed.

'Sorry, folks,' she said.

'For what?' Rhonda asked gently.

Kelly Anne tried to explain - tried to - because for once the words didn't come.

Rhonda leant over and pulled her into a hug.

'You've nothing to apologise for, honey,' she told her. 'We're all in the same boat.'

It took a couple of seconds but then Kelly Anne's eyes welled up.

She glared at me as she raised a hand to her face. 'Don't you laugh at me, Jonesy,' she snapped angrily as she tried to cuff the tears away. 'Don't you fucking *dare* laugh!'

'Why would I laugh at you? Like I said, I'm from a hockey family. We look after our own.'

'So, what, *I'm* one of yours?' She still had tears running down her cheeks as she spoke and dear God, but there was so much vulnerability in those words.

'Aren't you?' I asked.

She pulled away from Rhonda to raise a hand to fist bump and this time, instead of meeting her fist with mine, I reached over and hugged her.

For a moment she froze – like this was the last thing she expected – like a fist bump was all she was owed or all she deserved.

Then she lost it.

During all my time spent with her that was the only time she ever cried. She bawled her eyes out and I could feel her whole body shake as she sobbed.

Sometimes there's absolutely nothing you can do to take away the pain.

Sometimes all you can do is just be with someone.

And sometimes that's enough.

Let me tell you about Jane...

Watching the hockey became a thing at the Whyte Centre.

There were apparently some comments made about the ward not being the best place to put a big TV. The unfortunate administrator who was sent to make this observation to Stan was politely told to go and explain that fact to the ladies themselves.

He lasted about sixty seconds as Kelly Anne – this time aided and abetted by an equally vocal Rhonda and Sheila – told him how she felt about the notion of maybe moving the TV to a nice lounge, which was only a "five minute walk away".

'Never seen one of those admin guys move so fast!' Stan told me gleefully that night. 'Devil-girl told him she'd bounce pucks off his face if he dared touch it during hockey season. He actually told her he didn't think she was – and I quote – "in any condition to do something so physical".'

I winced.

'And how did that work out for him?'

Stan took a hockey puck from his pocket and bounced it in the palm of his hand.

'She didn't!' I laughed.

Stan laughed. 'In fairness, she aimed high but I think he got the message.'

'She going to wind up in trouble?'

Stan shook his head.

'Rhonda and Sheila will both swear it was his imagination and that no puck was thrown violently towards him,' he grinned. 'So will I if it comes to it. Stupid ass bureaucratic thing to do. If she'd smacked him square in the face with it, it'd have been well deserved.'

'Best not tell Kelly Anne you approve of her launching pucks at people who piss her off. If her dad's boss visits again he may not make it out alive.'

I meant it as a joke but the nurse's face became serious.

'Yeah, and wouldn't that be a shame,' he said.

'What's up Stan?' I asked.

'Look, man, you didn't hear this from me, okay? Russ doesn't pass this onto devil-girl because he doesn't want to upset her. He's so tired all the time what with having to work back a lot of the time he takes out to visit.'

'You've got to be kidding! The school doesn't just *give* him time?'

I was outraged.

'Way I hear it, Russ is a good teacher. A popular teacher. Hard to fire a guy like that – especially if his daughter is in here. So, if you want a guy like that gone, what you do is you put him under so much pressure that he quits. That way, you get rid of him but you don't get to be seen as the bad guy.'

I realised my mouth was actually hanging open.

'What did Russ do? Screw this guy's wife?'

Stan shrugged.

'The guy's a moron. He introduced all kinds of exciting, academic changes.' The sarcasm in Stan's voice was laid on thick as he spoke those last few words. 'Russ called him on it, embarrassed him I guess. He wanted to pound on Russ but, like I said, Russ is a good teacher. Then devil-girl got sick. Russ has had to practically beg for time off. Never, ever loses his cool. Hasn't stopped his boss making his life hell though. Truth be told, it's been a relief having you here man. I can get Russ to go home now because his daughter's got someone he trusts to keep an eye on her.'

Stan's words cut into me because I *wanted* to be the good sort of person he was describing but the truth was that I was a gutless wonder who was still planning to leave and the fact that it was going to cause her pain hadn't really changed my mind.

'She's got you too, Stan,' I said lamely.

'That she does, my man, that she does,' Stan replied. Then he handed me the puck. 'Ask devil-girl to make sure any more pucks she throws *don't* come through the ward doors. If she beans me with one, I'll make her wear a Wolves cap for a month.'

I went into the ward and very carefully put the puck back in its place in the little stack on her bedside table.

'Some comment you want to make, Mr Jones?' she asked acidly. 'Some problem with my behaviour perhaps?'

I glanced over at the pretty doll which was still suspended from the top of the bed frame by the noose around its neck.

I picked up the doll and then very deliberately bashed its head off the table before letting it drop again.

'No problem at all,' I said pleasantly. 'So, what game are we watching first tonight?'

The great thing about hockey season is that, once it starts, there's never a shortage of games to watch. We watched all the major teams play but top billing in the Whyte Centre went to any Sea Devils game.

After a chat with our PR guy, I'd been able to bring along more blue and green goodies for the ladies.

I'd started to bring them in sets of four - four tee shirts, four cups, and four jerseys.

I never offered them to Jane but I'd started to bring her a shirt or hat when I brought things for the others. Kelly Anne put them aside for her.

Once or twice when we had a game on, I'd notice Jane move – turning her head to watch some of the match.

About a week after the puck-throwing incident I caught her watching and she seemed to realise I was staring. She glanced my way and for the first time, she gave me a very faint smile before turning away again.

I was around her so often that I began to notice there were different types of silence from Jane. I began to look for those moments when all eyes were on the big TV – those moments when she thought nobody was watching her, when she thought everyone's attention was elsewhere, and she would turn towards us.

I noticed it once or twice and just knew instinctively not to make a song and dance about it.

One night, Kelly Anne – head in her hands as another goal got past Murphy and wound up in the back of the Sea Devils' net – was in full flow. She cursed, swore and beseeched the hockey gods to stop pounding on St Helens.

I stole a glance over at Jane, who had the faintest smile on her face, glanced at Kelly Anne, nodded at her, and then raised my eyes to heaven as Kelly Anne went into a rant about Robbie Dee.

Jane's smile got wider and then she stuck her tongue out at me – whether for my nod at Kelly Anne or not – I didn't know. She turned her back on me a moment later (as she always did) but I felt good about that short exchange and I mentioned it to Stan as I was leaving.

'That's a good thing, Davey,' he said, although he sounded hesitant rather than pleased. 'Just... be careful with Jane, okay?

That lady is fragile.'

'More fragile than Kelly Anne?' I asked.

He hesitated and seemed to be debating something with himself.

Finally he beckoned me to a corner – away from the door to the ward.

'Kelly Anne is pretty damn realistic, Davey,' he told me. 'She knows what's inside of her, she knows what her chances are, and she knows what she'll need to go through while she's in here. She's accepted it.'

'And Jane hasn't?'

Stan hesitated again.

I waited and finally he said, 'You see Jane turn away from everyone?'

I nodded.

'What side does she turn to?'

It was an odd question and I thought about it for a second, and then said, 'To her left?'

'That's right. Do you know why?'

'Because that way she can face the wall and completely blank us?'

Stan shook his head.

'It's so you can't see her left wrist, Davey.'

It took a moment for his meaning to sink in.

'You mean she...'

I couldn't finish the sentence.

'Day she arrived, she was calm enough. Then she had her briefing. She was told all about chemo and what that would do to her body. When she excused herself to go to the bathroom nobody saw anything wrong with her. Rhonda was the one who found her lying on the floor. Jane had a pair of scissors in her bag and she used them to open up her left wrist. Pain was so bad and her nerves so badly damaged she wasn't able to finish the job and cut open her right wrist too.'

'Jesus,' I gasped.

'By rights, someone suicidal shouldn't be on this ward but she needs to get treatment. She was so scared of the chemo and the way it was described to her that she had a bad moment – a *real* bad one – and lost her head. We try and keep it quiet around her. Not always easy with devil-girl in there but Kelly Anne always tones it down if it looks like Jane is getting upset. The two of them have the same kind of cancer but Kelly Anne's is more advanced. Jane sees her... and sees her future.'

I glanced back over at the door to the ward. Then back to Stan.

'I'll be real careful, Stan,' I promised.

'I know you will, Davey,' he said. 'For someone who plays for a second-rate hockey team, you're an alright guy.'

We bumped knuckles and I left. But over the next few nights I resolved to do whatever I could to be nice to Jane and see if I could coax her into joining into conversation with us.

For the following two nights, Jane seemed willing to make eye contact with me.

When the Sea Devils snatched a last-minute win over the Piranhas (and Kelly Anne more or less screamed the place down) Jane glanced over and seemed to be smiling a real, genuine, smile.

The next night, however, Stan took me aside before I could go into the ward.

'Be really gentle tonight, devil-boy,' he told me in a serious voice. 'Jane is brittle today.'

'Something happen?'

'Not in terms of her treatment,' Stan admitted. 'Her lawyer met with her earlier. She was okay when he arrived, but after...'

He nodded at the doors to the ward and I looked in. Kelly Anne was – as always – glued to her tablet although I saw her stealing glances over at Jane every now and again.

Jane was actually sitting up in bed. She had what looked like some paperwork in her lap and a pen in her hand but she wasn't actually writing anything – just staring at the forms in front of her with an oddly neutral – almost blank – expression.

'I've never seen her like this before, Davey,' Stan told me quietly. 'Far as I know, the lawyer had a few documents to give her – nothing dramatic – but she's been like this since he left. Now listen to me, if you see anything – and I *do* mean *anything* – about Jane that worries you at all, then you come get me. Clear?'

'Clear,' I replied.

Rhonda, Sheila, and even Kelly Anne were all much quieter than normal. All three kept stealing glances at Jane.

I pulled up a chair beside Kelly Anne and started to update her about my rehab.

I couldn't help it though when Kelly Anne glanced over at Jane and my eyes followed.

Jane set her pen to the thick-looking document once or twice but she always took it away again without writing anything.

I talked to Kelly Anne about how the team's recent win had changed the mood in the locker room. She told me she was almost finished a blog post on the topic of morale and asked if I'd like to read it before she posted it.

I nodded and she picked up her tablet and fussed about with it, looking for the document she had created.

I looked over at Jane while Kelly Anne's attention was elsewhere.

That blank look remained on Jane's face but her lips were moving as she stared at the papers in front of her.

Are you any good at lip reading? If somebody mouths a word to you, can you make it out?

Usually I'm pretty bad at it but Jane was doing it so pronouncedly that even I could pick it up. She mouthed that word over and over again. To this day, I'm not one hundred percent sure she even realised she was doing it.

The word?

No one.

I very gently nudged Kelly Anne.

Jane wasn't being melodramatic. Point of fact, I'm not sure she even realised there was anyone else there. Her attention was on those papers and nothing else.

We looked over at her and I turned to Kelly Anne.

'I'm going to get Stan,' I said as quietly as I could.

I was about to stand up when a tear appeared in Jane's eye.

Her expression didn't change at all. That dead look was still there but suddenly there was a tear trickling down her face.

I stood up.

'Jane?' I asked gently.

She didn't reply.

Just mouthed that word over and over again.

'Jane?' I raised my voice but she didn't look up. Stan appeared in the doorway looking concerned.

Another tear ran down her cheek.

I walked over to her bedside.

'Jane?'

She turned to me as if she'd only just noticed me which,

thinking about it, may well have been the case.

There were tears streaming down her face but her expression remained blank.

'Jane? What do you mean by "no one", honey?' I asked.

'No one.' She repeated the word aloud and then stared back down at the paperwork in her lap.

I glanced down at it and realised exactly what had happened.

The document was her will.

I felt a sudden urge to track down her lawyer and beat the living shit out of him.

The page in front of Jane invited the reader to list the people she would leave everything to. It suggested she think especially of family and friends.

'No one.'

Jane's voice was emotionless.

The tears were pouring down her face but her expression still hadn't changed.

She tapped the paper with her pen.

'Got no one,' she told me. 'No friends to leave things to. No family.'

I felt like somebody had kicked me in the heart.

And not for the first time, I found I had no words.

Luckily Kelly Anne did.

'You *do* have a family, Jane,' she said as she got up and out of her bed.

Jane shook her head.

'All gone,' she said in that dead voice.

'We're not gone, Jane. We're all still here. We're your family too.'

Jane was shaking her head but Kelly Anne had never exactly been the kind to give up.

'We're a family here, Jane. We're in the same situation. We've got each other's backs. That makes us a family in my book.' She turned and nodded at me. 'Like Davey said, we're a hockey family, Jane – we look after our own.'

I saw a flicker then. A slight change in Jane's expression. Pain and heartache trying to break free.

'I've got no one, Kelly Anne.' Jane whispered the words.

'You've got *us*,' Kelly Anne said simply. 'And I swear I'll beat the crap out of anyone that dares tell you that you don't!'

'I…' Jane struggled to get the words out. She licked her lips then tried again. 'I don't want to be on my own.'

'You won't be,' Kelly Anne told her and reached over and took her hand.

'We're a hockey family, Jane,' I said. 'And hockey families stick together. We're here for you.'

Jane stared at me for a second or two. Then she carefully wiped her fingers across her cheeks to get rid of the tears. After that, she very carefully and deliberately put the paperwork and pen down on top of her bedside table.

She closed her eyes.

Her breathing got shallower and louder and then she was suddenly crying and admitting to us what was probably her greatest fear as she told us over and over again that she did not want to die alone.

And Kelly Anne, then Rhonda, then Sheila hugged her as she cried and told her the truth.

That she *was* part of a family.

And she'd never be alone.

Let me tell you about the visit to practice...

The incident at practice came about because Robbie Dee was being a jerk.

I certainly never planned it and under any other circumstance it would never have happened but Robbie wasn't the kind of guy who could just let bygones be bygones and when he found out that we'd have a visitor to watch practice – Lady Kraken no less – he decided to pay her back for some of her less than charitable remarks towards him.

The fact that Robbie was a big, muscular pro hockey player and that the target of his little prank was a seriously ill teenage girl never seemed to occur to him as being the action of a bully.

But it did to me.

Rehab was going well for me. My skating and shooting were both almost back to normal and Coach Williams told me this would be my last week wearing the non-contact jersey.

Yeah, you can probably imagine how happy I was to hear *that* news.

However, there *had* been some genuinely good news. The second session of chemo Kelly Anne had gone through seemed to have had a positive impact.

The staff at the Whyte Centre never used phrases like somebody was "getting better" or "cured" because they knew how quickly their treatments could be rendered useless. Until someone was actually in remission, the language staff used was always neutral. An "improvement had been noted" or a patient was "responding positively to treatment".

You did not – under *any* circumstance – say anything that could lead to false hope for either a patient or their family.

So while there was no running up the flags, I did feel that the world looked a little bit brighter.

I realised I'd sort of accepted that I wouldn't quit St Helens straight away – I certainly couldn't do it while she was in chemo.

I'm a coward – not a sadist.

So I had started to get with the notion of playing again – at least until she was recovered a bit more.

153

When she was a little stronger, when she would be hurt a little less by the news, *then* I'd quit.

That was the plan anyway.

Since I wouldn't be in a position to do it for much longer, I began to talk to Russ about getting Kelly Anne to the King Centre to see a practice session.

Two weeks had passed since the night Jane had broken down in front of us and in that time Kelly Anne seemed stronger.

"Stronger" of course, was a relative thing and while Russ appreciated the gesture, he didn't know how practical it would actually be.

I told him to leave it to me.

The first person I spoke to was Coach Williams.

Kelly Anne wasn't happy at people knowing what she was going through – her comment about not being interested in joining the pity party had stuck with me – but I figured that if anyone could get it all organised, it'd be the Coach.

I was as nervous as hell when I asked him (I felt like I had "About to Quit" tattooed on my forehead when I was around any of the team) but when he heard my request he asked for the whole story.

I went through it and then asked if he could arrange for Kelly Anne to see a practice.

'Well of course I can!' he said indignantly.

I pointed out there was a whole host of issues involved in transporting someone from the Whyte Centre and back again but the Coach just waved his hand dismissively.

'If she's free Thursday we'll do it then,' he said.

So that's what we did.

When we sprang the trip on her, I honestly thought she was going to explode with excitement.

It took a lot of organising (she had to be taken there in a private ambulance) but once she was there, she was happier than I've ever seen anyone. Her eyes darted around her constantly as she tried to drink in every sight and sound.

Russ had desperately wanted to be there but had apparently been kept late (although he'd be there to take Kelly Anne back to St Elizabeth's).

Coach Williams' lips pursed when he heard about that but he said nothing. Instead, he welcomed Kelly Anne and her carer (Stan

– naturally) to the King Centre. He took her on the tour himself
and after about five minutes I think he'd forgotten that Kelly Anne
was just a kid. As I left them to get changed, they were deep in
meaningful conversation about the best tactics for the Sea Devils
to adopt over their next few games.

Kelly Anne had been star struck around him for all of thirty
seconds before telling him who she would play on what line and
why.

When I skated out onto the ice for that day's practice, I wasn't
at all surprised to see the Coach had brought Kelly Anne – now
wrapped in a blue and green fleece with "STAFF" emblazoned on
it – to the home team bench.

I skated slowly past and grinned.

'You finished telling our coach his job yet?' I asked.

'Don't make me kick your ass, Jones,' she snapped.

But she was grinning like a madwoman.

It should have ended that way – with no drama.

But Robbie decided to be a dick.

Truth be told, Robbie hadn't exactly been my favourite person
for a while. He made a point of ghosting me as I skated. He'd talk
about the day the non-contact jersey was removed and all the fun
we'd have then…

He skated past me as I was warming up and tapped me on the
shoulder.

'Someone told me our visitor is actually Lady Kraken,' he said.
'That can't be right, can it? She looks about sixteen if she's a day.'

'She's fifteen,' I replied. 'Guess we all got her age wrong.'

Robbie shrugged. 'Guess so, Jonesy,' he said and skated off.

I didn't give it much thought at the time. We were working
offensive drills that day and I was starting to feel part of the line-
up, getting used to the habits and rhythms of the guys I'd be
playing with.

Till I quit and left the team high and dry that is.

I crushed that thought down and got my head into the business
of the day.

I had made my first attempt on goal (a poor effort that Murphy
batted aside almost contemptuously) when I saw Robbie Dee
deviate from the formation he was meant to be in.

He skated real close to the bench where Kelly Anne was
holding her tablet up to film parts of the practice and then

furiously type up notes on it.

Have to give Robbie this much – his timing was perfect.

As Kelly Anne looked up, ready to lift her tablet again, Robbie swung his stick as hard as he could at the bench.

It missed her fingers by maybe an inch.

She dropped the table (her lifeline) and I hoped to God it wasn't damaged.

Coach Williams bellowed at Robbie to skate over so he could have a word. I skated over to Kelly Anne who was fussing with her tablet.

'Don't be broken, don't be broken!' she said to herself frantically.

Her hands were shaking badly.

Stan finally took it from her, checked it over and told her she was good to go.

She lifted it up but I noticed she sat all the way back in her seat this time.

'Jones!' yelled Coach Williams. 'Get yourself back on the ice, son!'

I skated away reluctantly. I couldn't help but notice that, despite having the coach chew him out, Robbie was grinning broadly.

'Problem, non-contact boy?' Robbie asked as he skated past me.

I said nothing (I'm gutless remember?) but I could feel the anger surge up in me.

We played for another half hour and my heart just wasn't in it. I missed an easy pass from Lief because my attention was on Kelly Anne whose day had been ruined by Robbie Dee.

I was wracking my brains to think of some way to ensure her day *did* end on a high when I saw Robbie Dee skating back to that side of the ice. The arc he was moving in would bring him right back to her.

He was grinning broadly once again.

I didn't think about what I did next.

I was just suddenly moving.

Robbie Dee could skate but he was a big, heavy guy and he just did not have my speed.

In the time it took him to line himself up to skate at Kelly Anne a second time, I'd crossed from one side of the ice to the other and I was still accelerating when Robbie's head turned ever so slightly and he realised I was on intercept.

I saw him start to sneer as I closed on him, and why not? After all, I hadn't made a single check on anyone even in pre-season.

He must have been positive I'd skate to the side at the last minute.

A perfectly understandable assumption.

And quite wrong.

My right shoulder hit him squarely in the chest and the force of the check took Robbie off his feet and put him into the Plexiglas head first.

To my own surprise, I kept my balance and skated slowly away with my eyes still on Robbie who had wound up in a heap on the ground looking equal parts winded and disbelieving.

Kelly Anne's jaw was actually hanging open as I skated past her. We bumped knuckles.

'Hockey families stick together,' I said and winked at her.

Then I skated over to the coach.

I expected the full force of Coach Williams' anger for what I'd done. After all, while wearing the black jersey I couldn't be touched – it sort of went without saying that you couldn't abuse that by checking other players.

As I skated past him and then stopped to take my punishment, the coach was noting something on his clipboard.

He glanced up at me.

'Keep your head up when you make the check,' he said. 'You need to be sure your shoulder goes where you want it to, clear?'

'Yes, coach,' I said, trying not to grin.

I skated off to get changed. Robbie would want words after that hit and, truth be told, that was fine with me.

He stormed into the dressing room as I had just taken off my skates. He marched right up to me and jabbed a finger in my face.

'Now, you listen to me, Jonesy!' he began.

He was still wearing skates as he towered over me but I knew that actually made it harder for him to move suddenly.

I stood up and grabbed his jersey and then twisted it. I shoved and then I spun Robbie around and slammed him up against the wall of the dressing room.

'Why do you think she's got a nurse with her, Robbie? Why do you think she's got no hair?' I yelled at him, getting right in his face.

'She's got hair!' Robbie wasn't used to being on the receiving end, especially not from me. 'She just has it cut short!'

'Guess again, genius,' I snapped. 'Think about what I just told you, Robbie, *really* think about it and then hazard a guess as to what's wrong with her.'

I let go of Robbie and shoved him away from me, letting him stumble then fall onto one of the benches.

He just sat there for a moment or two as I pulled off my jersey and armour.

Finally he said, 'I didn't know, Jonesy.'

'You didn't think,' I snapped.

He nodded.

'No, man, I didn't,' he admitted.

Lief was the next one off the ice and into the changing room. He looked across at me and Robbie glaring at each other.

'You ladies want me to come back later?' he asked.

'No, Lief,' Robbie said as he stood up. 'We're good.'

He took a step closer to me and I was tensing for a punch from him when he said, 'You think she'd let me come apologise to her, Jonesy?'

I was genuinely surprised.

'Guess you're not a full-time dick then, Robbie?'

'No, man,' he grinned. 'Strictly a part-time dick.'

'I'll go talk to her,' I said.

Robbie raised a fist and I slowly bumped my own against it.

'Adorable,' Lief grunted as he sat down. 'You ladies should just get a room and have at it.'

I gave Lief the finger as I left the room and could hear him laughing as I walked out.

Before she left that day, Kelly Anne got the autographs of everyone on the team. When Robbie approached her, the first thing he did was offer a very heartfelt (and public) apology.

He didn't have to. He could have left early or sulked about it but he genuinely wanted to make amends as best he could.

Kelly Anne accepted Robbie's apology with very good grace.

'If all it takes to get Jonesy to play like that is a few broken fingers then I'm up for it,' she said.

And I knew she meant it.

By the time Russ arrived to help ferry her back to St Elizabeth's everyone knew she was a genuine hockey Brainiac with an almost perfect grasp of just about every stat in St Helens' history.

They also knew that she had the big C.

Coach Williams told her she was welcome back at practice anytime and that he'd be offended if she didn't come back out next week before the team's big road trip – four road games against some of the best and the toughest in the league over the course of the next month.

Kelly Anne of course promised she'd be back and then Russ finally persuaded her it was time to head back.

I did my best not to dwell on the road trip as I made my way home.

The likelihood was (especially after that hit on Robbie) that I'd be signed off as match fit for the trip. We would be playing the Wolves twice and the Piranhas once but before any of those games there was the small matter of a re-match with the Dragons on their home ice in Douglasville.

I had gotten back to my apartment and was fishing my keys out of my pocket when my phone rang.

It took me a few seconds to dump my holdall and locate my phone in my jacket pocket.

The person on the other end of the phone didn't mind waiting.

Alec Hart – one of the most well-known and high-profile hockey agents in the league – was nothing if not patient.

Let me tell you about keeping secrets...

Can you keep a secret? I mean *really* keep it?

Most folk can't.

Think about it. If you were dating someone then you decided you had to break up with them, do you honestly think they wouldn't notice you being in an odd mood? Do you really believe that knowing you were about to break up with someone wouldn't affect your behaviour when you were with that person?

I'm the world's worst.

I've never been a good liar and keeping a secret isn't something I'm good at. As a rule I come across as sulky – given my frequent bouts of prima donna behaviour most people don't actually view that as unusual.

My conversation with Alec Hart couldn't have gone any better – provided I was committed to my original goal of getting the hell out of hockey.

If you had signed a one-year contract, would you know how to get out of it without penalties?

Lots of guys used hockey as a way into college and I'd run into one or two law students in my time, but I wasn't one of them.

I'd drifted into hockey as a career and been at best lukewarm about it since my dad had died. I'd always been a player and didn't have any idea about the business side of things.

Alec did.

He'd noted some interest in me from rivals – everybody assuming I wanted a quick step up to the next league.

When I told him I just wanted out of the contract he seemed nonplussed.

Alec explained that he didn't make any money from negotiating the release on my contract.

I assumed that would be the end of the conversation and was half annoyed and half relieved at that.

But it wasn't.

Alec knew of several off-ice roles including what he described as a "peach of a role" in PR.

Those *would* make him money. Any one of them would get me

161

off the ice and away from the danger of another hit like the one that got me hospitalised.

A few weeks back, I'd have called it a godsend and grabbed it with both hands.

But that had been before I got to know Kelly Anne.

Alec told me to think it over. He could make it happen and if I wanted that "peach of a role" he could more or less guarantee me it but the clock was ticking on that one.

Knowing I could have what I wanted, that I could ditch hockey and be safe, didn't make me feel good though.

The knowledge that I could do it actually weighed me down.

Throughout the following day I kept reminding myself that Kelly Anne was – to quote the doctors – responding well to treatment.

I tried to tell myself that if I stepped out of hockey then it wouldn't be *that* big a deal to her.

I almost didn't go to the Whyte Centre that night. I was sure that she'd sense me acting oddly and call me on it. She was sharp and, like I said, I'm a terrible liar.

But I did go.

It was a good night. The Sea Devils weren't playing but the Dragons were and when the Wolves tore them to shreds with a five-one demolition job it was almost as good as a St Helens win for Kelly Anne.

Watching the Ogre getting awarded a game ban for cross checking from behind didn't exactly upset me either.

I thought I'd pulled it off till I was leaving and Stan asked me for a word.

'Tough day at practice?' he asked me.

I shrugged and said, 'Yeah, something like that.'

He looked at me – looked me right in the eye – then said, 'That's the only thing that's bothering you tonight?'

'What do you mean?'

'I mean I haven't once heard you talk about hockey with any less enthusiasm than devil-girl does. She told us all about that session – every single detail. I had to remind her twice I'd actually been there too. Yesterday you were up for it. Tonight? Never heard you this quiet, Davey. What's up?'

I sighed, considered lying to him, but decided against it.

'Did you actually see the hit that landed me in here, Stan?' I asked.

'Over and over,' Stan replied. 'You think devil-girl missed an opportunity to show me it?'

'You know what the doctors said *could* have happened to me?'

He didn't reply.

He looked over at the door to the ward and then back at me and sighed.

'You need to tell her, Davey,' he said.

'I don't know if I can,' I admitted. 'You have no idea how badly I want to avoid hurting her, Stan but...'

'But you don't relish taking another beating like the last one you got handed.' Stan finished my sentence for me.

I looked at my shoes.

'I'm a coward, Stan. Everybody else seems to find it so easy to be brave, but not me. I've done all I can to avoid taking the bumps. I could've moved up to this league sooner but I knew damn well how much of a bruising I might take. I'm no tough guy – never have been and never will be. I finally drifted into it because it was the best offer on the table. Now I find that I can't decide what I'm more scared of – taking another beating or hurting her.'

'That's a tough spot to be in,' Stan said. 'Let me ask you this – you made your mind up yet? I mean, have you definitely made your choice and don't know how to break the news, or are you still trying to decide?'

'Still trying to decide,' I admitted.

'Tough place to find yourself in, Davey. You want to do right by her?'

'Of course I do. There's no question of that.'

'Then make a decision, be honest about it and then live with it. As soon as you've decided? Tell her. Don't try to weasel out of it – be honest.' He gestured around him. 'We don't go in for lies or false hope here, Davey. If you're going to leave, then tell her – she'll cope.'

'Not trying to be arrogant, Stan, but you sure about that?'

He nodded.

'I didn't say she'd like it and I didn't say it wouldn't hurt – I said, she'll cope.'

It was my turn to nod.

'She's... I mean, she *is* improving right now, isn't she?'

'Make your decision, Davey – don't use her health as a way to justify it.'

It was a blunt thing to say but it was also fair. I *had* been trying to justify.

'There isn't really a good solution that I can see here, Stan,' I said. 'I mean, if you can see something I've missed – some way to keep everyone happy – then feel free to share.'

'If I could conjure up some lies that might make you feel better, I wouldn't, Davey. And not because I dislike you, you understand?'

I nodded. 'Makes sense I guess.'

'Big C affects everything, Davey. Everything and everyone. Relationships and friendships tend to either become as strong as steel, or just disintegrate. We had a lady in here last year named Maria. She was divorced and had one kid – a girl in her late twenties named Teri. You could tell Maria and Teri were really close. Teri came in her to visit her mama every day.'

'But?' I asked.

'It got bad, Davey. Cancer ate that poor soul down to the bone. Teri had to watch her mama start to wither in front of her. At first Teri tried to tough it out. Slowly her visits started to get shorter and then one day – despite the fact she really did love her mother – Teri stopped visiting. She couldn't bear having to watch the inevitable any longer. Never forgave herself either. Her own marriage crumbled and she was in therapy last I heard. When the big C arrives, it damages more than just the sufferer, Davey.'

'The mother – Maria – what happened to her?'

'She died,' Stan said simply.

'Jesus.' I walked a step or two away from him.

'It was the cancer that killed her, Davey – not the lack of visits from her daughter. If Teri had been there every day to the end, it wouldn't have changed the outcome. Maria would still have died.'

'And if Teri *had* been there, then maybe Maria's last days might have been better?'

'Maybe,' Stan admitted. 'I'm not going to tell you that you being here isn't having a good influence, Davey. Fact of the matter is, I'm trying real hard not to say anything that'd pressure you one way or the other. It's you and *only* you that can make the decision.'

A moment passed and I finally said, 'Wonder what this makes me, Stan? Is there a name for someone so cowardly they're scared to even make a decision?'

Stan snorted.

'That doesn't make you a coward,' he told me.

'No?'

'No. That just makes you human. The only thing that would be cowardly would be to not make a decision. Think about it, Davey. And when you've made your mind up, tell her.'

It was good advice.

But hours after leaving St Elizabeth's I still didn't know what I wanted to do.

Sleep was a long time coming that night.

.

Let me tell you about the last black jersey session...

At the end of my last black jersey session, Coach Williams gave me a gift.

It was to all intents and purposes a "get out of jail free card" and under any other circumstances I'd have been elated.

The first game on St Helens road trip was the one I was most terrified of – the re-match against the Dragons on their home ice.

Danny's shoulder injury hadn't been as bad as first thought. Danny would be back on the ice for the game in Douglasville and while Coach Williams could have played me, he told me he'd list me as a healthy scratch – I'd travel with the team but wouldn't ice.

I thanked him but my voice was dead when I did so and I'm sure he would have noticed and wondered what was wrong.

It was a really thoughtful thing to do – especially as he must have needed the extra skater on the team.

Trouble was, he handed me the gift about ten minutes after I'd had one of the most painful conversations of my entire life.

It was the last skate at the King Centre before the road trip and a lot of the focus of that session had been on me.

Coach Williams had kept me in the black jersey right to the end. Some of the guys probably saw this as my punishment for checking Robbie but, as I told them, me and Robbie were good. Since I had bounced him into the Plexiglas, I'd gotten on a lot better with Robbie. Hell, I'd gotten on a lot better with everyone on the team. I'd popped my cherry and boarded someone, gotten physical and they all respected that.

If I hadn't been about to dump them all and leave, it would have been a good feeling to finally feel accepted by the guys around me.

That last practice had been all about offence, about scoring goals so that the Sea Devils could try and turn their season around.

And Kelly Anne was in the King Centre, seated where Coach Williams usually sat at the home team bench.

Coach Williams made a point of skating over now and again to ask her thoughts on the plays he was running.

'I started doing is as a joke,' he told me. 'But the truth is, she'd make a damn good bench coach. Her instincts are spot on!'

She did have to leave her seat once or twice. That bothered me a lot because I had a good idea why she was leaving. Her face was as white as a sheet when she returned with Stan each time and I found myself trying not to listen to her coughing in order to gauge if it was still as bad as it had been. She was meant to be getting better – surely that meant the coughing and vomiting would lessen?

But I kept my head in the game for most of the practice. Coach Williams had told the guys to buzz me – to skate right at me like Robbie had – as often as they could.

My flinch reflex – those moments where I basically shut my eyes, gritted my teeth and almost froze in place while waiting to be hit – had either been missed or ignored in pre-season.

The coach wanted me to lose that flinch now and he had everyone bar the goalie skate right at me whenever I won the puck.

It was brutal.

Even though I knew they weren't going to hit me, it was still terrifying because most of the guys were good enough skaters to be able to veer off at the very last second. I lost the puck more than fifty percent of the time that day. The times I kept possession were more down to Danny than to me. Danny was making me look better than I had any right to and was shouldering more than his share of the work – again.

Kelly Anne alternated between cheering and hurling abuse – mainly at me.

Her cry of "Don't make me kick your ass, Jonesy!" after I missed an easy pass had had the coach howling with laughter.

I endured it with a good grace (and why not, since I'd shortly have the opportunity to just dump the lot of them and walk away?) and silenced most of them with an almost perfect goal. A nice pass from Danny to me, a feign to get Murphy going the wrong way and then a neat slap shot that shot past Murphy's stick and thunked solidly into the back of the net.

Murphy glowered at me and our goalie's mood wasn't improved by Kelly Anne performing what could be best described as a one-woman Mexican wave in celebration.

It would have been so perfect if the day had ended there, but of course, it didn't.

Coach Williams had one more drill to run.

It was basically shooting practice – take the puck from the blue line and try and put it past Murphy.

Danny and I took turns and we did okay. We took two goals each off Murphy who, let's remember, was damn good.

I was skating forward, intent on getting at least one more, when it happened.

Robbie Dee actually screamed at the top of his lungs as he exploded towards me just as I had pulled my stick back to take the shot.

I froze.

You know what the first thing was that went through my mind? Wheelchairs.

Robbie didn't hit me, he shouldered me aside (taking the puck with him as he went) and Murphy raised his stick in triumph while behind me I heard a loud cry of "Fuck!" from an exasperated Kelly Anne.

Practice finished shortly afterwards.

We were skating off and I paused by the bench to say hi to Kelly Anne. Everyone else was still well within hearing distance as she pointedly said, 'You shouldn't have missed, Jonesy.'

I heard a few chuckles from the guys and tried to steer her onto a safer topic of conversation but she wasn't to be moved.

'You should have taken the shot,' she told me in a voice which carried. 'You'd have scored, Davey. You need to get the puck away when they blitz you!'

She sounded disappointed to put it mildly and while the guys were leaving the ice they all could still hear her.

'Everybody takes a hit from time to time,' she went on. 'They won't all be like the one Brooks laid on you, you know!'

My mind flashed back to my first game and wheelchairs raced through my mind again.

I found my eyes going over to the section of the Plexiglas the Ogre had thrown me up against.

Kelly Anne followed my gaze and then those piercing blue eyes swivelled back around to me.

She looked contrite and I tried to make a joke of it.

'Maybe I'm just not cut out for this?' I suggested lamely.

I hadn't been planning to tell her that day – mainly because I still wasn't sure myself.

I hadn't meant my words to be anything other than an admittedly feeble attempt to lighten the mood.

Those blue eyes saw straight through me.

She knew.

'Hey, Stan, could you get me some water?' she asked.

Stan got up without a word and I found I couldn't meet his eyes as he walked away.

Neither Kelly Anne nor I said a word.

Then, in a very quiet voice, 'You going to quit, Davey?'

She looked ready to cry but her voice was still firm.

At that moment, I think I'd have just about have sold my soul to be able to lie to her.

But I couldn't do that to her.

I just couldn't.

'I haven't decided,' I said. 'But... yeah, I'm thinking about it.'

'Because of the Ogre?'

'Because I'm a coward, Kelly Anne,' I told her honestly. 'Because I wake up at night in a cold sweat. And when I manage to calm down, do you know what I do? I walk up and down my apartment. I walk up and down and up and down and just fucking rejoice in the fact that I *can* walk and that I'm not in a wheelchair paralysed from the neck down. It's just a sport. A game. It's one I'm pretty good at but it's not one I plan to die for.'

She looked away from me. And I heard her swallow hard.

When she turned back she looked almost calm.

Her next words to me hurt more than anything else possibly could have.

I was bracing myself for anger, for swearing, for a verbal mauling.

But that wasn't what I got.

What she said was worse.

She told me she understood.

She told me she knew that the hits hurt, that bodies could be broken beyond repair in a contact sport like hockey.

She told me it would be alright.

In my whole life, I had never felt so low.

I tried to recover it, tried to remind her that I hadn't decided. Told her I'd still come visit. And she managed a smile, saying that would be great.

I tried one last time. 'I'll be taking this off.' I fingered the black jersey I was wearing. 'And I'm sure that I'll ice again, but...'

I licked my dry lips.

'Nothing is forever,' I said at last.

She nodded.

'Nobody knows that better than me, Davey.'

Stan returned at that point. I have no idea whether he had been listening and chose to stop things before they got really bad.

The day wasn't quite over.

The guys had wanted to make a fuss of Kelly Anne. And they did. They left her with blue and green goodies, including her choice of a game jersey with that player's name and number.

After our chat, I doubted it'd be mine she chose.

She seemed to have a good time and while she was with the guys, Coach Williams had handed me that "get out of jail free card".

I didn't want to be rude but after my conversation with Kelly Anne it felt meaningless.

Where her visit was done, I walked with her, Stan and Russ to the ambulance.

Stan nudged Russ and led him away.

Kelly Anne clearly still had something to say and didn't want an audience for it.

'Road trip to Douglasville,' she said. 'A chance to play the tadpoles on their home ice.'

'Yeah, doesn't get any better, does it?'

She reached out and hugged me.

'Whatever you do, Davey, I will still be your number one fan,' she said then she kissed me on the cheek. 'No matter what you choose to do, I'll be cheering you on, Jonesy, because that's what families do.'

She climbed into the ambulance.

'You make sure you come home safe from Douglasville, Jonesy,' she said. 'You come and watch the games with the girls and me, okay?'

'You got it.'

Then we bumped knuckles and a couple pf minutes later the ambulance pulled away leaving me feeling like the lowest, nastiest piece of shit ever left on the Good Lord's earth.

JOHN McKINSTRY

PART THREE
Blood on the ice

Goodness! So much testosterone! Any of you little tadpole
fans consider the possibility that Jones might just, you know,
play hockey?
#Jonesy #believe
Posted by user - Lady Kraken

JOHN McKINSTRY

Let me tell you about the decision…

About a year after that second game I played against the Dragons, I ran into Alec Hart.

We chatted for a few minutes and he told me he had no grudges over what I'd done. By that time, people knew about Lady Kraken and Alec was both respectful and genuinely curious.

The one thing he *really* wanted to know was, what it had been that had led me to make the decision I had.

'You had the easy option sitting right there in front of you, Davey,' he said. 'You could have walked away at any time. Why did you turn my offer down? I honestly thought you'd be the one who'd take that PR role'.

I figured Alex deserved the truth. So that's what I gave him.

I told him about how conflicted I'd been.

I told him about Stan's words – that the only cruel thing would be to not actually make any decision, but to just sort of drift along into things.

I had agonised over it.

In the end, I told Alec Hart I had weighed it all up and had decided to accept his offer and leave the Sea Devils as quickly as I possibly could.

Nights spent tossing and turning at the prospect of taking to the ice with people like Brooks and Fryar was no way to live.

Kelly Anne already seemed to have accepted my decision – it was a done deal.

Intrigued, Alec asked then, if that had been the case, what had changed my mind?

Because I *did* change my mind.

It happened in a rush and at the last minute but I called Alec to turn down the offer. Then the next night I went to Douglasville – but not as a healthy scratch.

I was the first out of the tunnel and onto the ice that night.

What changed my mind?

A letter.

I'd made my decision but knew it'd take some time to become reality. I would probably take a bit of abuse in Douglasville but I'd be safe.

I was packing my stuff – I don't know to this day how she pulled it off but Kelly Anne had written me a letter and somehow managed to get someone to slip it into my holdall. She couldn't have had much time to write it but then it wasn't a long letter. If you ignore her signature at the bottom it was exactly seven words.

Seven words that slammed into me like bullets.

I admitted to Alec Hart that, after I read it, I just sat on my bed for a long time – thinking.

I thought about my family.

I thought about what I'd done with my life to date.

I thought about my future.

I thought about being scared of everything and everyone all the time.

Then I folded the letter, put it in the drawer by my bed and made two phone calls.

The first was to Coach Williams.

I told him I had a little personal business to take care of. I wouldn't be able to travel with the team, but I would be in Douglasville for the game. And I *didn't* want to be a healthy scratch for it.

'You've got a free pass, son,' the coach told me. 'You don't need to ice – you sure you want this?'

'Absolutely positive,' I replied.

He told me he'd make sure they brought my game jersey and pads.

The second call was to Dennis.

I asked him if his long-standing offer of a few lessons still stood.

Alec Hart listened with rapt attention as I described how I'd prepared for the re-match against the Dragons.

When I was done, he shook his head and said, 'You know, I actually had tickets for that game? I gave them away to a client I was trying to impress. If I'd have realised what was going to happen on the ice that night, you would have had to pry those tickets from my cold, dead hands! It turned into one hell of a game, didn't it?'

I nodded slowly.

The memories of that night are still about the strongest ones I have.

One hell of a game?

Oh, it had been that all right.

That second game against the Dragons was both the bravest and the dumbest thing I ever did.

That was the night I stopped running.

JOHN McKINSTRY

Let me tell you about turning the other cheek...

I stoop.

You don't often notice it because I've done it for so long it feels natural to me. It's usually only when people see me deliberately stand at my full height that they realise how tall I actually am.

It started at high school.

Everybody wants to fit in – especially a kid who moved from Saskatchewan to New England because his dad picked up a contract to play hockey there.

So I hated the fact that I started to grow early and I started to stoop so I'd be closer to the same height as my classmates.

Partly it was to fit in more.

Partly it was to make myself less of a target.

With my dad's job, and my own weird (to them) accent, I gave the bullies at the school no shortage of reasons to pick on me.

You know the really bad thing about starting to grow? It's not just that you stand out. It's the assumption that, if you're a big guy, then you must also be a tough guy.

I was anything but a tough guy but people at high school just assumed I was – because I was tall.

Plus, since I grew up in a hockey family (and all hockey guys were assumed to be tough) it must have made sense to everyone that I'd be willing to fight.

Truth is, with my dad away so much it was my mom who really raised me and my mom always taught me that we should just turn the other cheek and rise above it when people gave us any kind of abuse.

All this was going through my head as I walked into the little gym in Casco, just outside of Maine, where Dennis was based whilst he got prepared for his next fight.

The gym was already busy when I got there.

There were lots of serious-faced men calling out instructions or advice to the people training there. One of the two full-sized boxing rings in the gym already had two young men in brightly-coloured head guards and gloves sparring ferociously in it. On the other side of the room there was a row of punch bags and speed balls and most of these were being worked on with a quiet intensity by the people there. I could hear the rhythmic tap-tap-tap as fists hit bags and it occurred to me then that while I had been struck repeatedly over the years I had never once made a fist and punched anyone back.

I had always, without exception, turned the other cheek.

When Dennis came through to greet me, I thanked him for taking time out from his schedule and he just laughed and told me he'd been waiting for me to accept his invitation to train with him since the Tommy Cates incident back at high school.

I asked him what we were going to do. I'd had an idea I'd spend most of the morning doing press-ups and sit-ups while some hard-faced trainer yelled abuse at me.

Dennis rolled his eyes at me and told me I'd watched too many boxing movies.

'Your fitness isn't the problem,' he told me. 'Your lack of technique however is.'

Boxing, Dennis explained, had as much to do with strategy and tactics as it did with punching power.

With that in mind, Dennis then led me, not to a locker room to get changed, but to a sort of meeting room which had a big-screen TV on the wall and a laptop on the table.

Dennis knew exactly who I was planning to fight so he had downloaded as much footage of Brook's fights as he possibly could.

My first reaction was that watching footage of the Ogre brutalising opponent after opponent wasn't going to be great for my morale and if I'd had to watch that little compilation on my own I'd have been right.

But with Dennis talking me through it, it became something very different.

'Big left hand,' Dennis noted as we watched the Ogre going to work on Pierre duBois from the Piranhas.

The same technique was used shortly thereafter to concuss Jimmy Tait, the Wolves top enforcer.

'Jab, jab then big left hand – every time.' Dennis noted clinically as we watched Brooks demolish player after player. 'He's strong and he can take a punch but he's predictable and I've met some beginners with a bigger repertoire of techniques than he has.'

As the fights, some shockingly brutal, continued Dennis had

some other observations.

'Look at him as he skates over to the penalty box,' he said. 'See how out of breath he is?'

I did.

'No question, he has a killer left hand but look how exhausted he is after. His stamina gets burned up really fast, Davey.'

When the footage was done, Dennis turned to me and said, 'He's predictable, he's human and he's beatable, Davey, but not if you just stand there and let him beat on you. I'm no expert but I'm going to go out on a limb here and suggest that the middle of an ice hockey brawl may not be the ideal place to practise a little Christian forgiveness.'

I laughed.

'I'm serious, Davey,' he pressed. 'You're going to have to be willing to shed a little blood here – you really ready to do that?'

'You're thinking about Tommy Cates, aren't you?'

He nodded soberly.

I thought back to Tommy Cates and my finger came up reflexively to the scar beside my eye.

'Yeah,' I told Dennis. 'I'm willing. I'm tired of running, Dennis.'

'Well halle-fucking-lujah for that!' he grinned at me. 'Alright, Davey, let's go hit the gym and I'll show you how to *really* mess up someone's day!'

And that's what we did.

Ask any commentator how they'd describe Dennis' style of boxing and the most likely reply you'll hear will be "clinical". That was what he taught me - short, vicious jabs and neat, well-aimed crosses that gave way into big, savage overhand hooks.

'You'll be scared, Davey,' Dennis yelled as I practised driving volley after volley of punches into a heavy bag. 'Scared, and if this guy has fouled you, which is likely, you'll also be mad as hell. The adrenaline will be absolutely pounding in your veins.'

He called on me to move round and I walked from the heavy bag to another piece of equipment which looked like a human torso and head-shaped punch bag. It had been carefully adjusted so it was at the same height as the Ogre stood.

As I began to pound my fist into the centre of the torso bag – right at where Brooks' solar plexus would be – Dennis continued talking.

'He likes fighting the angry ones because he rarely loses to them. That's because they flail away and they make dumb mistakes and, when they do, that big left hand descends on them and it's all over bar the bleeding.'

After just a couple of minutes, the sweat was pouring off me and I had an all new respect for just how fit Dennis had to be.

'And he loves it – just freaking loves it! – when they're scared. When they're scared they don't even *attempt* to attack him. They just sort of throw weak little jabs while covering up and praying they'll still have all their teeth when it's over. Oh, your pal Ollie loves the scared ones, Davey!'

At a command from Dennis I switched targets and started to aim punches at the head of the torso bag.

'You don't want to be either of those things, Davey. You just focus on what you want to get done. You don't flail away. You don't give off embarrassing little baby taps. You absolutely don't listen to any catcalls or jeers from the crowd. When the jackasses calling out abuse are actually on the ice going toe to toe themselves they get a vote in how things get done. Until that happens they don't. Only the man in the ring gets to say how the fight gets fought – not some pathetic heckler!'

By the time I moved back onto the heavy bag my arms felt like lead but this was just the warm-up. I went through drill after drill - all simple, basic stuff to someone at Dennis' level but new and unfamiliar to me.

My grandpa had given up trying to get me to throw punches early on. He taught Mason but not me because I never, ever used what he taught me.

I'd never really needed to.

I had my father's speed and, up till that point, I'd been able to skate away from any threat.

I probably still could – probably.

But not forever.

This fight was coming and to the Ogre it was just business. If I turned the other cheek with Ollie Brooks then he'd just punch me there and keep punching me till I was down and there was blood on the ice.

But for the first time in my life that had ceased to be the worst thing that could happen to me.

The worst thing that could happen wouldn't be losing the

inevitable fight – it would be not having it all.

Someone wanted to believe in me and I wanted to show her she could.

I ached all over by the time we were done but Dennis was a good teacher. We were cooling down at the end of the session and I thanked him again for his time and he told me I was more than welcome but that this was the easy bit.

Making it work for real?

"*That*," Dennis had told me, "is the hard part."

He pointed out an older fighter who was working out on a speedball at the other side of the gym.

'How would you describe his form?' Dennis asked. 'Does he look good? Confident? Competent?' I watched the guy work and after a moment or two said he looked pretty damn good. His movements and his punches all seemed sharp and fluid and he looked to be a lot closer to Dennis' level than mine.

'That's a pretty good summary, Davey. He has the moves and he looks good throwing them but most people wouldn't really rate him.'

'Why not?'

'Because he's never once gotten into the ring,' Dennis said simply. 'George over there is a pretty good technician when he's in front of a speedball or a punch bag but as a rule, Davey, punch bags just sit there and let you punch them. George has got the ability – point of fact he could have gone all the way – but he's never actually tested his skills on another man with ideas of his own and the desire to knock you out first chance he gets. Pretty much everybody else here has got at least a fight or two under their belts but not George.'

'So that makes him what? Inferior?'

There might have been a hint of anger in my words because I was feeling a bit too much empathy for the fighter Dennis had named as George.

Dennis shook his head.

'Not inferior, no. His skills really are genuinely good but until he actually steps in the ring he'll never know if they *really* work or not. Until he wins, until he loses, he'll never know what it's like to fight for real. Nobody does, Davey. The only way to find out is to do it.' Dennis nodded at George as the older man went flawlessly through some combinations on the bag. 'He was talking about

entering a seniors competition next month He might do it but I
doubt it. He'll come up with an excuse to avoid putting himself on
the line and then just keep sleepwalking through the rest of his life.
He has the skills, Davey, but whether he can make them work for
real is still up for grabs because he has never tried. Same with you.
You've got a little more knowledge now. As an athlete you already
had the speed and the strength and now you know what you
should do. The question now is can you take what you've learned
and make it work for real? If I could do that for you, brother I
would but it's something you can only do for yourself.'

I watched George as he moved to stand beside a mirror and
start to shadow box.

'The guys call him Gorgeous George,' Dennis added. 'Not
everyone who boxes gets their nose broken – I never have – but
plenty do especially by the time they get to George's age if they've
boxed for years like he has. No, George has kept his good looks
by never ever putting himself in a position where he might take a
punch that ruins them. Know what he told me? Said he was
coming up on a big birthday soon – just before that seniors bout
that we both know he won't attend – he told me life was passing.
Told me he wished he had more scars. Now isn't *that* a thing to
say?'

'More scars, huh?'

I watched Gorgeous George work out and I knew I was seeing
my future.

'I'll always have your back, Davey,' Dennis told me soberly. 'If
you get on the ice with Brooks and you don't fight then we'll still
be friends. Hell, if you skate away blubbering like a little girl you'll
still be my buddy. Fight or don't fight – it won't matter. All that
matters is that when you skate out there that you make a choice,
you make a decision and, whatever it is, I've got your back. But I
hope you do it, Davey. Put all those nagging little voices in their
place forever.'

I nodded over at Gorgeous George.

'You invite him to come workout especially for me, Dennis?' I
asked.

'Now, Davey!' Dennis said in mock horror, 'Would I do that to
you?'

'Without a second thought,' I said with a grin.

We watched Gorgeous George as he moved onto the heavy

bag. His punches looked good – sharper and harder than mine and I wondered if he had ever had to face up to anyone for real.

'More scars,' I repeated, almost to myself.

'All the skills in the world won't help you if you lack the desire to actually use them,' Dennis said. 'Nobody can help you with that one. That one's all down to you.'

Years after the rematch with the Dragons people set a lot of store by the fact that I spent a day before the match being taught to box by a reigning world champ.

Truth be told, I learned at least as much from watching Gorgeous George as I did from Dennis.

When I left the gym I was still scared.

But I knew exactly what I was going to do when I got to Douglasville.

Let me tell you about the TV spot...

Everyone loves a rematch, right?

The Dragons' PR team did themselves proud when Douglasville Ice Arena hosted St Helens for the first time that season. In addition to the usual blitz of promo on their website and social media they recorded a short TV commercial.

They did it at very short notice since Coach Williams only listed me as a player (rather than a healthy scratch) a couple of days before the game but, given the short timescale, they still came up with a short TV spot that was picked up and played to death by the local stations in the run-up to the game.

The TV promo started with a black screen.

After a second you could hear a regular thud–thud–thud along with the sound of chains jangling.

Then the black screen gave way to a picture of the Ogre, stripped to the waist, pounding on a punch bag.

You couldn't miss the huge, powerful arms the Ogre had or the almost casual way he threw punches into the bag so hard he was sending it flying each time he struck it.

Then the screen faded to black (although the sound of the punches being thrown, that rhythmic thud–thud–thud, continued) and a caption came up on the screen in neat, white lettering.

The caption read, 'Someone has unfinished business with the Ogre.'

After a second that faded and was replaced with a new message.

'Body bags are on standby at the DIA.'

This then faded to the Dragons logo and a number for the box office.

St Helens staff had appealed to the league as soon as the TV spot aired but there wasn't a lot that could be done and Douglasville didn't much care if the league fined them because, thanks in no small part to that advert, they sold out the arena and made the game available on cable for a decent PPV fee that made the club a fortune.

From the money-making point of view it seemed that Douglasville was welcoming my appearance with welcoming arms.

The hard-core Dragons fans online however were another thing altogether.

My old friend Born_In_D-Ville led the charge by posting "Here comes the pain!"

He was quickly joined by a flock of others and most of the jibes from the keyboard warriors were about how gutless I was (not exactly original) and how vicious the Ogre could be (hardly something I was unaware of).

DragonFire82, a fat, tattooed guy in his mid-fifties by the look of the photo on his profile, sort of nailed the growing social media storm by posting – "You're a gutless wonder, Jones! When are you going to just man up, drop the gloves and take your damn licks?"

I was in my hotel room packing up my gear before heading out to the bus for the short ride to the arena for the big game when I saw that one.

I actually clicked on 'reply' and was trying to decide how best to respond to my admirer when someone beat me to it.

'Gosh! All you little tadpole fans really *do* have your panties in a bunch, don't you?'

Lady Kraken had logged in and didn't appear to be in a taking prisoners sort of mood.

DragonFire82 had immediately posted back "Jones is a gutless wonder! Ollie B is going to open him up tonight!"

Born_In_D-Ville added "Jones isn't in the Ogre's league! They're going to be taking him off the ice with a spatula!"

"Tut tut boys" Lady Kraken replied, "We have a division of labour on the St Helens team. Jonesy doesn't handle the taking out of the garbage – we have Frankie and Robbie Dee for that. Jonesy's job is to score goals. You remember goals, right guys? It's just that your team haven't been all that productive at scoring them of late…"

The abuse got pretty heated after that.

I could imagine Kelly Anne sitting on her bed, grinning to herself as she chirped and belittled her online opponents.

She seemed to stop after a few minutes though.

Lady Kraken usually stayed online to fight her battles for as long as it took but after pointedly putting Born_In_D-Ville down she seemed to go silent for quite a while. I thought back to how she'd been when I'd last seen her. She hadn't been great but she *was* meant to be improving, right?

Forty minutes passed before she posted again.

I had images of her throwing up blood as I waited and it was a relief to see her return online.

Her post was a photo.

It had probably been taken by Stan and it was of Kelly Anne. She had her back to the camera and you'd be very hard pressed to guess much about her identity from it as all it showed was the back of the hockey jersey she was wearing.

It was a game jersey – the one she would have chosen when she went along to that second practice session. It was a Sea Devils away jersey, a light, almost sky blue with green lettering and numbers.

Specifically the number twenty one - my number - and above that the name Jones.

My throat felt tight when I saw that.

Even after she knew I was likely to leave she had still chosen a jersey with my name on it.

Below the photo she had added the message: "Tonight's top scorer."

The keyboard warriors didn't appreciate that at all.

Most of the comments were of the "He'll be too busy being unconscious to score goals" variety but quite a few were very personal attacks on Lady Kraken.

One – from DragonLady29 – was a bit different. DragonLady29 posted "Where was the photo taken? Is that a hospital room? Are you okay honey?"

A couple of others posted along similar lines and I was starting to revise my opinion of the online Dragon fans when Born_In_D-Ville weighed in again.

"It's going to be a count of three devil-girl" he posted. "One, two, three and your boy is down, out and on his way back to intensive care!"

I hit reply at that point.

"You like counting?" I posted. "First puck I put past Gagnon is one. Second one is two. Follow the pattern tonight buddy, I'll give you some practice in counting all the way up to double figures."

Our PR guy would be pissed at me doing it and the club might even fine me but I didn't much care.

I would've gone further but that was when there was a knock on my door.

'Game time, superstar,' Frankie called. 'Be downstairs in five.'

I was a little concerned at the lack of any reply from Kelly Anne but she was, I forcibly reminded myself, responding well to the treatment. On a whim when I turned my tablet off I stuck it in my gym bag.

Then I walked down to the lobby to get the bus out to the DIA and settle the unfinished business I had with the Ogre.

Let me tell you about the locker room...

I've played in some hostile arenas in my career but very few can match the DIA in Douglasville. It's the only rink I've ever been to where the home fans turned up early so they could boo at us as we skated out for the warm-up.

They take their hockey as seriously in Douglasville as they do in St Helens I guess.

The boos and the catcalls were accompanied by home fans banging the palms of their hands or their fists on the glass as we skated past them. If you win at the DIA then you deserve the win because you're in a war of attrition with the Dragons fans from the moment you arrive. It's a loud, hostile environment that it's almost impossible to be unaffected by. I missed the first pass sent my way in the warm-up – much to the delight of the red and gold-clad fans who laughed their asses off at that.

'Friendly bunch, aren't they?' Lief noted dryly as he skated up to me.

I snorted with laughter.

'They're loud as hell, Lief, and the rink's not even half full yet!' I said.

'Yeah but these guys only sing when they're winning, Davey. Put a couple of goals past them and they go quiet awful fast. That's why they're going after us now, they want to pound on us before we get the chance to score on them. Can you imagine how it'd feel to be the one to silence *this* place?'

He winked and skated off.

I dropped back into the practice and after a few minutes was starting to motor despite the noise.

Danny was on fire already. The boos and the noise seemed to be having the opposite effect on him to the one intended. He was setting up against Murphy and sent puck after puck at him. I skated to join him and we started to put some of the pre-season training to good use. Danny blitzed our goalie and I followed him up, looking for the rebounds. When the buzzer went to signal the end of the warm-up we had taken maybe twenty shots at Murphy and buried eight of those in the net.

As we skated off I could see Brooks – who I'd studiously avoided looking at over on the other side of the ice – staring at me.

He gave me that big, evil, shit-eating grin of his as we made our way off.

And despite all that I'd done, all the decisions I'd made that had brought me to the DIA that night I suddenly wanted to tuck tail and run.

When we got into the locker room I stowed my helmet and gloves then tapped Frankie on the shoulder and asked for a word with him.

When we had moved a little away from the guys I asked Frankie a question that I'd actually pretty much always wanted an answer to.

How do you be brave?

It would have been more relevant to ask "How do you not be a coward" but since Frankie wasn't one I didn't think that would have been the right question.

His reply – and he did take a moment or two to mull it over – took me by surprise.

'You don't,' he mumbled.

'Seriously?' I asked surprised.

He nodded.

'It's got nothing to do with bravery, Davey,' he said. 'It's about knowing how far you want to go and what you're willing to pay to get there. Get it fixed crystal clear in your mind what you want then walk towards it.'

'That's it?'

He nodded again.

'Of course,' he added, 'if you wanted to *give* yourself a reason to do it you could draw a line in the sand for yourself, make a commitment about what you're going to do here tonight.'

'A line in the sand,' I mused.

'A statement,' Frankie said. 'Words to the effect that you aren't backing down – no matter what. Although to be fair just pulling the green and blue jersey on at the DIA pretty much does that! But maybe tonight you need to sort of emphasise the message?'

I was starting to grin as I walked back to where my gym bag was and pulled my tablet from it. A couple of seconds later I was typing furiously.

When I'd done, I showed it to Frankie.

'How about this?' I asked.

It was a short post for the bulletin board which I'd addressed to Lady Kraken.

It read "Every goal I put past these second-raters is a thank you for all your support, devil-girl."

Frankie began to laugh.

'PR team is going to be looking for your head on a plate, Jonesy!' he chuckled.

Several of the guys asked what I'd written and I passed the tablet round so they could see. Robbie was just handing it back to me when Coach Williams walked in.

He took the tablet from me and read it.

For a moment my heart was in my mouth and I expected a mouthful from the coach.

Then he nodded as if to himself and handed me the tablet back.

'Yup,' he said. 'That'll piss them off alright.'

I hesitated because he hadn't said it was okay to post it and I looked at him uncertainly.

'Post it!' Robbie Dee suddenly shouted.

'Push the button, Davey,' Danny added.

Suddenly everyone was clamouring at me to push the button.

So I did.

Coach Williams checked his watch.

'I give it about two minutes before the screams of the keyboard warriors are loud enough to be heard in here.'

We laughed.

I could feel the adrenaline beginning to surge as Coach Williams went through the game plan.

We were a battered, frequently defeated team at that point but for the first time since the season began, every player was there. No injuries and no suspensions to damage our chances.

We talked about what we were going to do and how we were going to do it. The Dragons wanted a bloodbath. We wanted to frustrate that every chance we could.

'Everybody knows Brooks is gunning for Davey tonight,' Coach Williams noted as he got to the end of his pre-match talk. 'You guys watch each other's backs and do what you can to keep that animal from cheap-shotting Jonesy.'

He didn't say stop the Ogre.

Everybody in the locker room knew that it wasn't going to be

Frankie that Brooks went after that night.

There was a fight coming. All the coach could do was tell the guys to keep me safe from an ambush or getting back-stabbed.

'Sure you're ready for this, Jonesy?' Coach Williams asked. When I nodded he said, 'Good because I've got an idea for how we can further tweak the noses of our hosts.'

There was a glint in his eye when he said it and I told him I was intrigued.

And that was how – to howls from the red and gold faithful - the first person to skate onto the ice at the DIA that night wasn't Murphy but me.

A bigger statement that I wasn't backing down that night could not have been made and I can't tell you how good it felt to have Frankie skating just behind me.

The boos were deafening as we lined up and waited for the home team to make their appearance.

I knew they'd seen what I'd done.

Traditionally, the goalie is always the first man onto the ice but that night it had been me.

I was ending a message to the Dragons, their fans and the world that I hadn't just come to play hockey that night.

I'd come to fight.

Let me tell you about Born Into Battle...

The lights don't go down at the DIA when the home team skate out – instead they all go red.

Then a siren sounds and the opening strains of "Born Into Battle" come thundering out of the PA system as the Dragons take to the ice.

Born Into Battle is to the Douglasville fans what Cruel World is to the St Helens supporters. It's a loud, aggressive track whose chorus goes, "Blood going to fly!" repeated over and over.

As one hockey pundit famously noted, the song's chorus pretty much sums up the team's strategy for winning games in three short words.

The Dragons skated on one at a time as Born Into Battle thundered out. It was interesting to note which players got the biggest cheers. Gagnon was first out and the crowd went wild for him. The next player the crowd raised the roof for was - unsurprisingly - the Ogre.

But the next player whose appearance sent the home fans into a frenzy of applause wasn't an obvious one.

It was Billy Fryar.

He was one of the shortest players in the league and had only dropped the gloves once that season but the fans loved Fryar because they were well aware of just what he was capable of.

At first glance, Fryar didn't look dangerous but, as I was well aware, he was a danger to me on the ice.

I had never, ever considered the smaller players to be any less of a threat than the big guys – quite the opposite in fact.

As Fryar lined up, his eyes fixed on me.

I'd seen that look before.

My gloved finger touched the scar at the side of my eye.

As Born Into Battle continued to thunder out I was reminded of a kid I had gone to High School with named Tommy Cates.

Tommy made my life hell for months.

He was a little guy, short and fat and he was okay to me when I first met him but over time he got mean.

I think at first he assumed, like just about everyone else, that I must be a tough guy. When he saw other people pick on me and get away with it he realised that wasn't the case and he quickly became my tormentor.

I always turned the other cheek and Tommy just lived for that. For a little guy he could hit really hard and he often did. Dennis would remind me that I was a head taller than Tommy and that I should just step in on him and squash him like a bug. Tommy told me if I ever hit him back he would go straight to the Principal and claim I was picking on him. Given the difference in our height and build, Tommy had laughed, "Who do you think they'll believe?"

I think Tommy really saw hurting me as a challenge. I just didn't react most of the time – just took the punch or the shove or elbow and moved on – trying not to show how bad it hurt.

I made it into a game for him I guess.

Then one day he arrived at school with this big, fat, gold sovereign ring on his finger. He was showing off to everyone and telling one and all that he stole it.

I always tried to avoid Cates when I could but that day in particular he made a beeline for me.

'Hey! Canuck! You see what I got here?'

Tommy had a whiny, nasal sort of voice and it carried. I should have realised he wanted an audience. I should have seen trouble coming but back then I wasn't exactly street smart.

'Yeah, that's nice,' I had said in as bland a voice as I could manage. It was halfway through lunch and all I really wanted to do was get to the end of the break and get back to class and away from this jerk.

'Nice?' he almost exploded. 'Just nice? That's it? What, do you think I would steal any old piece of crap?'

'It's very nice, Tommy,' I told him in as placating a voice as I could manage.

He thrust his hand out aggressively.

'You didn't even notice the design on it, did you? You didn't even look at it!'

Dennis, who had been in the crowd, was a whole hell of a lot smarter than me even back then. He shouted 'Don't!' at me just as I (like the sucker I was) turned and leaned in to inspect the ring on Tommy's hand.

A second later, Tommy's hand flew up and back-handed me hard across the face.

He'd spent time sharpening the edge of the ring and when it hit me it missed my eye by a fraction of an inch. I've never known if that was luck or not. I couldn't believe back then that someone would want to take an eye out just for kicks.

My hands came up to my face and I felt the thick, sticky wetness on my palms as the blood began to pour out and the panic set in.

Tommy was laughing.

'Did you see?' he yelled at some of the onlookers. 'Did you see what this moron did?'

I saw other people in the crowd laugh too.

Dennis had pushed past a couple of the onlookers and got a handful of tissues.

'Hold this in place, Davey,' he commanded.

I did.

'You need to get to the first aid room,' Dennis said, steering me in that direction. 'And then you should go back and stand on that fucking insect.'

Tommy heard that last comment and followed after us.

'Oh but he won't! Canuck boy here doesn't want any trouble from me, isn't that right, Canuck boy? He's a good little Christian, turns the other cheek every time! Isn't that right, Canuck? Isn't it?'

He shoved Dennis aside, spun me around and hit me again.

'Isn't it, Canuck boy? Isn't it?'

Another punch.

I never forgot the look on Dennis' face – the disbelief that I would just stand there and not protect myself.

When Tommy hit me a third time and I still didn't retaliate, Dennis practically screamed, 'Davey – hit him back!'

But I didn't.

I was turning the other cheek.

And more than that, I was just plain scared.

'He won't!' Tommy actually began to sing the words in that nasal voice of his. 'He won't, he won't, he won't hit me back!'

He took a step towards Dennis and gave him a shove.

'He won't,' Tommy giggled.

Dennis was nearly sixteen at that time and had been boxing since he was about six. The punch he unloaded on Tommy was a short, powerful uppercut to the jaw that landed with sufficient force to shatter two of my tormentor's teeth and leave him in an unconscious heap on the ground.

Dennis hadn't said anything as he stepped over Tommy's unconscious body and took me to the first aid room and nobody else had gotten in our way as we walked.

As the lights went back to normal at the DIA and we listened to the last strains of Born Into Battle, I saw Fryar eyeing me and the look was so like Tommy Cates that I shivered.

We all skated over to our goal and huddled up around Murphy.

Usually Lief or Frankie would be the ones to talk but that night it was me that spoke up.

'Too loud in here for me tonight, guys,' I said then nodded at Danny. 'What's your thoughts on an early goal and shut these idiots up, Danny boy?'

'Gets my vote!' he grinned. 'You want to work the corners?'

I shook my head.

'No perimeter hockey tonight – straight down the line, into the crease and right in Gagnon's face.'

'Their D-men are going to have you in their sight, Jonesy,' Robbie Dee chimed in. 'Sure you want to play the puck straight at them?'

'Their D-men are coming for me no matter what I do tonight Robbie, so screw them. We storm the crease every chance we get tonight.'

I glanced over at Danny, 'Right?'

'Right,' Danny agreed eagerly.

Robbie glanced over at the Dragons D-men.

'Jonesy, you sure about this man?' he sound genuinely concerned.

I was saved from replying by Frankie who slammed a hand against Robbie's shoulder.

'He's sure,' Frankie growled.

Robbie Dee nodded slowly.

'We've got your back, superstar,' Frankie told me. 'Work your magic.'

He extended his gloved fist and I met it with my own. Robbie touched gloves too and after a second so did Danny and then the whole team, one after another touched gloves with Frankie and me.

For a heartbeat, none of us moved.

The Dragons fans were booing, jeering and pounding on the Plexiglas but I swear I hardly heard them.

Then one of the linesman skated past yelling at us that it was time for the face-off.

We broke neatly, taking up our positions as the referee held the puck high up in the air and looked left and right to check everybody was in place.

My heart was hammering as Lief and Billy Fryar set their sticks and braced themselves.

Then the whistle blew, the puck dropped and we were off.

JOHN McKINSTRY

Let me tell you about what Frankie describes as applause...

We couldn't have gotten off to a much worse start.

Fryar beat Lief to the puck at face-off and was accelerating forward before anyone could stop him.

Robbie Dee had been expecting a push forward and so was out of position. Fryar had nobody except Frankie close to him and Frankie was too far away to get to him before he took a shot at goal.

Fryar let fly and for one agonising moment I was sure we were about to start the game a goal down after only a few seconds of play.

The save Murphy made wasn't a good one.

He got his glove to it but couldn't catch it and although it didn't go in Murphy lost his grip on it and the puck flew back onto the ice – right in front of another red and gold clad attacker who had followed in Fryar's wake hoping for the rebound.

Murphy was off balance from the first save and Sullivan – the Dragons player who had followed Fryar – should have scored an easy goal.

It's hard to be accurate when someone of Frankie's height and build crashes into you though.

As Frankie's shoulder hit Sullivan the shot went wide and the chance for an easy goal for the home team vanished.

Sullivan wasn't happy with the shoulder check.

He yelled over at the referee and I heard him shout 'Elbow!'

He was accusing Frankie of an elbow shot not a shoulder check. The latter was legal but the former wasn't.

But the referee shook his head.

'Clean hit,' he said then skated off.

Sullivan turned and glared at Frankie.

He was a little shorter than Frankie but looked to be heavily built and strong as an ox.

Frankie blew him a kiss.

'You don't like that, tadpole?' he called. 'You got a problem with it?'

Sullivan skated slowly forward.

If he thought his slow, deliberate approach and murderous glare were intimidating then he'd badly misjudged the situation.

'You want to go, sweetheart?' Frankie bellowed.

Sullivan held Frankie's gaze for a second or two then skated away.

All around us the Dragon fans were booing and hurling abuse.

Frankie caught my eye and suddenly grinned, 'Hear that, Jonesy? I don't believe the good people of Douglasville like me!'

I couldn't stop the sudden snort of laughter.

'*That's* your applause, Jonesy,' Frankie rumbled. 'When you're playing at the DIA and they hate you *that* much? That's applause!'

As we skated into position for the next face-off I realised that Frankie was absolutely right – abuse from the home fans really was applause.

And it was time for me to earn some.

Let me tell you about first blood...

We seemed to do nothing but defend for the next few, frantic moments.

Murphy earned his money denying Fryar's next shot on goal with a peach of a glove save and then - finally – the puck was sent to the other end of the ice and St Helens were finally on the attack.

We faced off in the Dragons' zone and I fully expected to see the Ogre make his appearance but to my surprise Ollie Books was still on the home team's bench.

'Ogre hasn't iced yet?' I asked Lief as we moved into position.

Lief shrugged, 'I don't think so – can't say I'm exactly unhappy about that but I thought they'd play him early'.

If I'd had time I might have wondered why the Dragon's top enforcer hadn't skated out to play defence at that point but you don't get a whole hell of a lot of time for reflection out on the ice.

So I put the Ogre from my mind, set my stick and got my head in the game.

When the puck dropped it was Lief who won it and snapped it off to his left where Danny was waiting.

As soon as he had the puck, Danny blasted it forward at goal. I could hear the crack as it hit the post and came off at an angle.

I was already chasing after it and could see in my peripheral vision that Danny was skating hell for leather towards me and that Lief was also dropping back so that he was right in front of Gagnon – blocking the Dragon goalie's view and stopping him from getting ready to defend.

I caught the puck and accelerated as I went behind the back of Gagnon's net.

As I rounded it, I could see Sullivan was shoving Lief, trying to barge him aside so Gagnon could see clearly.

Lief however wasn't budging.

The smart play as I turned would have been to pass the puck to Danny. That was what the Dragons would be expecting.

Instead I twisted and let fly with my first shot on goal.

Truth be told I never had any expectations it would find its way past someone with Gagnon's level of skill and it didn't. Gagnon caught it on his stick and knocked it away.

But Danny was there to catch it.

None of the St Helens players had given an inch. Danny propelled the puck forward and Lief, who was still screening Gagnon, shoved Sullivan aside hard and managed to get his stick to the puck as Gagnon – almost miraculously – managed to clear Danny's shot.

Sullivan skated back in – clearly aiming to shoulder charge Danny. Before he could connect with him, however, he got knocked off his feet as Robbie Dee crashed into him.

St Helens didn't generally commit all five skaters to an attack and the Dragons didn't know how to stop us as Danny blasted another shot at the Douglasville goal.

You have to give Gagnon the respect he deserved – he saved that third shot and tried desperately to keep hold of it but he couldn't and the puck ricocheted off his stick.

I had read the angle and was already in position as the puck bounced off of Gagnon's stick.

I was maybe two feet away from goal when the puck hit my stick and the instant I felt the puck come into my possession I aimed at the top left-hand corner of the net and launched the puck into the air.

The light behind the goal went on, the siren sounded and it was one-nil.

And the Dragons really, really didn't like it.

There was some pushing and shoving and some very harsh words from them. The Dragons wanted a brawl but we weren't biting.

Fryar tried to get in Danny's face but Danny was already skating away.

I was heading over to our bench with the intention of line changing so I could catch my breath when someone slammed into me from behind.

It was Sullivan.

'You think you're hot stuff?' Spittle flew from his mouth as he snarled at me. 'That what you think you are? Hot stuff?'

I skated towards him.

When I didn't slouch but stood up straight I was actually a little taller than he was and I waited till he was right in front of me and I had eye contact with him before nodding.

'Tonight's top scorer,' I told him as I pointed my finger at my chest. 'Get used to the sound of the siren, Sullivan – you'll be hearing it a lot tonight.'

Then I turned my back on him and skated away.

I was trembling a little but I had gotten the words out and damn it had felt good!

That good feeling lasted maybe five seconds which was the time it took Sullivan to skate after me at full speed and slam his shoulder into my back.

Let me tell you about Frankie's views on backstabbers...

I'm not sure if it was luck or reflex but either way my chin came down onto my chest as I was hit and as a result when my head hit the Plexiglas my helmet took most of the impact.

I was seeing stars for a second or two but that wasn't the bad part.

The bad part was the sudden rush of memories.

Wheelchairs.

My mind was suddenly filled with images of wheelchairs.

A hand caught my shoulder and I nearly threw a punch, but it wasn't an attacker, it was Danny.

'Skate on with me, Jonesy,' he said. 'Never let an idiot like Sullivan see that you're hurt – skate on with me.'

Across the ice, Coach Williams was bellowing abuse at Sullivan and demanding a game ban for him. The referee was conferring with a linesman and there were two big Dragons players separating a grinning Sullivan from Frankie who was calling the Dragons player a gutless backstabber and promising to tie Sullivan's skates around his neck with his feet still in them.

'Skate on, Jonesy,' Danny persisted.

Dragons fans were jeering, pounding at the glass and I could hear a chant of 'Watch him break and cry!' starting up.

'Skate with me, Jonesy!' Danny repeated.

I did.

It took a moment or two for my vision to clear and my head to stop ringing but as I skated with Danny my body's habits took over.

By the time the Dragons had launched their own protest to the referee (they apparently claimed I'd spat at Sullivan before skating off) my natural rhythm was back and I was moving normally.

I was terrified all over again.

But I was also furious.

It wasn't enough that I was going to end up going toe to toe with Ollie Brooks but I had to eat cheap shots from Sullivan as well?

Oh yeah, I was pissed off.

When the referee finally announced his decision (checking from behind was his call and it cost Sullivan two plus ten) the Dragons fans booed and the travelling supporters from St Helens erupted with applause.

Except that Sullivan didn't want to actually leave the ice and go into the penalty box.

'PLENTY more where that came from!' he yelled at me as the linesman physically blocked him from skating over to me. 'You hear me, Jones?'

Frankie skated slowly in front of me.

He tapped the linesman's shoulder and motioned for him to step aside.

'Want to know what I do to back-stabbers, Sullivan?' Frankie had murder in his eyes but the linesman wasn't budging.

'The penalty has been given,' the linesman snapped bluntly, 'So you back off and you,' he gave Sullivan a shove, 'Penalty box – now!'

Frankie was not happy at this but we could hear Coach Williams bellowing at him to stand down.

'Be right hear waiting for you, Sullivan!' Frankie growled as the Dragons player finally allowed himself to be escorted over to the penalty box.

Sullivan was laughing and the red and gold faithful were jeering at us but the truth of the matter was Douglasville had just been handed a penalty that would lose them a skater for two minutes of the game.

St Helens were on the power play and I was pissed off and wanted to ruin Douglasville's night.

I was tired and my head ached but you know what? You couldn't have gotten me off the ice at that moment if you'd put a gun to my head.

The blue and green machine was bellowing support as I skated to the centre to take the face-off.

Fryar skated up to stand opposite me.

He fidgeted with his helmet strap and when he saw he had my attention he tapped the side of his neck and grinned at me.

'Was St Elizabeth's a good hospital?' he leered.

St Elizabeth's, home to the Whyte Centre which in turn was home to someone who wanted to believe in a worthless, gutless jerk like me.

Fryar couldn't have said anything more likely to inspire me.

I set my stick.

Fryar still wanted to trash talk till the ref pointedly mentioned an additional penalty for delaying the game, then he finally set his stick as well.

When the puck dropped I beat Fryar to it.

He was more focused on hurling abuse at me than taking care of business and I put the puck between his legs, shouldered past him and found myself skating behind the back of Gagnon's goal at top speed.

I glanced up once as I turned.

I'm a selfish player, a diva.

Gagnon saw me pull my stick back and he positioned himself perfectly to handle it.

Except that for once I didn't care who scored – just so long as the puck went into the back of the net.

So instead of a full-force slap shot I tapped the puck almost lazily at Danny who had exploded forward and was coming in from Gagnon' s blind side.

All the Dragons D-men had been focused on me and had handed Danny room to manoeuvre and he punished them for it with a short, beautifully accurate shot that went into the bottom left corner of the net and had the blue and green machine up out of their seats cheering.

Two-nil St Helens.

Let me tell you about the five on three...

Any notions that the Dragons might have had about playing an actual hockey game vanished when they conceded that second goal.

After that, things *really* got dirty.

Lief was tripped from behind – going face-first into the ice – by Fryar about a minute after that second goal.

The referee missed it and so, despite Coach Williams bellowing loud enough to probably be heard at the other side of the DIA, no penalty.

A new guy in the Dragons line up – Ray Campbell - came on with nine minutes left in the first period and managed exactly fourteen seconds of ice time before being called for tripping.

In point of fact the Dragons spent most of the rest of the first period on the penalty kill as they wound up a man down for tripping then as soon as that penalty was done they were caught almost straight away for a blatant slash aimed at poor Lief again.

Between them Campbell, Fryar and Sullivan seemed to be competing to see who could commit the nastiest foul of the night.

When the Dragons played dirty, it was usually the Ogre who led the way but Ollie Brooks did not ice during that first period.

He stood up a couple of times as if he was going to get onto the ice and each time he did I felt my stomach clench and wondered if this was it but each time he sat back down again.

Ollie Brooks looked relaxed and calm – like he was just another fan there at the DIA to enjoy a good, physical game of hockey.

Even without the Ogre you had to accept that the Dragons were good – *really* good – on the penalty kill.

Being a man down didn't seem to demoralise them at all - in fact it just seemed to spur them on.

The Dragons were ferocious when on the kill but no team can survive penalty after penalty.

The reason the Dragons made it to the final three minutes of the first period with the score still at only two-nil was Gagnon.

Gagnon was playing out of his skin that night. He denied us a third goal over and over again. With any other keeper I figure the Sea Devils would have gone five-nil, maybe even six-nil by the end of the first but Gagnon denied us over and over that night. He was like a machine and nothing seemed to get past him.

But, as my dad always used to say, your goalie is only as good as the D-men in front of him and with just over three minutes on the clock in the first, St Helens were piling on the pressure.

Which was when Lief was tripped and this time the referee saw it and sent a red and gold clad player to the box.

St Helens was on the power play again and Lief shouted at us to set up fast.

Hockey is all about momentum. We had been on the attack and Lief wanted us to keep going and get back into the play.

The Dragons, needless to say, had other ideas.

Fryar launched the appeal to the ref and was quickly joined by Sullivan.

It had been a blatant trip and a fair call by the ref. What Fryar was doing was wasting time – blunting that momentum we'd had.

It was frustrating as hell.

We could all see what he was doing, as could the crowd. The blue and green machine was loudly demanding the referee restart play while the Dragons fans had started chants of "Hear the man out! Hear the man out!"

The referee said something to Fryar who shook his head and went on talking.

Then the referee blew his whistle, pointed at Fryar then brought his right hand across his chest before snapping his hand back out to the right again.

The signal for a delaying-the-game penalty.

The Dragons fans went berserk as the referee awarded the penalty and handed St Helens a two-man advantage.

Five on three for two minutes.

It still took another minute to get the Dragons to actually send someone else to the box but when they finally did we were ready to put the puck in the net. We faced off as fast as we could and threw everything we had at Gagnon.

If you ever want an example of coolness under pressure then take a look at the video of that five on three. We logged thirteen shots on goal and the Dragons' goalie got a hand or stick to every single one of them.

The puck came to me with six seconds of our five on three left and I passed it to my left as Lief drifted into Gagnon's blind side.

He would have scored if he'd been able to get a shot off, I'm sure of it.

Sullivan seemed equally sure that Lief was about to score and didn't wait for him to take the shot. He charged him from behind and sent him flying.

There were sixty one seconds left in the first as I helped Lief up.

It was a step too far for Frankie.

The Sea Devils enforcer tossed his stick to the ground then gave Sullivan a shove.

'You know what I do to back-stabbers, Sullivan?' Frankie yelled.

Frankie tossed his helmet onto the ice then promptly dropped his gloves.

Sullivan dropped his gloves and tore off his helmet and made to toss it away.

But he didn't lose his helmet, instead he got a grip of the chin strap and as Frankie skated in on him he swung the helmet hard as he could at Frankie's face.

My heart was in my mouth.

Dear sweet baby Jesus, I thought, don't let that have hit him in the eye.

Sullivan didn't hesitate.

When Frankie's hands came up to cover his head, Sullivan went in for the kill, grabbing Frankie's jersey then raining down right hook after right hook on his opponent.

The linesmen were already trying to break it up. Sullivan's illegal use of equipment was going to get him a ban and they probably assumed Frankie was already too badly injured to go on after that.

Sullivan kept punching as he drove Frankie back up against the Plexiglas with the Dragons fans cheering him on every step of the way.

'Blood going to fly!' they chanted, 'Blood going to fly!'

And a second later it did.

A hockey fight ends when one of the combatants goes down. Sullivan wasn't actually being very smart therefore in pushing Frankie up against the glass because it allowed him to catch his balance and, once that had happened, the fight became an even one.

Frankie drove a right upper cut straight into Sullivan's jaw. It

was enough to halt Sullivan's assault for a second and that was all
Frankie needed. He grabbed Sullivan's jersey and unloaded a big,
brutal right hook into Sullivan's jaw.

Then another.

Then another.

And another.

Suddenly the linesmen were separating the two of them as
Sullivan slumped to the ice and the blue and green machine were
on their feet, howling and cheering, as Frankie was led off the ice,
the victor.

When the game finally restarted we put another nine shots on
the Douglasville goal before the buzzer announced the end of the
period.

Gagnon – coolness personified – denied us every time.

It was two-nil St Helens at the end of the first and the Ogre still
hadn't iced.

Let me tell you about goalie interference...

When we got back to the locker room at the end of the first period, we all thought that we'd seen every dirty trick that Douglasville were capable of.

We were wrong.

In hockey, there's one thing you absolutely cannot do and that's deliberately target the other team's goalie.

You can't check them, charge into them or try and knock them out of your way. If you get caught doing anything that could be classed as goalie interference it's a penalty and your ass is headed straight for the penalty box.

The Dragons had had no joy provoking our forwards and had had their asses kicked by our D-men. The only person in blue and green they hadn't gone after was Murphy.

It never came up as an option when Coach Williams took us through his team talk during the break. None of us seriously considered a deliberate attempt to put Murphy off his game.

While we listened to the coach and chugged down bottles of water or juice I couldn't resist pulling my tablet from my bag.

No reply from Kelly Anne.

I was going to message her again but the coach saw me with the tablet and snapped, 'Head in the game, Jonesy! Post your message later!'

I obediently put the tablet away and gave him my full attention as he outlined the game plan for the second period.

A two-nil lead in hockey – especially going into the second period – is far from unassailable. The coach wanted a quick third goal and when we skated back out that was our plan.

We weren't expecting Fryar to break away early and skate up to stand almost shoulder to shoulder with Murphy.

St Helens had pushed all our skaters forward and been denied by Gagnon.

It was as we turned (a red and gold defender had iced the puck after it bounced off Gagnon's stick) that we saw where Fryar was.

At that early point all Fryar was doing was trash talking. There had been no D-men there to shove Fryar away from our goalie so there he stood, hissing abuse and threats at Murphy.

Fryar vanished promptly when Frankie and Robbie Dee both skated over but it set the pattern for the second period. Every time he was left unmarked Fryar would somehow find his way up beside our keeper.

In hockey you can't stand in the crease – that little blue semi-circle in front of the goal – unless you've got the puck or you're just travelling through it. Fryar danced in and out of it. He actually stood right in front of Murphy – blocking his view – until a linesman noticed and ordered him out.

But Fryar was a clever player who picked his moments really well.

Eleven minutes into the second period and Robbie Dee picked up a penalty for charging (probably a fair call, truth be told) and St Helens was on the penalty kill for the first time that night.

The face-off was in our zone and when the puck dropped Fryar exploded forward – making a beeline for Murphy.

Frankie and Lief both moved to block him.

A heartbeat later we realised we'd been suckered.

Campbell rushed forward as soon as Frankie and Lief moved. The two of them going after Fryar had left a hole in our defence and Campbell punished us for it with a textbook slap shot that went straight past Murphy.

Two-one.

The Dragons fans went wild.

The grin Fryar treated me to as he skated away was enough to make me want to use my hockey stick to wipe it off his face.

'Heads up!'

Frankie bellowed the words and I glanced across at him.

'Our heads never go down, superstar!' he barked. 'It's one of the golden rules. Only people it serves if we get depressed and lose heart are the ones wearing red jerseys and I'm damned if I'm going to do any of them a favour so get your head up and let's get goal number three!'

And for the next seven minutes of the second period that's what we did.

Fryar dropped back again and again to trash talk our goalie. When Robbie Dee came back on, he chased Fryar out of the crease only for Campbell to skate up and start mouthing off at Murphy.

Coach Williams turned the air blue as he screamed at the ref or the linesman to take some action against the Douglasville players but the Dragons were clever. They danced in and out of the crease and they didn't actually touch Murphy. They were skating right up to him as if to land a hit then veering off at the very last instant.

There was just under two minutes of play left in the second when Douglasville decided to take their harassment of our goalie up a gear.

Fryar skated into the crease but this time he shouldered into Murphy – not hard enough to knock our goalie down (that would have been noted by an official) but hard enough to jolt him and make sure that Murphy's full attention was on the person intruding into his zone.

I heard Frankie swear and saw him drop back.

Fryar was already moving away as Frankie skated back to the St Helens goal. Frankie's eyes were on him – watching to make sure actually left.

Frankie never saw Campbell skating towards his unprotected back.

'FRANKIE!' I yelled as I dropped back myself.

It was warning enough.

Frankie spun and Campbell – seeing he no longer had an unprotected target – veered away from him.

'Next time, Frankie boy!' Campbell called as he skated past.

'Try your luck, rat boy!' Frankie replied bluntly, 'You've seen what I do to backstabbers!'

Next face-off was in the Dragons' zone.

Frankie dropped back straight away, ready to protect our goalie.

Campbell and Danny fought for the puck and Campbell won it – sending it to Fryar who was off down the ice in a heartbeat.

One of the Dragons other D-men – a big, blond-haired guy named Lewis – tried to block me from following but he was clumsy and I feigned left then promptly went right and left him in my wake as I chased after Fryar.

Frankie was already back in St Helens' zone, sweeping his stick back and forward to block any shot Fryar might take.

But Fryar didn't shoot, instead he passed the puck backwards to Campbell.

I lost sight of Fryar as I turned to Campbell who was the immediate danger. As Frankie moved in to block I happened to glance up and saw Fryar jostle our goalie.

I skated straight at him.

Fryar was laughing at me as I chased him out of the crease.

Campbell didn't take a shot on goal, instead he circled the net.

There were two more red and gold jerseys about to arrive in our zone. I chose to go after Campbell.

I was quicker that he was and managed to catch him and shove him up against the wall as I tried to use my stick to take the puck off him.

As we fought for possession I could hear pandemonium breaking out behind me.

I caught the puck cleanly and iced it – sending it past the halfway line towards the Dragons' zone again.

As I turned I could see a furious Frankie chasing Fryar out of the crease again.

Lewis was still in our zone and yelling at Frankie as the St Helens enforcer physically shoved Fryar away from our goalie.

Frankie then gave Lewis his full attention – asking loudly if Lewis felt strong. Did he want to go?

He'd assumed Fryar would skate round the goal and head back up the ice to his own zone.

Fryar did indeed circle the St Helens goal.

But instead of going up the ice he went straight for Frankie.

I could hear a whistle blowing – the ref had clearly seen what was going on – but it was too late.

Lewis practically jumped aside as Fryar shoulder charged our enforcer from behind.

The impact – as Frankie's head hit the Plexiglas – was sickening.

And I was suddenly skating forward.

Me.

Gutless, useless, stick-to-the-rules-at-all-costs me.

Fryar was shouting something as I bore down on him. Something about what Frankie did to backstabbers I think.

I couldn't make it out clearly.

It didn't matter anyway.

I cannoned into Fryar at full speed and, if I'm being honest, I'd have to admit it wasn't my shoulder but my elbow that I used to make the check and drive the vicious, back-stabbing little bastard backwards into the wall.

As Fryar slumped to the ground I couldn't help but think that my grandpa would have been proud of that hit.

Chaos reigned on the ice.

The referee was blowing his whistle while the linesmen were frantically trying to keep the two sets of players apart.

It took nearly ten minutes for the referee to restore order. In that time it was made clear that neither Frankie nor Fryar would be back on the ice that night.

When the game finally restarted there were thirty-nine seconds left to play in the second period. I was in the penalty box for checking from behind and the Sea Devils were on the penalty kill.

And that was when the Ogre finally took to the ice.

JOHN McKINSTRY

Let me tell you about the Ogre's entrance...

The Douglasville fans went apeshit and Born Into Battle began to play as Ollie Brooks skated slowly, purposefully onto the ice.

All eyes were on the Ogre as he skated into position.

Face-off in the Dragons zone.

A blur of movement, sticks lashing at the ground to get control of the puck then a hard shot drove the puck all the way forward - icing the puck and stopping the clock.

Twenty-two seconds left in the second.

As they moved up the ice, the Dragons all skated slowly past the penalty box.

As Brooks glided towards me I felt like a diver in the shark cage who looks out and sees a Great White slowly swim past.

Brooks raised his stick and banged it hard against the penalty box door as he skated by.

He mouthed something at me as he went past.

Normally, I'm no good at lip-reading but I got that one.

'Soon'.

He mouthed the word.

Coach Williams was furiously questioning the referee's sanity as the ref indicated that the next face-off would be in the St Helens zone.

Robbie Dee had clearly taken charge of our defence. He faced off against the Ogre and when the puck dropped Robbie made sure he was right in the Ogre's face.

Everyone was looking at Brooks.

Nobody was paying proper attention to Lewis.

Campbell tapped the puck backwards to Lewis and then skated right into the crease – blocking Murphy's view.

Murphy shoved Campbell aside and stepped a little too far forward as he did so.

Lewis couldn't miss.

With eight seconds left to play in the second Lewis buried the puck in the back of the net and it was suddenly all square at two-two.

Brooks made a point of skating past the penalty box before he left the ice.

'Soon'.

He mouthed the word at me again.

When the buzzer finally brought the second period to an end I was practically shaking with a mix of fear and anger.

There was a twenty-minute break before the start of the third and final period.

As I made my way to the locker room I knew that those twenty minutes were going to feel like the longest ones of my life.

Let me tell you all about the tripping call...

It may sound crazy to say but as I took up my position for the start of the third – deliberately facing off against Brooks – it was with a feeling of relief.

The break between periods had been hell.

My brain played through every nightmare scenario imaginable and all I did was pace up and down the locker room.

Finally Robbie Dee grabbed my arm and dragged me to one side. He then held up both hands - palms facing me.

'Jab,' he said.

I stared at him for a second and he waved his right hand at me.

'Jab!' he repeated.

I got the idea and threw a weak jab at his right hand.

He nodded then held up both hands at about face height.

'Jab, cross!' he instructed.

I threw a jab, cross, harder the second time, earning loud smacking sounds as my fists hit the palms of his upraised hands.

Within a few seconds I was absorbed in the practice – firing off punches on command.

Minutes passed.

Finally Robbie lowered his hands.

'Feeling better?' he asked.

I nodded.

'Now you know why Frankie beats up the wall before he ices against Douglasville,' Robbie told me. 'Guys don't fight well when they're all messed up with nerves. Ogre's going to try and drag this out for you. He won't come after you straight away, he'll want you on tenterhooks waiting for it to happen, you understand?'

I remembered Dennis' remark about boxing being as much about strategy and tactics as it was about punching power and I nodded.

'If I get the chance, Jonesy, I'll put the ugly son of a bitch into a wall and save you the job,' Robbie promised.

I shook my head at him.

'Appreciate it but not tonight, man,' I said. 'This is on the cards and I'm done running.'

Robbie opened his mouth to reply but before he could say anything one of the DIA stewards banged on the door of our locker-room and yelled that it was time for the third period.

Sad to say Robbie was spot in his appraisal of how the Ogre was going to act.

After we faced off he shadowed me.

Lief had run the puck forward and had turned to pass it to me, noted the Ogre right at my back and sent it to Danny instead.

A few seconds later the Dragons line changed and the Ogre left the ice.

We began to build a little momentum, to get our game going again but as soon as we did Brooks reappeared and all eyes were on him and me.

He shouldered past me as we skated forward and when we faced off he immediately shoved his stick into my chest to stop me from going forward when the puck dropped.

One of the linesmen saw it and barked at the Ogre to knock it off and he did with that same evil, shit-eating grin on his face.

Precisely one minute and thirty-one seconds of the third period had been played when he tried to trip me.

Danny had passed me the puck and, as soon as I felt it hit my stick, I began to accelerate up the ice.

I felt a sharp pain in my leg as the Ogre deliberately swung his stick at my ankle and I stumbled and slipped.

I didn't actually fall though so I was a little surprised when I heard the referee's whistle.

Lewis was already skating over to the ref to argue the call and, if I'm honest, I had some sympathy with him. It was a soft call for the referee to make and everybody knew it.

Especially Brooks himself.

He made no move to skate to the penalty box.

He just stood there, staring at me.

A dozen thoughts danced through my mind.

We needed a goal. Letting Brooks be taken off to the box would give us a two-minute power play.

More importantly, my tormentor would be off the ice and out of my face for the duration of the penalty.

A linesman had skated over and he tapped Brooks on the shoulder and gestured to the penalty box but the Ogre ignored him.

He only had eyes for me.

It would have been easy – oh, so easy! – to allow Brooks to be removed from the ice.

And you have no idea just how tempted I was.

But I couldn't.

I just couldn't.

The linesman was starting to yell but the Ogre wasn't listening to a thing the man said.

He knew what was about to happen.

I reached up and pulled my helmet off.

The linesman glanced over at me, realised what was happening and skated prudently away.

The blue and green machine surged to their feet screaming encouragement as I skated slowly towards the Ogre.

I looked that tormenting son of a bitch right in the eyes.

Then dropped the gloves.

Let me tell you about the fight...

The Ogre skated slowly to my left as he tossed his helmet then dropped his gloves onto the ice.

I mirrored his movement and let myself skate round to his right.

Brooks brought his hands up but more like a wrestler than a boxer. His hands were open not closed so that he could grab me (preferably getting an unbreakable grip on my jersey) then pull me close and beat me bloody.

And he was grinning at me.

I hated that grin and was getting really sick of seeing it.

'Was it just the one ball that finally dropped?' his tone was conversational as we circled each other. 'Or did they both finally pop for you?'

My fists were clenched and I held them close to my head.

He likes fighting the angry ones Dennis had warned because they do stupid things like throw, big clumsy punches.

I didn't respond to him.

Man, I wanted to just turn and run!

As we circled, we were getting steadily closer to each other.

'How many teeth you think you'll have when you leave here tonight, Rookie?' He drawled the words and I could see the glint in his eye. He loved this, lived for it.

We were just outside touching distance and I'd seen from the video of his fights just how fast the Ogre could move.

He liked fighting the scared ones. Well I was freaking terrified out there. My bladder felt full and I was absolutely sure that when the first punch connected I'd piss my pants.

His left hand flew towards me lazily. He was grabbing for the jersey but I held back from throwing a punch, just skated a little to the right.

I saw his right shoulder tense then relax as I moved.

It had been a fake.

He'd wanted to panic me into making a stupid error.

I was breathing out in relief when the real attack came.

His hand shot out again but quick as a snake this time. He practically lunged at me, got hold of the jersey with his left hand

and was cocking his right back for a big right hook.

If someone like the Ogre grabs you I can confirm that your reaction is to pull away and try to go backwards really fast to get away from him.

And that – since he already had a hold of me – would have been fatal.

Which was why Dennis had drilled into me that - when you're grabbed - you don't pull away.

You go forward.

As Brooks pulled me forward I let him and as I did so I drove my fist into his jaw.

My knuckles stung as they connected but the grin vanished from Brooks face.

As the big right hand flew at me I grabbed him and pulled him into me as I punched again and again.

I caught him across the cheek and I wasn't quite on balance so it didn't connect with full power but it wasn't a weak, half-hearted punch by any means.

Then the Ogre hit me.

My head was spun by the force of it and I tasted blood in my mouth and knew my lip was split.

I spat the blood onto the ice and unloaded punch after punch on Brooks.

Right hand after right hand.

The momentum carried us naturally backwards and as I felt Brooks back hit up against the Plexiglas, I found my balance and instead of a hook I threw a straight right jab and drilled my fist squarely into the Ogre's nose which smashed under the blow and sent blood everywhere.

The Ogre's head banged against the glass and when he righted himself the look in his eyes was furious.

He didn't punch back – just grabbed me with both hands and then, with a guttural yell, spun me around and threw me against the glass.

I felt the wind whoosh out of me.

Before I could recover he pulled me forward then spun me round again - clearly planning to rag doll me against the boards.

I grabbed him and pulled in as close as I could. He tried to force me away so he could board me again but I'd managed to shove my left foot between his legs and I kicked at his skates as he moved, doing all I could to stick to him like a limpet till I could get some air back into my lungs.

After a second or two of this he changed his grip, pulled me away from the wall and tried to force me backwards.

He wanted to unbalance me and get me down on the ice. That would be a win for him – all he had to do was knock me down.

And Jesus was he strong.

By clinging to him I was forcing him to burn up energy rapidly. I could hear how laboured his breathing had already become.

Then pain suddenly slammed into me.

Tiring of trying to wrestle me onto the ice, the Ogre had pulled his left hand (his favourite weapon) back and driven a punch into my side.

I slipped.

One skate flew backwards and for just a second I was down on one knee.

I saw the look of triumph cross his face but before he could land another punch on me I dropped my right hand to the ice and as the big left hand flew towards my face I braced myself as I threw myself backwards. His punch missed me and he was off balance.

I pulled him into an uppercut.

I felt the crunch as I drove his teeth together.

Suddenly the Ogre – the unbeatable enforcer – was skating backwards as blood poured down his chin from his mouth and I was going forward, beating on him.

A right hook.

Then another.

He ducked his chin and neither punch landed cleanly but I knew they would still have hurt.

His hands came up to grapple again and I slapped one away then threw another right hook.

That one connected cleanly.

He stumbled.

I cocked my hand right back to throw another but, before I could, he grabbed at me. His left hand smothered the punch I'd been about to throw, then his right hand caught the front of my jersey and hauled me forward into a head-butt.

I was seeing stars.

I didn't have to think about it. I knew my nose was broken and I opened my mouth to take a big, panic breath as my feet almost went from under me.

That was - despite the pain – when I saw just how badly hurt my opponent was.

His arms still had a grip on me but he was stretching forward, his arms further forward than his feet and he was holding onto me for balance.

For a moment we were both grappling as we both tried to catch our breath.

Then he pulled me close again and tried for another head-butt.

I let out a scream of anger as I used my elbow to send him stumbling back up against the glass.

I took two more shots to the body as I wrestled with him but neither had the power of that first punch he had hit me with.

As his back connected with the Plexiglas I let go of my grip so I could use both hands.

Jab!

Jab!

His already damaged nose was ruined.

Cross!

His head was turned to the side as I drove that punch home.

I thought that was it.

I thought he'd fall over, that he was done.

But this was the Ogre we're talking about and while I saw his legs shake he didn't go down.

Instead he unloaded that big left hand and I felt it connect with my right ear.

I gritted my teeth and changed target.

A low uppercut to the ribs just like Dennis had taught me.

Then another.

His head came down as he doubled over and I went for another right hook to the jaw.

He shoved me and the punch missed but I went straight back on the attack.

Jab!

Jab!

He ate those punches as if they hadn't hurt and shoved himself off the wall.

I took a hit to the right hand side and then another to the left.

I could hardly breathe.

I grabbed hold of him and as I did his hand – that lethal big left hand – cocked back again.

But in that same moment he exposed his chin.

If I'd missed or if I'd not gotten enough force behind it then that would have been it for me because at that point I had virtually nothing left.

But I didn't miss.

I practically threw myself at him as I launched that punch. My fist connected right into his jaw and his eyes glazed over as his legs went from under him.

He still had a hold of me and dragged me down to the ice with him.

I wound up kneeling beside him, ready to unload another punch as I desperately tried to draw in a breath.

But there was no need.

The Ogre was out cold on the ice.

I'd won.

Let me tell you about the chant...

Here's what I remember about the rest of that game.

I remember the blue and green machine going absolutely berserk as I was led off the ice.

I remember the medic at DIA telling me what I already knew – that my nose was broken – and telling me that there was no actual law against ducking or at least keeping my chin down when the punches were flying.

'Good fight, man,' he said as he finished doing what he could to patch me up.

I remember the moment I sat back down with the rest of the team and Coach Williams just glanced over and gave me a nod. Just a quick up and down gesture but it implied a lot more than that.

More than anything, I remember Gagnon's performance in that third period.

I swear that Gagnon must have had ice water instead of blood pumping through his veins – the guy was just unflappable.

He blocked shot after shot with a skill that even players at the very highest levels couldn't have matched. None of us knew it then but we were watching a future Olympian. Gagnon was noted by one of the scouts who kept an eye out for new talent and two years later it was Gagnon who pulled on a Canadian jersey at the Winter Olympics and shut out Sweden in the semi-finals.

Even when the Dragons conceded another five on three to us nothing got past the Dragons' goalie.

There was a little under two minutes of play left in the third and we looked on course for overtime and maybe penalty shots.

Then the chant started.

It built slowly until it seemed that the blue and green machine was all chanting it together.

Danny – who had just line changed and came off the ice – nudged me.

'You hear that?'

Truth be told, my ears were still ringing and I really wasn't hearing the words. I told Danny that and he grinned at me.

'Listen real hard, Jonesy,' he told me.

The puck got iced at that point. Play stopped and I heard the chant properly.

'Send! For! Jonesy!'

My dad's chant.

I understood then – finally – why my dad did what he did, pushed himself as hard as he had and gave all that he gave.

I can't really explain it properly but hearing it just made me want to win for them.

'Send! For! Jonesy!'

I looked over at Coach Williams.

'You don't have to ice again tonight, Davey. You've more than done your duty tonight. You can sit it out here.'

'What if I *want* to play, Coach?' I asked.

The medic at the DIA hadn't had me whisked off to the nearest hospital and he hadn't told me I couldn't ice.

Coach Williams just looked at me for a second then he said, 'First hit I see that I don't like, you come off – no arguments.'

I stood up and grabbed my stick.

As they saw me get up, the St Helens fans erupted with cheers.

Coach Williams nodded over at the Dragons who were gathered around their goal waiting for the ref to make a call.

'Make them cry, son,' he told me.

As I skated out onto the ice, the boos echoed down on me from all around the DIA.

I took it just like Frankie told me to – as applause.

But it incensed the blue and green machine.

The referee was still trying to make the call and was deep in discussion with one of the linesmen when the blue and green machine decided to make their feelings clear.

One of them close to the glass started it.

He raised a hand and slapped it against the Plexiglas.

It only took seconds for the entire away support to join in – either clapping or pounding on the glass.

Clap!

Clap!

Clap-clap, clap-clap!

I took the face-off against Lewis.

'You ready for another beating so soon?' he sneered at me.

Behind us the sound of the blue and green machine was actually drowning out the jeers of the Dragons fans.

Clap!

Clap!

Clap-clap, clap-clap!

'You hear that, Lewis?' I asked him.

The linesman skated over with the puck for face-off and I saw Lewis glance up once as the blue and green machine continued the chant.

'It means the Devils are coming,' I told him.

Lewis opened his mouth – no doubt for a little more trash talk – but at that precise moment the puck dropped and I hit it away from Lewis and towards Lief before the Dragons player could even get his stick to it.

Seventy-one seconds on the clock as Lief took the puck off towards the left wing, looking for an opening.

He found none as the Dragons pulled all their guys back to play defence so he circled the back of Gagnon's net.

A short pass to Danny then straight back to Lief.

Fifty-nine seconds left.

As Lewis practically threw himself at Lief in an attempt to break up our momentum Lief passed the puck backwards to me.

I took it forward – skated around Campbell - then tapped the puck neatly across to Danny, who blasted it at Gagnon.

Gagnon slapped the shot away almost contemptuously,

Forty-five seconds left.

Lewis chased the puck as it careened across the ice towards Lief. The two of them clashed – their sticks cracking against each other – as they furiously fought for possession.

Thirty-four seconds left.

Lewis forced the puck past Lief and managed to get it about a foot away when I swooped in, intercepted the puck and passed it neatly over to Danny who promptly slap shot the puck and I actually heard the clang as it hit the post and bounced.

Bounced straight towards me.

Twenty-nine seconds left.

Lief had the better angle so I passed the puck sharply to my left.

Twenty-two seconds left.

I didn't budge after I passed to Lief – I lurked near the goal like a good sniper should.

Lief played the puck forward, looking for someone to pass to. Danny was changing position but I held my ground.

Nineteen seconds left.

The puck went from Lief to Danny then back to Lief again who blasted the puck forward.

I watched the shot almost with detachment.

I knew as soon as he hit the puck that he was going to miss.

That didn't matter.

All that mattered would be the angle it came off at.

I moved slightly left as Gagnon's stick knocked the puck aside.

Sending it almost straight to my stick.

No sooner had the puck touched my stick than I let fly. It was a short, clinical shot that put the puck past a desperate attempt by Gagnon to stop it and sent the puck into the top right hand corner of the net.

There were just eight seconds left to play in the third when the score board changed to display the legend St Helens three, Douglasville two.

The blue and green machine cheered the place down and eight seconds later - when the whistle finally blew - they were all out of their seats applauding the team.

Even now, as I look back I'd still describe that moment as one of the sweetest, most perfect moments I ever experienced.

We shook hands with the Dragons players and left the ice to cheers from the blue and green machine.

I felt absolutely invincible as I made my way to our locker room, absolutely on top of the world.

I enjoyed the moment, (Hell, I revelled in it!) It was such a great feeling.

I'd been in the locker room maybe a little less than five minutes when one of the DIA staff knocked on our door and told me I had a phone call.

And that was when everything changed.

Let me tell you about the call...

My phone call was from Russ and I couldn't have been any happier to hear from him.

I was babbling, talking far faster than I normally did and asking him what Kelly Anne had thought and did she cheer when that third goal went in?

Dear God in Heaven but I have so much respect for Russ. I was basically talking about myself and all the good things I'd just done and inviting him to congratulate me for them. In his shoes, I don't know how I would have coped with someone doing that to me.

Russ waited patiently for me to pause for breath before telling me why he was calling.

His voice was always so calm that at first I didn't understand that something had to be very wrong for him to call me post game while I was still at the arena.

He gave me the news gently.

Avoided adding any drama, just explained the facts.

The embolism, the collapse, the frantic attempts to save his daughter.

On the ice, I'd just won the fight of my life.

Off the ice, another battle had taken place.

Kelly Anne had beaten the odds again and again and had never stopped fighting.

And despite the best efforts of the people around her, that was the night when she finally lost her battle.

I heard and understood Russ' words but they didn't really sink in. Not really.

They didn't make sense; they couldn't really be real, could they?

When I put the receiver down I stood there not moving for a minute or two.

I felt confused.

I knew that Russ wouldn't have lied to me but I couldn't possibly process this, I just couldn't.

My stomach felt like I'd just been punched and my head was spinning.

The big moments in your life – the ones that crash into you like a wrecking ball – don't come when you're ready for them. Life doesn't often give you the chance to brace yourself for the impact it's about to deliver.

No, the big moments often arrive out of the blue and with no warning.

I didn't want to accept what Russ had just told me but that didn't make what he had told me any less true.

Kelly Anne had lost her fight.

She was gone.

Let me tell you what happens if someone believes in you...

My dad once told me that nothing – absolutely nothing – beats the moment when you know the crowd is behind you. It was, he said, like being Superman - only better. It was a gift, he said, a chance to repay their faith in you by doing those things they believed you were capable of doing.

When thousands of people call out your name, when thousands of people cheer you on, it's an unbelievable rush but you know what? It doesn't need to be thousands of people.

All it takes is one person.

When one person genuinely believes in you it changes you.

If you're ever lucky enough to meet someone who truly believes in you, then thank them with all your heart and promise yourself that you'll never, ever let that person down, because I'll tell you that if you don't do that, if you take that person lightly, or if you blow them off, then you'll regret it forever after.

Kelly Anne had believed in me.

Me.

A gutless, childish, selfish prima donna.

And how did I repay her for that?

I told her I was going to quit.

You know something? I didn't shed a single tear at the DIA or when I was travelling back to our hotel that night.

Not a single one.

I was doing everything on autopilot. I handed my kit to one of the assistants and I went to get checked out at the hospital so I didn't see the team on the way back.

When I got to the hotel room I packed my bag, ready to check out early next morning. Then I ordered a meal from room service.

No tears.

Just a heavy feeling in my gut and the absolute knowledge that I should be feeling something but I wasn't.

I felt numb and I told myself that was a good thing.

I'd never had many friends and I'd never done anything much to change that. If people come into your life, then they can also leave you, or be taken away from you.

My dad and big brother had both left me a long time ago and I could remember crying my eyes out then.

My mom was gone. So were my grandparents.

I found myself thinking back to all the funerals I'd already been to and realised that I'd need to go to Kelly Anne's.

I wondered idly if I still owned a black tie?

And once I'd gone to the funeral that would be that. Done and dusted. I'd gradually forget about the little girl who believed in me and life would move on.

My tablet was lying on the bedside table and I picked it up.

I logged on and found Kelly Anne's last post – the photo of her wearing the jersey emblazoned with my name and number and with the prophetic words "Tonight's top scorer" below it.

Below it, DragonLady29's comment, "Where was the photo taken? Is that a hospital room? You okay honey?"

I hit reply and began to type.

After a couple of minutes I took my fingers off of the tablet and raised them to my face.

To my surprise I could feel wetness there.

I brought my hands up in front of me where I could see them and was surprised to realise I'd wiped away tears.

I reminded myself that I was a cynical, selfish person.

I was an adult not a child.

I couldn't really be crying when just writing down a post, could I?

But I was.

It was like the trigger that my brain had been waiting for. Suddenly the heavy feeling, that sense of unreality, that this couldn't really be happening, evaporated.

And I cried.

It wasn't manly or tough or macho – I broke down and I bawled my eyes out like a child.

It took time for that first storm of crying to pass. When it did, I tried to return to what I was writing. The tears ambushed me over and over again as I tried to write but I did finally get it done.

You can probably imagine how busy the forum was and how vicious the comments were that night. After most Sea Devils and Dragons match-ups the comments often flew thick and fast till the early hours of the morning.

My post did the almost impossible. After I pressed send I

practically silenced the forums. For a good few minutes nobody replied, the forums just stood still.

This is what I wrote.

"Somebody missed the big game tonight. If you use the forum regularly – especially if you were on here just before the game – then you might be wondering why she isn't on here now, chirping and cheering and tirelessly flying the flag for the sport and team she loved. Whether you wear blue and green or red and gold, a lot of you will have encountered her on here – she wasn't exactly shy. On here she posted under the name Lady Kraken and her real name was Kelly Anne. She was fifteen years old.

"A couple of you saw her last post and asked if it had been taken in a hospital. Asked if she was okay? It had been. And she wasn't.

Kelly Anne was being treated for cancer at the Whyte Centre in St Elizabeth's hospital. She did not want anyone's sympathy or pity – all she wanted was to watch her hockey. But she missed the big game tonight because, a few moments after her last post, she collapsed. Despite the staff's best efforts, she died.

I'm not sure if I've got the words to come even close to do this justice, but I'm going to try. I didn't know Kelly Anne for very long. There are lots of things I could tell you about her but right now the only one I can focus on is she believed in me. She believed in me and now she's gone. And I feel like somebody has torn my heart out.

She would have loved that game, I think. I was looking forward to talking with her about it, sharing what it was like to play against the Dragons and how it felt to drop the gloves with the Ogre. It's a story I'll never get to share with her now and I can't describe how much that hurts.

RIP Kelly Anne – I will never forget you."

It took a few moments before anybody replied.

The first one to do so was DragonLady29.

'Hands are actually shaking as I write this,' she wrote, 'I'm so sorry, Jonesy.'

A moment later Born_In_D-Ville posted 'This is a joke, right? Seriously, this is just a bad joke?'

'I wish it was,' I replied.

'Fuck,' he replied, 'Fuck, fuck, fuck - I am so sorry, Jonesy. I had no idea.'

He ended his post with the tag #RIPKellyAnne – something that fans from both clubs began to add to their posts.

The comments began to absolutely pour in after that.

Within five minutes the story seemed to have spread to both sets of fans.

Within ten it had become the most posted-about story on the forum.

I fielded questions from fans from both camps for a while. The tag #RIPKellyAnne flashed up constantly as I did.

Eventually though I started to feel a little overwhelmed. I apologised to the people online but said I needed to log off and get my head together.

After another minute or two I turned the tablet off.

I remember sitting there feeling both utterly exhausted but still too alert to go to bed.

I wondered just how many nightmares would be waiting for me when I did finally get to sleep that night.

The knock at my door jolted me out of my thoughts.

I walked over and opened the door to find Coach Williams, Danny, Lief, Robbie Dee and (clearly just back from the hospital) Frankie all waiting for me.

I felt suddenly guilty. I'd posted publically about Kelly Anne but hadn't told any of my own team first.

'Guys, I ...' the words dried up in my throat. 'She's...'

'We saw your post,' Danny said.

'I should have told you guys first. I just...'

'Sometimes it's best to be on your own,' Coach Williams said. Then he held up a bottle of Scotch. 'Other times? Other times it's better to have people around you to talk to.'

I shut my eyes tight.

I will not break down, I told myself.

'If you need to be by yourself, Davey, then that's cool,' Danny said. 'But if you want a little company then we thought you could tell us a bit more about Kelly Anne. I mean, we only met her a couple of times and I'm betting there's a few other stories you could tell us about her?'

I could feel one treacherous tear trying to leak out and I dashed it away with the back of my hand, then opened the door wider.

'You just wouldn't believe some of the stories, Danny,' I told him.

It took another call to room service to get enough glasses and then the Coach poured everyone a drink and we raised them in a toast.

I told them the story of how I'd first met Kelly Anne and about Stan and the other women at the Whyte Centre (they especially liked the story of Kelly Anne throwing a puck at the administrator).

We all got very drunk and when I finally stumbled into bed there were no nightmares.

The Coach was right.

Sometimes you just need to be alone.

Other times you need to be with your family.

Let me tell you about the priest...

To understand the events that took place at Kelly Anne's funeral properly it helps if you know a little about the priest.

It was after all the look on his face and the comments he made afterwards that helped put it all into context for me.

The priest who would be saying the funeral mass for Kelly Anne – one Father Michael O'Brien - was a very well-known figure in St Helens.

When Russ had contacted him to tell him the news that Kelly Anne had passed away and ask about the funeral arrangements the elderly priest had promptly cancelled a vacation he'd planned to be sure he could be there to do the funeral for her. Father Michael had been the one to baptise Kelly Anne. He told Russ that while it broke his heart to also be there to say the final mass for her that there was just no way he could leave that responsibility to some stranger who'd never met her.

It was the kind of gesture that people had come to expect from Father Michael.

If you talked to people in St Helens you'd find lots of people would describe the priest – whether they agreed with his views or not – with the same four words.

He gives a shit.

And Father Michael really did.

He was a smart guy. In addition to his degree in Divinity he had another in law. It had been widely assumed that when young Michael O'Brien took his vows years ago he'd wind up as a bishop at least.

But Father Michael wasn't remotely interested in climbing the church's hierarchy – he had much more important things to do, like looking after the people in his parish.

He gave a shit about them – even when other people just didn't.

A local politician had once (rather unwisely) accosted Father Michael at the shopping mall. The politician had had a camera crew with him as he was being interviewed about all the great things he'd allegedly done for the local economy.

He latched onto the priest – clearly assuming that Father Michael would say only vague, positive things.

But Father Michael gave a shit about his parishioners and he knew what the reality was.

He tore into the politician with question after question: about tax breaks for big companies that vanished as soon as the tax break was gone, about the lack of support for local businesses and about lack of opportunities for the young.

The politician's interrogation had (much to the camera crew's delight) gone on for several minutes before the politician finally remembered an appointment he had and fled.

Father Michael gave a shit about the people in his parish and woe unto anyone who tried to have a go at his parishioners.

It would have been both fair and accurate to call Father Michael an older guy but I'd probably have avoided saying it to his face, because even at the age of sixty-two, I'm fairly sure he could have beaten me black and blue if he'd felt the urge to do so. Shrink Coach Williams down a couple of inches, age him by twenty years and give him iron-grey hair and a broken nose and you've pretty much got Father Michael.

I liked the priest from the moment I met him.

Normally my involvement at a funeral extended only as far as turning up on the day to pay my respects and say goodbye but with Kelly Anne it was different.

Russ had invited me to speak at the funeral.

There would be a eulogy by Father Michael of course but - given her near-fanatical love of hockey - Russ had asked if I'd also say a few words.

Russ had actually invited the whole team to attend if they were free. I think he'd met pretty much all of us when he turned up to collect Kelly Anne from the practice sessions she'd attended. He probably assumed that maybe one or two might turn up to represent the club.

The funeral was on a Thursday morning.

It was the day after our road trip. After the Dragons we'd beaten the Piranhas but then been beaten twice by the Wolves – although we ran them close in the first game and forced them into overtime on the second. We were all exhausted and that Thursday was actually our only rest day.

Not one single member of the team chose to take their rest day – we were all going to be there to say goodbye.

I got to know Father Michael when I went along to the church on the Wednesday night. I'd gone to support Russ – solid, dependable Russ who never seemed to be ready to quit – and the priest had asked me if I'd decided what I was going to say.

I admitted I didn't have a clue and that I was actually terrified of getting up to speak and then finding that no words came out.

The priest just chuckled at that.

'That won't happen, son,' he assured me.

'No?'

'No. I've known people who thought nerves would destroy them but, when you just remember the person who's left us, it's almost impossible not to conjure up a few memories and stories. And that's all you have to do – share your memories. Besides,' he said with a twinkle in his eye, 'I knew Kelly Anne and if you were to mess it up then I have a strong suspicion that she would get up from the coffin so she can kick your backside for you.'

It was a lame sort of joke but I smiled anyway.

'If that's all it takes to bring her back, Father,' I said, 'I'd be happy to screw it up.'

He clapped my shoulder.

'I know you would, son. Don't worry about tomorrow – you'll be fine.'

When the next morning dawned I don't think I've ever been more nervous. Even the moment when I skated out at the DIA was less stressful than the moment when I and the rest of the St Helens team – all dressed smartly in blazers, shirts and ties – arrived at the little church where Kelly Anne's funeral mass would be held.

The service was being attended by Kelly Anne's friends and family. Turns out her mom had passed away when she was little but she had lots of friends – some from school and some from the different hospitals she'd been in. Stan was there along with a couple of other nurses who'd treated her over the years. The church – Our Lady of Hope – wasn't a big one and we filled maybe three quarters of the pews. It was, as both Stan and Coach Williams noted, a good turnout.

The incident happened just before the mass was due to begin.

We'd been talking, sharing stories, when one of Kelly Anne's friends glanced out of the window then said (perhaps a little louder than she'd intended) 'Who are all those people?'

A second later another girl asked, 'Why are they dressed like that?'

I was sitting at the front of the church and so couldn't see anything but, like the others, I could hear the excited comments from behind me.

'Is there a problem?' someone asked.

'Why are they all standing out there?' someone else asked.

I looked over at Russ but he shook his head. Whatever was happening outside Our Lady of Hope was news to him too.

That was when Father Michael appeared.

The elderly priest looked quietly furious as he strode down the aisle towards the doors of his church.

Father Michael gave a shit about his parishioners and the very notion that somebody might try to create a scene at a funeral had clearly pushed all of his buttons. Father Michael wasn't the kind to let other people fight his battles for him. It was his church, being used for a service for one of his parish and if someone was trying to disrupt things, then they were going to have to answer to him.

Russ and I exchanged a look and then both of us got up and followed in the priest's wake.

We had almost caught up with Father Michael when he reached the doors and yanked them open.

'What's the meaning of this?' the priest barked, 'Who are you?'

As Russ and I pulled level with the priest we suddenly saw what he was seeing.

I glanced over at Russ.

He shut his eyes tight as if in pain but then a second later began to smile and then to laugh.

Unlike Father Michael, Russ understood what it was he was looking at.

'Davey,' the priest asked, 'who are they?'

We never did do a headcount but – conservatively – we reckon there were close to two thousand people standing outside the little church.

They'd organised themselves, met up at the bus station and then walked the short distance to the church from there.

They weren't shouting or jeering or behaving badly. As a group they were quiet and respectful.

'Davey?' Father Michael pressed.

The strange clothes they were wearing were hockey jerseys.

I could see every team in the league represented there but

overwhelmingly the colours I saw were blue and green.

'Davey,' the priest's voice was filled with a genuine concern, 'who are these people?'

I looked over at Father Michael and smiled.

'They're family.' I said.

JOHN McKINSTRY

Let me tell you about my eulogy...

Before I left for the church that morning I'd taken something from my home and put it in the pocket of my blazer.

I hadn't been sure if I'd need it or want to refer to it and the idea of sharing it didn't occur to me till I was actually in the church itself.

Truth be told, I had absolutely no idea how to deliver a eulogy and was really scared I was going to make a mess of it. I'd brought the item with me as a sort of talisman – a rabbit's foot to bring me luck and stop me screwing things up.

As Father Michael began to organise things so that some of our new guests could come inside and speakers were passed back so the rest could hear I felt my mind go blank.

I just didn't know what to say.

The mass, once it started, moved far too quickly and before I knew what was happening it was time to stand up, walk up onto the altar and say something about Kelly Anne to the people gathered there.

As I walked up, I caught Father Michael's eye and he nodded at me as if to say "You'll be fine".

Except I didn't feel fine.

If you've never been to a funeral mass before then I can tell you that almost every moment of it feels different to any other situation you'll ever find yourself in. There's a sort of nervous tension in the air from the start to the end and in most churches the coffin will be on display – usually just in front of the altar.

When I got to the little lectern, that's what I was looking at – the small, white coffin where Kelly Anne lay.

I leant towards the lectern, licked my very dry lips and opened my mouth to say something - but no words came out.

There was silence in the church as I tried to think of something – anything – to say.

I opened my mouth again then closed it again.

Somebody coughed at the back of the church but, apart from that, there was silence.

I sighed then said, 'I'm no good at this folks,' into the microphone on the lectern. 'I'm a hockey player. I hit pucks across the ice for a living – I'm not clever with words and I've never done anything like this before.'

I looked up and stared out at the congregation.

'I didn't know Kelly Anne for long. In the short space of time I did know her, she'd say things – personal stuff about her illness and her chances of having a future – and I just wouldn't know how to reply to her. I hated myself for not having the words then. And I hate it right now.'

I took a deep breath and gathered my thoughts before continuing.

'If I told you Kelly Anne was an inspiring person, it'd be an understatement.' I paused then added, 'Of course, if she heard me say that, then she'd probably laugh and warn me not to embarrass her or she'd kick my ass.'

A few people grinned or laughed.

'Which doesn't make my comment untrue – she *was* an inspiration.'

People were nodding and I could feel the memories as they danced through my mind.

'I can't do her justice so I'm not going to try. Instead I'm going to share something with you.'

I could feel a tear beginning to form in my eye and I cuffed it away, reached into the pocket of my blazer and took out her letter to me.

I told them how – despite her illness – she had been thinking of me and not herself. I told them that reading her letter had hit me like a wrecking ball.

Then I read it to them.

It didn't take long, like I said before, beyond her signature it was just seven words long.

Those seven words were – "I'm not quitting and neither should you."

Everybody seemed to be nodding their heads as I read it out because Kelly Anne never did quit – the very idea was just alien to her.

I told the audience that before meeting her I could never have said that about myself and that now it was the quality I most wanted to possess.

When I finally sat down I felt physically drained.

Russ leaned over to me and – speaking very quietly - thanked me.

'She'd have been touched, Davey,' he said.

I nearly lost it when he said that but Father Michael distracted us with his own eulogy and spared me from embarrassing myself.

As the priest talked about her life, I looked across at the little, white coffin.

I hope you approve, devil-girl, I thought. I hope you can see how much everyone loved you.

The mass was a short one – as Russ had requested – and it flew by. One or two people had a tear in their eyes but that was it.

Until we moved the short distance to the crematorium.

For most of us that was when the tears came.

That was where we really said goodbye.

Let me tell you about the song...

Two of the funerals I'd attended prior to Kelly Anne's had also been cremations.

At both of them, when the coffin was slowly slid behind the curtains, they played music.

I suppose it was meant to be soothing but I always hated it. It was piped in, impersonal and vaguely religious. At my grandmother's funeral, my grandpa had told me that he didn't mind people singing a hymn, but the piped-in organ music we were treated to (it was Amazing Grace if I remembered rightly) was awful and I absolutely agreed with him.

The crematorium staff (who were actually wonderfully sensitive to the situation) had offered a range of songs which could be played as that little white coffin was taken behind the curtains.

Russ thanked them but told them that no music would be played.

We already – thanks to Coach Williams – had a much more appropriate option.

I was honoured to be one of the pall bearers to lift the coffin and carry it gently to the crematorium (which was practically next door to Our Lady of Hope).

As people moved that very short distance I saw more and more of them beginning to tear up.

People know that the funeral mass is almost the end and they're upset. They know that the crematorium however is the end; it's the final stop.

Russ was doing well. He wasn't just holding it together; he was helping other people do the same.

Watching Russ that day made me change my mind completely about what a tough guy was.

Russ was a tough guy.

It wasn't Frankie. It wasn't the Ogre. It was Russ.

The only opponents people like Brooks or Frankie had to fight were other hockey players.

The opponent Russ squared off against was far stronger and fought far dirtier.

Russ' opponent was life.

255

And Russ – quiet, calm, gentle Russ - hadn't ever backed down an inch.

I remembered what he'd said to me in the Whyte Centre – "Not today, you will not break me today."

There were children from Russ' class present that day and it dawned on me as he spoke with them, cheered them up and allowed them to lean on him for support, that they were the same age as Kelly Anne. I wondered how he did it. Taught them, encouraged them and helped them grow when he must have known that his own daughter would never get to do the things his pupils would.

Oh God, I thought, please let me grow to be even one tenth as strong as this guy.

The only time Russ stumbled that day was when he laid the coffin down.

He held onto the handle, hand clenched tightly around it like he was never going to let go.

He stood there for a long moment then he bent down, said something so quietly that probably only I could hear and finally, with an apologetic look at the other people around him, stepped back.

We stood there quietly as a tall, middle-aged man walked slowly forward.

He paused when he came to Russ then extended his hand. Russ shook it and after a moment the tall man stepped past Russ.

He stared at the little coffin for a moment as if he was waiting for something.

He was.

He was waiting for the first person to start to clap.

He was waiting for his intro, because the tall man was Jimmy Crowe himself.

It turned out that he and Coach Williams had been good friends back in the day and had kept in touch.

There was only one song we could have sung to say goodbye to Kelly Anne.

The first person to clap was our Coach.

It was taken up almost immediately by everyone in the crowd.

Clap.

Clap.

Clap-clap, clap-clap.

The crematorium had offered Jimmy a microphone but he'd just smiled and assured them that he wouldn't need it and he didn't.

I watched as the singer took a couple of deep breaths and then began to sing Cruel World.

And as he sang, the blue and green machine joined in.

You know something? Singing is another talent I just don't possess. Fact is, none of the team could really carry a tune.

But we all sang.

The people who had gathered outside – whether they were wearing blue and green or red and gold – sang.

And Jimmy Crowe led our choir.

He changed the lyrics from time to time.

When he got to the second verse – our wings will be broken to prevent us from flying and our lives will be pain till our moment of dying – Jimmy changed those lines and instead sang that her wings were broken but it never stopped her flying and though her life held pain, she never stopped fighting.

People all around me were in tears.

I didn't break until I saw the little coffin start to move.

My voice cracked and I could feel the tears, knew people would be watching and I didn't care.

Jimmy Crowe's voice soared as he sang that she'd been told her life shouldn't be prized, told that she shouldn't rise.

As the coffin vanished behind the curtain it took more strength to keep singing than it had to face down the Ogre.

'She will rise!' Jimmy sang.

The sound of all those people singing and clapping had risen to a crescendo.

'See her rise!' Jimmy sang and we all added our voices to his. 'SEE HER RISE!'

When he reached the big final line of the song Jimmy didn't bellow that the Devils were coming.

He waited for quiet before saying – softly but clearly – 'An angel is coming.'

I wiped my tears away and almost managed a smile.

Kelly Anne would have laughed at that – she knew she was no angel.

But I think she would have approved of how we said goodbye.

When the service drew to an end, I was one of the first to leave the crematorium.   Russ was busy thanking people for their kindness and Father Michael was helping organise the flow of people past Russ, stopping him from getting overwhelmed.

As I waited for people to pay their respects I walked a little away.

I looked up at the pale blue sky above St Helens and thought of Kelly Anne.

Rise devil-girl, I thought, rise.

Let me tell you about endings...

Nothing is forever.

Kelly Anne knew the truth of that better than anybody else. Every story has an ending, some end happily while others don't.

Just over a week after his daughter's funeral, Russ finally quit his job at Blue River High.

The principal – Mr Sanderson – apparently accepted his resignation with a certain degree of glee and insisted on Russ leaving the school premises immediately with the Principal personally escorting Russ off the school grounds.

It's probably unrelated but there was a persistent rumour that the real reason for Mr Sanderson having to take a couple of weeks off shortly afterwards was to have treatment for a broken nose and cheekbone after somebody picked a fight with him in a bar and beat the living crap out of him.

I'm sure there's no substance to those rumours though. I'm equally sure there was an entirely innocent reason behind the bruising on Coach Williams' right hand – mainly around the knuckles – a couple of days after Russ quit.

Russ' new job?

He came to work at St Helens Sea Devils Ice Hockey Club. He joined our PR team in a newly-created post – charity event organiser.

I don't know what Russ was like as a teacher but in his new role he's like a man on a mission. Every dollar – hell, every cent – raised is a way of hitting back at the disease that took away his daughter and Russ absolutely lives for his work and is damn good at it.

The charity match – St Helens against the eventual winners of the league the Wolves – was his first big project.

We raised a shed load of money and we also managed to get Stan both VIP tickets as well as a chance to meet his hero, Wolves captain, Timur Volkov. It's the only time I've ever seen Stan star-struck and I still rib him about it when I see him. He still works at the Whyte Centre. When he bitches about it ("The hours are long and the pay is short!") we invite him to come work at St Helens. I doubt he ever will though. He makes a genuine difference to the patients there and he knows it.

St Helens didn't win the league that year but we did manage a very respectable third place behind the Wolves and the Piranhas.

I stayed on.

I can't tell you hand on heart that I'm no longer a coward because that would be an absolute lie. I'm still absolutely terrified right before every single game.

I hate the very idea of being hurt but I've also discovered I hate the thought of losing even more.

The nightmares still happen and my hands still shake when I'm in the tunnel waiting to ice.

But I'm done running.

And I fully intend to bring the league title home to St Helens where it belongs just as soon as I can.

I think my dad would have liked that.

I talk to people more now. I run the risk of building friendships with people.

Kelly Anne taught me that.

We aren't here for long and if we don't make each day count then we're not living – instead we're just sort of existing and what a waste that would be.

I want to say the story ended happily for everyone. I want to but I can't.

You don't get many Hollywood endings with the big C.

Sheila, the first lady I saw when I walked into the ward at the Whyte Centre, has been in and out ever since. For a while it looked like she was in remission but before they could issue an all-clear it came back. She had another course of chemo and – so far – it looks good and she told me she's hopeful for the future.

Rhonda, dear sweet Rhonda, lost her battle about five months after Kelly Anne did.

I met her brother at the funeral. He told me she had expected me to stop visiting after Kelly Anne had passed away and had been touched when I kept popping in.

He told me I'd helped make her last few days just a little bit brighter.

If I ever win the Stanley Cup it'll mean less to me than that single comment from him.

And that just leaves us with Jane.

When Kelly Anne passed away everybody thought Jane would

give up the fight. To see your own possible future (Jane was right there when Kelly Anne collapsed and was actually the one to raise the alarm) must be a terrible thing.

But Jane didn't give up.

In point of fact, Jane told me she was done with being a 'poor little martyr.'

Seems Kelly Anne had a massive effect on her.

'If I'm going down, I'm not going without a fight,' she told me.

The odds were stacked against Jane but, as Coach Williams was fond of saying, the odds only tell you what's *likely* to happen – not what's actually *going* to happen.

Jane came through chemo successfully.

I bought her a bottle of ridiculously expensive champagne on the day she was told she was in the clear.

We stayed in touch and I was delighted for her when she told me a few months later that she'd met someone.

A few months after that I got a call from her.

She told me she had something really important to tell me.

For a second my heart jumped into my mouth.

When any cancer survivor tells you they have something important to tell you, your first reaction is always a momentary fear that the disease has somehow found a way to get a hold of them again.

Jane knew I'd assume that and she immediately told me not to worry – it wasn't the cancer.

It wasn't anything bad in fact.

It was something wonderful.

She was pregnant.

She'd waited till she was sure before telling anyone and (other than her boyfriend of course) I'd been the first person she'd told.

When she had her scan to determine the baby's gender she was told she was going to have a daughter.

A few months later Jane became the mother to a beautiful, healthy baby girl.

You can probably guess what she called her.

261

Let me tell you what I've learned...

Here's what I've learned so far.

Life is a contact sport and there's absolutely nothing you can do to change that. There is no black jersey you can pull on to somehow avoid the hits – it just doesn't work that way.

There will be bad moments, there will be painful moments and there will be moments so cruel that you'll be sure they're going to break you.

But you need to remember there's joy as well. There are friends, there is family and there is hope.

So when the cruel moments arrive – and they will – don't back down.

And when you take a hit, don't stay down.

Look life in the eye and tell it, "Not today, you will not break me today."

I shall rise.

Just fucking watch me.

Acknowledgements

Thanks first of all to Janice for transforming the chicken scratchings I call my handwriting into a proper, legible document (no easy feat!).

A massive thank you to Lynne, my proof reader and secret weapon, and James over at Humble Nations for creating yet another great cover for me.

Thank you to my test readers Jayne and Jillian (your comments and enthusiasm meant the world to me!) and a massive thanks (as always) to the real life Coach Williams, my best friend Craig, without whom I'd never have discovered hockey in the first place.

Lastly, a big thank you to all of the wonderful lunatics I've met since starting to follow ice hockey, especially my own hockey family at Braehead (you all know who you are!).